THE LIES HE TOLD

VALERIE KEOGH

BLOODHOUND
— BOOKS —

Print ISBN 978-1-914614-15-6

ALSO BY VALERIE KEOGH

For Jenny O'Brien
Great nurse... writer... friend.

1

MISTY

Toby Carter stood in the open doorway and waved to get my attention.

I dragged myself away from the characters that were coming to life under my fingers, took off the headphones I used to shut out the world when I was working and dropped them on the desk.

London had been struggling in a heatwave for over a week but Toby looked cool in his summer-weight suit, his white shirt still as crisp as when he'd left early that morning, his tie still in the Windsor knot he preferred. As always, his fringe fell across his forehead in an artfully casual way that I knew cost him a fortune to maintain.

I was stressed with a looming deadline but, as ever, the sight of him was the perfect antidote and as my tense shoulders slumped, the corners of my lips tilted upward in an automatic smile.

'Hi, have you been home long?'

'I don't love you anymore.'

The words were said without inflection and for a second I

thought I'd misheard. I had to have done... we were perfect together. A tinny, demented bumblebee buzz came from the discarded headphones. I wanted to be distracted, so picked them up and stared at them, anything rather than look across the room, anything rather than try to make sense of words that were baffling.

'I don't love you anymore,' he repeated, a little louder, each word clearly punctuated.

I dropped the headphones, my eyes sliding reluctantly across the room. It was the bulging holdalls bracketing his shiny shoes that I saw first. I stared at them so that I wouldn't have to look at his face and see the truth written in his eyes.

'I'm sorry.'

Sorry. Was that what it came down to – a reduction to that one damn, miserable, pathetic word?

I was still staring at his bags as if the answers were in them struggling to get out. Maybe they were. Maybe he'd packed up all the answers... I should rush over and release them.

But before I could move, he bent and slipped his fingers through the handles. Long, strong fingers that had worked their magic on me so many times. He was taking them away... his fingers, the bags full of dreams, hopes and promises. All of it. Leaving me.

It was only then that I looked up and met his blue eyes. Startlingly blue and intense. Coloured lens. I discovered this the first night he'd stayed over and taken them out, the real colour an unremarkable pale blue. It was a touch of vanity that had amused me. I'd thought it had shown his vulnerability and had found it endearing. Now, I wondered if they were as fake and unreal as his promise to love me forever.

'Here're your keys.' He held out the key ring I'd bought him. The one I'd had made for him. Our initials cut into stainless steel. M and T entwined together and designed to last forever. Like we were supposed to.

Two keys. One for the back door, one for the front. Lying together, as we'd done. Fitting neatly, as we had.

If he didn't have the keys, he couldn't come back. Couldn't slip in beside me in the quiet of the night the way he'd done recently when he'd been delayed by meetings at work. Slip in beside me, wrap an arm around my waist, deliberately disturbing me so that I'd turn in his arms and he'd make love to me when I was barely awake, knowing the buttons to press to make me moan.

Couldn't come back and surprise me in the middle of the day when he'd insist I needed to eat. He'd lure me away to a restaurant where we'd eat and drink and the remainder of the day would be lost in lust and love.

Couldn't arrive home unexpectedly, open the door of my office quietly and slip across the room to wrap his arms around me, making me shriek in fright and dissolve in laughter as he howled with glee having caught me out again.

I stared at the keys and wanted to tell him to hold on to them... in case he changed his mind... in case he remembered the words he'd whispered, the ones where he swore he loved me and couldn't live without me.

Instead, I held out my hand in an automatic response.

My chipped nails were a stark contrast to his perfectly manicured ones. Was that it? Had I let myself go? Too busy to be the perfect woman he'd met that first night... the successful, almost-famous girlfriend. Perhaps he'd finally realised that success... like fame... cost. My approaching deadline had meant longer hours recently, fewer expensive dinners out and weekends away. I'd explained and thought he'd understood. Perhaps he hadn't... or maybe he had and decided the cost wasn't worth his effort.

He dropped the keys into my outstretched hand, taking almost exaggerated care not to touch me as if afraid I'd grab him in a final desperate attempt to hold on. The entwined M and T were cold. I curled my fingers around them.

'I'm moving in with a friend. I've sent the address to your mobile so you can forward any post, okay?'

Okay? Did he expect me to say yes, that everything was hunky-dory? I suppose he expected me to say something though, not simply sit there staring at the keys, the metal cold and hard, like the weight in my chest.

I was a bestselling author. One of my books optioned for a movie, another for a TV series. Words... they were my forte. But for the life of me I couldn't find one appropriate thing to say bar the one word I refused to utter, the plaintive pathetic *why* I knew would release a dam of tears and recriminations.

Better to say nothing rather than that, to remain quiet rather than to beg him to reconsider and stay with me. Anyway, I could see by his set grim face that no words of mine no matter how suitable or erudite were going to change his mind.

The next few seconds were blank and numb. Only the pain from the keys and entwined-forever initials pressing into the soft flesh of my palm brought me back. The marks remained long after the echoes of his leaving had faded – the leather soles of his shoes slapping on the wooden hallway, the clunk of the front door as it shut behind him.

The words came then. A string of invectives and derogatory terms I usually reserved for the use of the worst of my fictional characters. The words echoed around the room and bounced off the walls, deafening and futile. I shouted until I was hoarse, then I released my clenched fist and threw the keys and the now-redundant key ring across the room. They crashed against the wall and slinked to the floor, landing beside the chunky glass paperweight I'd been given by my publisher the previous year.

What that was doing on the floor, I couldn't think. But then nothing was the way it was supposed to be.

Leaving the keys and paperweight on the floor, I put my headphones back in place, turned the music up so loud it drowned out everything and went back to my book, to my characters, to playing God in a world where I had control.

2

MISTY

It took me several hours to get back to my work after Toby cracked my world apart. Hours when I came up with the perfect words I could have said to him, words that would have sliced him and made him bleed. All too late, of course, the way those words frequently are.

The shade of my desk lamp was a green glow in the dark room, the light it threw over the keyboard a cold yellow. It would have made sense to get up and turn on the main light but I was afraid if I did, I'd not sit down again. And I needed to finish this book. It was due in by 8am and I'd hoped to have had it done hours before. Instead, it was almost 7.45 before I reached the last word, my eyes gritty with tiredness and the tears that had come after he'd left. Not before. I'd taken some pride in that.

Needles of pain pricking my right shoulder told me I'd been hunched over my keyboard for too long. I lifted my arm, rolled it and felt the muscles and tendons crunch. Today, along with all the other million and one things I'd been promising to do for the last few weeks, I might try to fit in a massage.

But first, I needed to send this manuscript to my publisher. It took a minute to frame a brief friendly email apologising for the very-last-minute delivery then, with the completed manuscript attached and after a few second's hesitation where, as with every book to date, I wondered if I'd done enough, if I should maybe change the last paragraph, the first paragraph, the characters, the whole damn thing because I knew *this* time the book was rubbish, I hit *send*. And that was it. My eighteenth novel was done.

With a weary sigh, I dropped my headphones and glasses on the desk, switched off the computer and lamp and struggled to my feet feeling stiff from too many hours in one position. Too tired to do anything else, I left the small bedroom I used as an office and went next door to the room that had euphemistically been described as the master en suite in the sales details. Reality was a room swamped by a king-size bed and an en suite that was too small to be anything other than adequate.

Built-in wardrobes covered one wall. I'd made space at one end for Toby's clothes, pushing mine to the far side. My clothes had become squashed, his taking up more space as the weeks had passed and he'd added to his extensive wardrobe on each of our frequent shopping trips. I'd considered buying a wardrobe for the spare bedroom but hadn't got around to it. Luckily. I tried to sneer but failed and pressed my lips together to stop the tremble that would make me feel even more pathetic.

Toby had left the wardrobe door hanging open, the empty hangers inside a testament to my newly single status. Single... again. A slam of the wardrobe door set the hangers rattling. I don't think I've ever heard a sound so lonely.

I was dressed in what I referred to as my writing garb... a loose, comfortable kaftan which didn't constrict as I hunched over the keyboard. I didn't bother to remove it and dropped onto the bed behind. It was exhaustion that was turning me maudlin, making everything feel worse than it was. After a few hours' sleep, I'd be saying 'Toby who?'

With that optimistic thought in my head, I shuffled up the bed and dragged the duvet around and over me. Covering my head with it, cocooning myself. Tears prickled when I remembered other nights when I'd slept wrapped in Toby's arms. *I don't like to let you go*, he'd said. And I'd thought how lucky I was to meet a man so honest, so loving.

Now it was the weight of the duvet rather than his arms that comforted me and, despite everything, I drifted off to sleep.

~

It was the shrill ring of the phone that woke me, the sound only slightly muffled by the duvet. It took a few seconds to untangle an arm to reach the phone, searching fingers pulling it off the stand and under the covers to my mouth. 'Hello.'

'You got it done?'

It was Ann, my older sister. I pushed the duvet off my face and pulled a pillow down to prop up my head. 'I did, with minutes to spare.'

'As long as it's gone. Welcome back to the land of the living.'

If it was the land of the living, why did I feel so dead inside? My head might have been hoping for *Toby who?* after a few hours' sleep but my heart was still crying for loss it didn't understand.

'Hello, earth to Misty!' Ann's laugh tinkled down the line.

'Sorry, I'm not quite awake yet.'

'Get yourself into a cold shower, that'll do it. It's almost twelve. Lunch at two? Ursula is free, too, so we can do a big catch-up.'

I never argued with my sisters. There was no point, they were unstoppable forces, I never won. Agreeing to meet at our usual lunchtime haunt, I hung up.

Ann and Ursula, my sisters, were my best friends. Married in their early twenties to decent, hardworking, kind men who still adored them, they lived only a short drive or a long walk from my home in Hanwell. They tethered me to the normality I craved when, before Toby, I'd buried myself in my writing, living a fantasy life populated by make-believe characters. I'd argued with my sisters that it was safer, that the real world could be viciously painful.

But then I'd met Toby.

I curled up, pulling the duvet over my head again. I hadn't really wanted to prove myself so spectacularly right. The real world was both vicious *and* painful.

'Toby Bloody Carter.' I almost spat the words out as I threw back the duvet and scrambled from the bed. It was good to have a reason to get dressed otherwise I'd have stayed in bed drowning in self-pity.

The frantic and always last-minute rush to get a manuscript completed by deadline was generally followed by a certain lassitude that would be harder to shake now that I was alone again. *Alone.* What a horrible word.

A minute later, I was under the shower, water as hot as I could stand it beating down from the large square shower head. *Built for two.* Toby's words were so clear, I switched off the shower to listen for him, shivering foolishly as water cooled on my skin and memories of our naked entwined bodies floated on the steam.

'It's a cliché,' I'd said to him the first time when he suggested joining me. 'Every second-rate romance story has the couple showering together whereas the reality can't possibly be romantic.'

He'd laughed and taken great pleasure in proving that cliché or not, sex in a shower with the right man was a magically unforgettable experience.

The right man.

I refused to cry but neither could I bring myself to sing a chorus of 'I'm *Gonna Wash That Man Right Outa My Hair*' as the water cascaded over me. The time would come when I'd accept I was better without him... but that time hadn't come yet.

My pixie-style haircut needed nothing more than a rub with a towel and a comb through to look good, but I spent time choosing what to wear. It didn't matter that Toby wouldn't see me; it was important to show the world what he was willing to throw away so carelessly. Black trousers, white silk camisole, black linen jacket. And, of course, sky-high stilettos, the ones I'd been careful not to wear for fear of towering over the five-foot-nine Toby and thereby denting his ego.

It was a good look. Classy, slightly edgy, the dangling chandelier earrings I'd bought in India the previous year adding an arty touch. I dabbed concealer on the shadows under my eyes. Nothing I could do could hide the sadness that tugged at my lips and I hoped my all-seeing sisters wouldn't notice.

I had a few minutes to spare before the taxi I'd ordered was due. Switching on my computer, I did what I'd been longing to do all morning. I pulled up Google Maps, checked the address Toby had sent me and typed it into the search. A street view showed me exactly what kind of salubrious address he'd moved to. Beaufort Gardens, Knightsbridge.

It took a moment for the tooting of a car horn to break through my seething and irrational envy.

When the taxi, double-parked on the narrow road outside, tooted a second time, I grabbed my oversized leather clutch bag and hurried out walking on the balls of my feet to prevent my stiletto heels catching in the cracks in the pavement.

I was always so damn careful so how did I get suckered in by Toby's lies?

3

MISTY

It was only a short ride to Tentelow Lane where the Three Bridges Restaurant overlooked a park of the same name. It was a favourite place to meet my sisters and normally I'd have dressed more casually and walked the mile or so in flat comfortable shoes enjoying the luxury of being outside, away from whatever I was working on. But that day, I needed the armour of fine clothes and heels.

Ann, my eldest sister, lived in Hounslow, and Ursula in West Ealing. About two miles away from the restaurant for both but they'd walk in flats, raise eyebrows when they saw my heels and shake their heads.

Then I'd tell them about Toby and they'd understand. They always did.

~

As usual, I was first to arrive. The waiter showed me to a table that overlooked the park and I sat with the first hint of pleasure in the day. It was the best time of year: the tall trees were in full leaf with lime-green leaves that shimmied in the slight breeze.

I ordered a bottle of Chenin Blanc without looking at the menu and it came almost immediately. The waiter left it sitting in the ice bucket as if assuming I'd wait for whoever was joining me at the table for three. *Silly man.* I reached for it, tossed the screwcap on the table, poured a glass almost to the brim and swiftly downed a couple of mouthfuls to reduce it to a more refined level.

The glass was almost empty before Ann came through the door, her mouth curving into a smile as she crossed to the table. 'I'm not late, am I?' She bent to give me a kiss on the cheek. 'Aren't you melting in that jacket?'

'I didn't walk here.'

'Even so. It's been the warmest July on record.' Ann sat on the chair opposite, picked up the menu and fanned her face. 'I walked, maybe I shouldn't have.' She was wearing a sleeveless cotton blouse, the smooth stretch of her upper arm marred by a telltale tan line. Ann was, at heart, a polo T-shirt and chinos type of woman.

She was also a woman of habit. I took the menu from her and wafted it back and forth gently. 'I bet you left home late then had to hurry to catch up.'

'You know me too well.' Ann reached for the wine bottle. If she was surprised to see how much I'd already had, she said nothing and poured a small measure for herself before holding the bottle towards me. 'More?'

'Sure.' I edged the glass closer to her, amused when she barely quarter filled it. Picking it up, I raised it towards her. 'Cheers.'

'To the success of your book!' Ann tipped her glass against mine, took a sip and put it down. 'So, are you taking a break before you start anything new?'

Maybe I was imagining things but the question seemed to have undertones. I was about to query it when my other sister arrived. Ursula was a year older than me and the wildest of the three of us. Certainly the most eccentric, describing her style as bohemian. She strolled across the restaurant in an off-the-shoulder blouse and matching floor-length skirt. Her mousy-brown hair was streaked with pink, and multiple bracelets on each arm created a noisy jangle as she waved wildly. Other diners raised their heads, then their eyes.

Ursula looked like she should be the artistic one but, in fact, she was an accountant. Her style, she insisted, was a survival mechanism to counteract what she referred to as her daily nine-to-five drudgery. In a cloud of floral perfume, she enveloped me in a hug before she flopped onto the third chair and reached for the wine bottle. Less reticent than Ann, her eyes widened at the little that remained and she darted a look at me. 'You're knocking it back a bit, aren't you?'

Although she was right, I was irritated at the assumption. They thought they knew me so well. 'It might have been Ann!'

Ursula laughed. 'I bet Miss Sippy is still on her first glass.'

Ann lifted her wine. 'You're right!'

'Fine, fine, yes, I've had a couple.' I picked up my half-full glass, emptied it in two long gulps, then waved the empty glass and smacked it down on the table so hard the cutlery rattled. 'Toby and me...' If I said it, it made it real didn't it, and I'd have to face up to it. 'We've split up.' I expected them to look shocked... stunned... to wail and gnash their teeth, to join with me in mourning my loss.

But it was I who was stunned when Ann raised a clenched fist and mouthed *yes!* and Ursula dramatically wiped her hand across her forehead with a loud *whew!*

'Oh, don't look so surprised, Misty.' Ann reached for her glass and this time took a large mouthful of wine as if in celebration. 'You've been a different person since you met him... and not in a good way.' She pointed her index finger at me and waved it up and down. 'That outfit, for instance, who are you trying to be?'

Ursula held the empty wine bottle up for the attention of a hovering waiter who took it and returned moments later with a replacement. It wasn't until their glasses were full that she spoke. 'Toby wasn't good for you.' She twirled a hand around in the air, sending bracelets jangling and ruffles flying. 'He was a fake, all hot air and waffle.'

I felt a lump in my throat and swallowed. I expected sympathy, for my sisters to join in with my tears of sorrow. Not this. They hadn't liked him. How had I never known?

'And there was that whole thing with his ex-girlfriend.' Ann screwed up her mouth. 'I still think you should have gone to the police about that, you could have been seriously hurt.'

'Definitely,' Ursula agreed.

But then she always did agree with whatever Ann said. My two older sisters were closer, linked not only by sisterly love but by their children, Ann's two and Ursula's three. It was a common denominator which excluded me despite my love for my nieces and nephews. Close as they were, I knew when I'd told Ann about what happened with Toby's ex-girlfriend that I was really telling both. They'd no secrets from one another – at one time that would have included me.

The whole *thing* with the ex-girlfriend – how unthreatening that sounded... *a thing*!

In fact, it had been a terrifying experience.

4

MISTY

It had happened two months before. Toby had been living with me for a month at that stage. He'd moved in a scant five weeks after we'd met at one of those cultural events I'd been invited to on the back of the success of my last book. Introverted by nature, crowded functions weren't my thing and only my publisher's declaration that they were important made me accept.

The venue was the function room of a restaurant in Shepherd's Bush. It was too small for the crowd who were no doubt attracted more by the free drinks and canapés than by the procession of worthy people making dull speeches. I had pasted on what I hoped passed for a suitably intelligent expression and posed for photographs with fellow authors, agents, editors, and people whose role I didn't know.

When the photographers had left, when the crowd divided into smaller groups, little cliques where everyone appeared to know everyone else, my store of small talk became quickly exhausted. I excused myself without difficulty, my words lost in the snappy back and forth of conversation between others in the circle, the gap I left closing as if I'd never been there.

I pushed through the overcrowded room towards the exit, skating around people, eyes down to avoid anyone I might know and be dragged back into yet more superficial chat. At the exit, another group had congregated, one man with a hand outstretched resting on the door frame blocking the way. 'Excuse me,' I said, raising my voice a little to be heard over the cacophony. When there was no reaction I tapped the man's shoulder to get his attention.

He did turn then, a question in vivid blue eyes, an appreciative smile curving his perfect mouth as he stared without moving. 'I think I'd probably excuse you anything.' He laughed and shook his head. 'Although you might never forgive that cheesy comment.'

'I've heard worse.' I hadn't but he didn't need to know that and anyway, I'd have forgiven him anything. I wasn't a believer in love at first sight, but lust, that was something else altogether. Any thought of my leaving the event vanished in that moment. Instead, I joined in with the band of people he was with, looking attentively at the man who was speaking without hearing a word, conscious only of the man at my side who stood so close I could feel the heat coming from him, could smell the musky masculine scent of his cologne.

There were three glamorous women in the circle. I wondered if one was his partner. But none were shooting wary *keep away from my man* looks in my direction, their attention on the older man who was holding court, a writer I'd heard of but had never read.

I was suddenly aware, as I'd not been before, that the black dress I was wearing was several years old. It was my go-to dress for every semi-formal occasion, close fitting and low cut with spaghetti straps baring enough flesh to be suitably fashionable. I'd put on a few pounds since I'd bought it, though, and had struggled to fasten the zipper when I'd slipped into it earlier. I resisted the temptation to look down to check my belly wasn't bulging and clenched my abdominal muscles instead, just in case. The following week, I promised myself, I'd get back to that exercise regime I'd started but abandoned after a few days.

The exit sign, neon bright, beckoned. A gap had opened near the doorway and feeling suddenly foolish I smiled at no one in particular, turned away, and edged around the man to make my escape into the reception lobby.

I handed my ticket to the bored-looking woman in charge of the makeshift cloakroom. She was chewing gum with bovine intensity and looked at the slip of paper as if she wasn't quite sure what to do with it. Then, without a word, she disappeared into the room behind and returned moments later with my coat.

It had been so hot inside that I greeted the chill outside with pleasure and left my coat draped over my arm. The heat had driven others from the venue. Small groups of people stood about chatting and laughing. A couple hiding in the shadows were kissing passionately. Two women, having obviously made the most of the free bar, were hanging from one another, giggling.

And I was standing alone, taking it all in, wondering how much of it I could use, my thoughts already drifting back to my fictional world.

There was a taxi rank across the street. I wasn't surprised to see a queue and prepared for a long wait. There was the underground, of course, but I was nervous about using it late at night. My attention was on the passing traffic as I waited for a gap to cross, so when I felt a hand touch my bare shoulder I squealed, twisted away, and turned with my mouth open ready to scream for help.

I shut it again with a snap when I saw the blue-eyed man from inside, an apologetic smile tilting his lips.

'I'm sorry,' he said. 'I didn't mean to startle you. You're not leaving already, are you?'

I was thirty-two... old enough and wise enough to know better... but neither age nor wisdom were sufficient to enable me to resist the mesmerising eyes that bored into mine with obvious appreciation, the width of his shoulders, the lock of hair that fell just so, the absolute total *gorgeousness* of him.

He jerked his thumb towards the door. 'It's a bit noisy and hot in there, isn't it? If you're done with all the publicity stuff, d'you fancy going somewhere quieter? We could get something to eat, if you like, those canapés didn't fill much of a gap.'

I'd stuttered out a *yes* almost before he'd finished asking, then laughed in embarrassment feeling unaccustomedly gauche.

Maybe my descent from successful professional to tongue-tied ingénue had amused him too, or maybe he'd found it endearing because instead of laughing he leaned in and kissed my cheek. It was the barest touch, but his lips had lingered, the warmth of his breath tickling the fine hairs at my hairline, erotically charging each one.

He cupped a hand around my bare elbow and suggested a nearby pub. 'It does good food and isn't usually too noisy.'

He was right on both counts. We found a quiet nook inside, ordered food and a bottle of wine and ate, drank, talked and laughed till closing time threw us out.

We were still chatting as he walked with me back to the taxi rank. Now, when I'd have been delighted with a queue a mile long, there was only one person. 'I won't be waiting long,' I said as if I were pleased, as if I hadn't wished for a hundred people to suddenly appear and barge ahead of me demanding taxis.

'Good,' he said. 'It's getting chilly.' He put an arm around my shoulder to draw me closer. 'I'd love to see you again.'

His warmth, the scent of him, was intoxicating. 'So would I...
see you, I mean.'

'How about dinner tomorrow?'

I pretended to consider it, then laughed. 'Dinner sounds
good.'

'I'll pick you up at seven, if that suits?'

Of course it suited and by the time a taxi rolled up alongside
we had it organised.

I sat into the taxi and smiled all the way home, my phone
with his precious number input by his long, slim fingers, clasped
in my hand. I remember I felt bewitched.

Dinner the following night in a French restaurant I'd never been
to before, was followed by dinner three nights later in an Italian
we both knew and liked. The days in between, he rang me two
or three times a day, and always last thing at night, whispering
goodnight before he rang off.

Our kisses became increasingly erotic. 'You're a witch,' he
said, shaking his head and putting me at arm's length. 'You've no
idea what you do to me!'

He made me feel powerful, feminine, sexy. And I loved it.

Two weeks later, I invited him back to mine for coffee. 'And
dessert.' I'd never been so daring, never taken the lead, but this
felt so right. He empowered me like no man had ever done.

In the following three weeks, there were nights of passion
that left me gasping, and days lost in dreams where I struggled
to write a word. And when I did, my criminals were suddenly
uttering words of love in situations where such words had no
context. I deleted with a chuckle and tried to concentrate on the
murder and mayhem that was required.

When I lay sated in his arms, the velvet darkness of night a warm blanket around our naked bodies, I knew it couldn't get any better than this. 'Why don't you move in with me?' The whispered words shimmered and floated away in the night. Unheard, I guessed, and I wondered if I should repeat them. Wondered if I'd lost my mind for asking.

It was several minutes later before I heard him say, 'Yes, I think that's a great idea.'

And that was it, five weeks after we met, Toby Carter moved in with me.

5

MISTY

I had thought it would take a while for Toby to organise moving in and assumed he'd need to give a month's notice to the landlord of the apartment he had in Streatham – so when I opened my front door the following day to find him standing there, two holdalls on the step beside him and a couple of boxes on the garden path behind, my delight was tinged with surprise. There was no sign of a car or taxi on the short street... it looked as if he'd simply materialised out of nowhere. The thought made me smile and fling my arms around his neck, dragging him inside, words of delight tripping from my lips. It didn't matter... nothing mattered except he was there with me. This amazing, loving, gorgeous man.

Toby wasn't the first man I had shared a home with, but he was the first in a long time, and the only man I'd invited to share the house in Hanwell I'd bought two years before. I anticipated having to make some compromises. My schedule was often manic, with twelve-hour days coming up to deadlines. I was aware, too, that my writing consumed me, that often the characters in my books felt real to me, their lives more interesting than mine, their world safer, better than the world I lived in.

But suddenly, with Toby in my life, everything seemed different. It was as if I was seeing my life through a kaleidoscope... everything... everyone... every word was shot through with colour.

If it was different to what I'd expected, if the reality of living with this gorgeous man was more difficult than I'd hoped and if there were more compromises than I'd planned to make... with more *give* on my part, more *take* on his... that was simply a matter of adjusting, wasn't it? *That's what I told myself. What I kept telling myself as the weeks passed.*

The 'thing with his ex-girlfriend' that Ann was referring to happened two weeks after Toby moved in. I was engrossed in my writing, headphones in place, classical music calming my brain and oiling the words that tripped off the ends of my fingers. Lost in what I was doing, it was several minutes before the sound of the front door being pounded wormed its way into the music... drum rolls out of place in a piece which should simply have been strings. I took off the headphones and listened. Maybe I'd been imagining it. But then it came again. Not the polite, if frustrated knock of a delivery person, but the loud hammering of someone desperate to gain my attention.

I frowned at my computer screen and typed two words before saving the document and pushing my chair back, the wheels rolling noisily on the wooden floor.

The hammering came again... longer and louder... I swore softly and hurried down the stairs, taking the last few steps in a leap while shouting, 'I'm coming, hold your horses!'

Twisting the doorknob, I pulled the door open, ready to give whoever was there a piece of my mind. I was completely unprepared for the open-handed blow to my face that stunned me and sent me stumbling backward into the hallway, my arms windmilling as I tried to keep my balance.

'You bitch!' A wild-eyed woman stood in the doorway. Slightly smaller than me but bulkier with long hair loose around her shoulders and brown eyes narrowed in hatred.

My first thought was that I was the victim of a misunderstanding, my second that some reader really hated my books. I lifted a hand to my face, feeling the stinging heat of the slap. 'I think you must have confused me with someone else.'

The woman curled a lip and clenched her hands into fists. She kicked the front door shut, then took a step closer to me.

I was waiting for the adrenaline rush I'd read about... that I'd written about... the one that gave you the strength to fight or the speed to run. I must have been the exception to the rule because shock had frozen me into immobility.

'Misty Eastwood, semi-successful writer of rubbish novels. That's you, isn't it?'

I bridled at the *semi-successful* and lifted my chin at the *rubbish novels*. Attacking me was one thing, casting aspersions on my skill and my books was something else. I wasn't a physical person, words were my usual ammunition, but before I'd time to think of something suitable to diffuse the situation a clenched fist shot out and hit me on the other side of my face.

The pain was excruciating, the strength of the blow sufficient to send me tottering back against the wall where I lost my footing and slid to the floor.

It took this blow, this terror, to send the adrenaline sizzling through me. I had to get away but my head was still ringing from the punch, making it hard to focus. The living room was a few feet away. If I could get inside, I could lock myself in and phone for help.

My attacker's mouth was wide as she screeched foul words. When her eyes squeezed shut in anger, I rolled onto my knees and scrabbled for the door but the adrenaline rush wasn't enough to counter the steaming anger that was driving the strange woman. A kick to my side made me gasp. Instinctively I curled into a ball as the kicks and blows came relentlessly, each accompanied by grunted accusations I couldn't understand.

Would the attack have continued until I was unconscious, maybe even dead? I'd never know because the woman stopped her assault when the front door opened.

'Toby!' I shouted, fearful for him, for what this crazed woman would do. I uncurled, ready to leap to his defence, staggered anew to see the woman melt into his arms, a look of pure confusion on his face.

'Babs, what...' He pushed her away and looked down at me in horror. 'Shit, Babs, what have you done?'

Babs? I groaned and scrambled to my feet, wincing in pain. Toby hovered, trying to help. I took his arm. 'Help me inside to a seat.'

'Maybe I should ring for an ambulance,' he said as I struggled into the living room and lowered myself onto the sofa.

Shock was wearing off quickly, anger riding in to take over. 'Maybe you should ring for the police.' I flexed my arms, moved my legs, took a few deep breaths. Nothing broken. Not for want of trying. I guessed the soft shoes my attacker was wearing had prevented more damage. I'd have multiple bruises but nothing worse. The woman stood in the doorway, eyes only for Toby. I held his hand and glared at her. 'Who are you?'

But it was Toby who answered. 'My ex-girlfriend.'

His ex-girlfriend? Still lost in the honeymoon phase of our relationship, we'd not spoken about past loves. I shifted in my seat, grimacing when the tassel of a pillow dug into my bruised ribs.

Toby, on his knees beside me, shifted backwards and got to his feet. 'I'll go and get a cold compress.'

I wasn't keen on being left alone with the crazy Babs but a cold compress might help with the swelling I could feel rising on my cheek. I held a hand to it while keeping my eyes on her. 'It wasn't an amicable split then, I'm guessing.'

'Four years.' The words were barely a whisper.

I stared. *Four years!* I couldn't imagine losing Toby after a few weeks... How would I feel after four years? 'That was a long time. But it's not my fault, is it? You can't go around attacking people because your relationship fell apart.'

Babs shot me a pitying look. 'Four years. They ended two weeks ago. On the 1st of May at 4.15pm when he walked out, taking all his belongings with him.'

6

MISTY

I wanted to laugh off the woman's words because it couldn't be true... could it? This wonderful man I'd fallen in love with couldn't have moved in with me straight from another woman's home... another woman's bed. Had he been sleeping with the two of us at the same time? I turned my head to look at him as he came back, the wet towel in his hand dripping splodges of water onto the wooden floor where they would mark it and remind me of this moment forever. 'You came to me straight from her?'

Toby looked from me to Babs and back again, his free hand creeping to his face and running down it as if to wash the guilt away. 'I can explain.'

My head was reeling. The physical attack had been bad enough but this onslaught of emotions was threatening to overwhelm me. Maybe he could explain, but I didn't want to hear it then. I didn't want to call the police either although I certainly had cause. *But four years!*

Babs was still standing there, staring at Toby with the adoring eyes of a whipped puppy. What kind of a name was *Babs* anyway... a nickname, a lover's name.

I reached a hand for the towel and pressed the cold wet cloth to my face, hiding from the sight of both of them. 'Get her out of here.' From the safety of the darkness, I heard their footsteps recede, his heavy ones, hers a mere whisper, voices raised in the hallway, angry words fading as they moved away; on the doorstep, on the garden path, the pavement outside, then disappearing into the distance.

I lay back against a cushion, lifted my feet onto the sofa and stretched out. Every movement hurt. My cheek was the worst. I opened my jaw wide and felt the swelling. In the morning, it would be multicoloured proof of the vicious attack.

Four years.

I tried to remember what Toby had said about where he'd lived. He hadn't lied to me. Not exactly. He'd said he lived in an apartment in Streatham. He never said he lived alone. *Never said he was living with his girlfriend of four years either.*

Too agitated to sit still, I slid my feet carefully to the ground and stood. Time to have a look at the damage. In the hall mirror, I took stock, my fingers gently palpating my cheekbone. It was swollen, shiny, already starting to colour. I was going to look a mess. Luckily, we had nothing planned. It would be dinner at home for the next week or so, none of the nights out in cocktail bars and restaurants that Toby preferred.

Back in the living room, I picked up the towel and frowned at the wet patch it had made on the cotton material of the sofa. I hoped it would dry out without leaving a watermark. Hoped everything would revert to normal... that I could turn the page, write a new chapter.

Where was Toby? He should be here looking after me. I took the towel into the kitchen, lay it on the counter, and searched in the freezer for the ice cube tray. With several ice cubes knocked into the middle of it, I folded the ends of the towel over and held the makeshift cold pack against my cheek.

Feeling beaten, mentally and physically, I went back and slumped on the sofa again, my head against the cushion. The room was west facing. It was May and the temperature had been unusually high for the last few days. The setting sun captured the gaps between houses on the opposite side of the street and the heated beams of light melted the ice before it could do any good. Cold water oozing through the towel ran down my neck and soaked into the cushion.

Shock is exhausting. The post-adrenaline dip weighed me down and shut my eyes.

'Hey.'

The softly spoken word woke me; my eyes flicked open and looked straight into Toby's intense blue ones. I was clutching the towel to my chest, the wet had soaked through my T-shirt and the chill of it made me shiver. The chill of it, not the sudden frightening thought that I didn't know this man at all.

A finger gently touched my cheek. 'I'm so sorry.'

'You should have told me.' I pushed his hand away, dropped the wet towel on the floor and sat up. 'You left her for me?'

Toby shoved his hands into his jacket pockets. 'It isn't as simple as that. Babs is...' He walked to the window, fiddled with the catch, and pushed it open wide. 'It's this damn heat,' he muttered.

'Sounds like a line from a Tennessee Williams play. *Cat on a Hot Tin Roof*, maybe.'

Toby turned to look at me. 'What?'

'Nothing, I was...' I shook my head and bent to pick up the wet towel. It was still cold; I wiped it across my face. 'Babs is what?'

He came over and sat, close enough to touch me. I thought he might, that he'd caress my arm or leg with his long fingers. I shivered at the thought... at the betraying thought that I wanted him to... despite everything... despite Babs... I wanted him to touch me.

'I should have told you, but what we have is so precious, so special, I didn't want to ruin it.' Toby ran his fingers through his hair. His perfectly cut hair fell instantly back into place, a lock falling to kiss the edge of one eyebrow. 'Babs is emotionally fragile. I didn't realise it for a long time and by then I was living with her in her apartment. I loved her... or I thought I did. Over the months it became increasingly exhausting to have to keep bolstering her ego, constantly having to tell her she was the most important, beautiful, intelligent woman I'd ever met.'

He reached out to grasp my hand, sandwiching it between both of his. 'Almost three months ago, I told her it was over. She went ballistic. You've seen the way she gets.'

I looked at him in horror. 'She hit you?'

He looked down, embarrassed. 'She attacked me with an empty wine bottle. Luckily, I was able to get it from her before she did too much damage.' He put a hand up and brushed a finger across his cheek. 'She only caught me a glancing blow. The bruise faded in a few days.' He covered my hand again. 'She was so hysterical that I was worried. So, reluctantly, I gave in and said I'd stay, but it was never the same and we both knew it was only a matter of time.'

I remembered the anger that had driven Babs, the hate that twisted her face. 'You might have known, but I don't think she was that aware. She seemed like a woman who'd been completely caught off-guard.'

'She's good at that. At making you feel you're in the wrong. It's an art she's cultivated and she does it so well.'

I looked at the sensitive fingers that were caressing my hand. Fingers that the previous night were caressing more intimate parts of me. I had to know. 'Were you still sleeping with her?'

His eyes widened. 'Wow, no! How could you think such a

thing! I swear, I hadn't slept with her for a couple of months before I left. That's why I thought she knew it was over. I even suggested that I pay her rent, for goodness' sake. As far as I was concerned, we were flatmates.'

I lifted my free arm to show the dark splodges that already coloured my fair skin. 'Flatmates don't generally beat up the new girlfriend.'

Toby reached for my arm, leaned closer and planted kisses on each mark. 'I'm so sorry,' he said, sitting back. 'I gave her your address so she could forward any post. It never entered my head that she'd come here and make trouble.'

Make trouble seemed a gross dismissal of what I had been through. I opened my mouth to say that it was more serious than that but stopped at the stricken look on his face. It wasn't his fault. Not really. Or not all of it anyway. 'You should have told me about her, Toby. Mentioned that your last girlfriend was unstable. You certainly should have told me you were living with her before you came here.' I tried to pull my hand away but he tightened his grip. 'I don't like the feeling of being the *other* woman.'

'You're not the *other* woman. You're the *only* woman. I love you.'

I wrote stories, used words every day... I knew how empty they could be. 'How can I believe you?'

He pulled me closer, ignoring my wince of pain. 'I swear to you. She means nothing to me. I felt sorry for her and stayed with her out of some desire to be a decent guy.' He pressed his lips to my cheek then, ever so gently, brushed them down to that angle of my neck where every nerve in my body seemed to wait for his touch to explode in a dizzying mix of sensations.

And in that second, I didn't care if I believed him or not.

7

MISTY

I looked out the window of the Three Bridges restaurant ignoring the exchange of worried glances between my sisters. Getting beaten up by Toby's crazed ex-girlfriend had been a terrifying experience but it hadn't left me feeling as defeated as I did now that he'd left me.

'Did he go back to her?' Ursula reached across and laid a hand on mine. 'Is that it?'

Would it have been better if that had been the case? If he'd suddenly decided he couldn't live without the unstable Babs. It might have been better than the truth that was becoming glaringly obvious. 'No, he didn't go back to her. I think he's moved in with someone else.' I could feel the corrosive bite of bitterness. Was this how Babs had felt? Perhaps my next step was to go around and launch an attack on this unknown, unnamed woman.

Nice though my home is, I was under no illusions. The salubrious-looking apartment Toby had moved to in Beaufort Gardens was a huge leap upward. His designer suits would fit right in with the Knightsbridge clientele. He'd enjoy fine dining in the local restaurants, drink cocktails and expensive wines in the chic bars. And he'd never put his hand in his pocket for any of it. Reality. It was a cold awakening.

I wasn't sure how it had happened... how it had changed from his insistence on paying for everything the first few times we'd gone out, to my paying every time since. I had a vague memory of laughingly demanding to pay one night and his reluctance to let me, then I wanted to pay to celebrate my last book hitting the number one spot, then to celebrate signing a new contract... and suddenly it was every time. I hadn't minded, it was the twenty-first century after all and I earned more as a writer than he did as a marketing executive. No, I'd not minded... and it was only in retrospect that I realised how much money I'd spent on him. He encouraged me to buy new clothes – smarter, more chic, sexier – and every time we went shopping, it seemed natural for him to buy clothes, too, and instinctive for me to pay.

I felt Ursula's hand tighten its grip and I looked up with a smile. 'I'll be fine. It was a bit of a shock, I thought...' *What had I thought? That this was it. Happy ever after.* I gulped a mouthful of wine. 'I thought we were perfect together.' *We were. My money, his style. A perfect combination.*

Ann tutted with motherly concern. 'He seemed perfect and was gorgeous to look at but he was like a china doll sitting on a shelf waiting to be admired. They're not meant to be played with or to have fun with.'

I had to smile. There was no point at all in telling her that Toby had been great fun to play with... the sex had been mind-blowing... I knew that wasn't what she meant. Ann was talking about the more ordinary things: the long walks hand in hand, the nights in by the fire watching TV, cooking together, planning a future together. Things Toby and I had never done. But, despite everything, I still hurried to defend him. 'You didn't know him really. After all, you only met him once.'

'And whose fault was that?'

I felt the quick heat of colour on my cheeks. I hadn't realised my sisters had disliked Toby but I knew how he'd felt about them. *Fuddy-duddy, middle-class bores* was how he'd rated them after dinner in Ursula's house a few weeks into our relationship, both sisters desperate to meet the man who'd put a smile on my face.

As a result of his dislike, he refused to go to Ann's husband's fiftieth birthday party at their house the following month. I'd gone without him, making a vague excuse that he was feeling unwell that I knew wasn't believed but wasn't questioned. I could have stayed away, too, and made another excuse. But these were my sisters, I loved them and wasn't going to miss an event that was so important to them.

Ursula, the middle-child peacemaker, jumped into the uneasy silence that followed Ann's remark with a change of conversation. 'Now you can go back to writing romances.'

I dragged my eyes from Ann's critical ones and looked at Ursula with a confused frown. 'What?'

'Romances.'

Repeating one word from a sentence that didn't make sense in its entirety was a foible of my sister's that never ceased to irritate me. 'Romances what?'

Ursula waved a hand – *jingle jangle*. 'Go back to writing them. I much preferred them to these psychological thrillers. All these twisted individuals, stalkers, and creepy characters. I swear you're different since you started writing them.'

I tried to laugh but it came out wrong, sounding forced and fake. 'Honestly, you two. Ann thinks I've changed because of Toby, you think because of the books I write! Maybe I'm simply older and wiser.' I brushed a hand down the front of my Armani linen jacket. Did it smack of desperation? Was I – that awful condemning phrase – *trying too hard*?

'Anyway, Toby is out of my life now. And no, Urs, I'm not going back to writing romances. I make a much better living from my twisted tales.' I reached for the menu. 'Maybe we'd better order before we drink any more?' Before I drank any more... before alcohol, irritation with them, my situation and the realisation of my utter stupidity, made me say something I'd regret.

After we'd made our choice from the extensive menu and placed our order, I directed the conversation to safer channels by asking Ann about her youngest child, Teddy, who was having a tough time at school. The chat flowed organically to her other child and from there to Ursula's three and when it flagged, when there was the slightest danger that it would twist back to me, I asked another leading question.

Their children, their husbands, their perfect lives. There was always something to ask.

8

MISTY

Back home, I changed into one of the many kaftans I had bought over the years. It was time to start my next book. I sat at my desk, opened a new page on an A4 pad and sat it on the desk to the right of my computer. On the pad I'd keep a rolling total of my word count every day. It kept me focused which was necessary for the tight deadlines I worked under. It was the end of July. My next deadline was the end of October. I should have finished the last one and started this one days before. But life... for that, read 'Toby'... had got in the way.

It was time to get back into the rhythm of writing, the three or four thousand daily word count I was used to doing, sometimes staying up till after midnight because I couldn't abandon my characters mid-catastrophe.

Sufficient alcohol imbibed over lunch had loosened my thoughts but didn't affect the speed at which my fingers flew over the computer keyboard. Headphones in place, relaxing music kept external distractions to a minimum. But it wasn't the car noises, shouts and laughter from people passing outside that disturbed me that afternoon. It was Toby who forced himself into my head, appearing before my eyes until I blinked him away. Even my fingertips were complicit, my eyes widening when I saw his name appearing on the screen.

Delete.

If it were only that easy to wipe the memories.

All of the memories, the good and the bad.

When I'd written Toby's name instead of Peter for the third time, I crashed my hands on the keyboard and sent a stream of random letters shooting across the screen. I left them there, saved my work and shut down. My hair caught in the headphones as I tugged them off roughly. It was the pain that made my eyes water.

Before I stood, I reached for a pen and filled in my word count for that day. A miserably low six hundred. I had a fairly good idea, too, that what I'd written was rubbish and would probably need to be deleted in the morning.

It was almost midnight. The house was quiet. No sounds drifting from the street outside. Bunching the hem of the kaftan in my hand, I went downstairs. The stairway was uncarpeted, the wood rough under my bare feet. Scandinavian style, I'd explained to Toby who'd asked why I'd not carpeted it.

I'd thought the cream track painted down the centre of the stairway was chic and classy, but he'd turned up his nose and suggested carpet would look better and give the house a more luxurious feel. Toby never seemed to be happy with the way things were. Maybe if I'd agreed to get a carpet... I stopped that thought before I completed it.

In the kitchen, I opened the fridge and took out a bottle of wine. Then with a sigh, put it back. Getting drunk was too easy an option and I'd never been one for taking the easy way out. I shook the kettle. Enough water sloshed against the sides for a cup of tea. With a flick of my thumb, I turned it on, then twisted around with an ear cocked. Without looking I snaked my hand out to switch off the kettle and listened again.

Seconds ticked by. A chill from the floor tiles crept over my feet and I shivered in the thin fabric of the kaftan. The house was silent. I'd imagined the sound.

Tea seemed suddenly too much trouble. I turned out the lights and went back upstairs.

Toby was gone but I could still smell him in the bedroom. His scent. It was there. Lingering in the air, in the fabric of the chairs, the mattress, the summer-weight duvet, the wallpaper, the bedroom carpet. *Every-bloody-where.*

There were fresh sheets on the bed. The pillows, piled one on top of the other, seemed to be taunting me. *Sleeping alone again, Misty.*

With a groan, I pulled off my kaftan, threw it onto the chair and, naked, moved to the window. The room was in darkness. The curtains open, the bottom of the sash window pulled up far enough to allow the cooler night air to slip into the room and over my skin. I shivered but didn't move away or shut the window.

The road outside was quiet. It was a residential road of mostly older and retired people, all of whom would be tucked into bed at this hour. The sash window rattled as I pushed it up as far as it would go. I bent to rest my elbows on the ledge and leaned out, craning my neck to look up at the sky. There was too much light pollution for stargazing but the moon was there, full and fat and looking down on me. He looked amused or was that a sneer on his faraway face.

It was the slightest of movements that dragged my eyes from the man in the moon to a figure on the other side of the street. Partially hidden in the shadows, it was a tilt of the head that had caught my attention as if the person were trying, with a stretch of the neck, to get a better look at me.

I pulled inside, flattened against the wall and pulled the curtain around me, suddenly conscious of my nakedness. Myrtle

Road wasn't a shortcut to anywhere, wasn't a road to attract a late-night footfall. There was no reason for anyone to stand there... and none to be standing there staring up at my bedroom.

I took a steadying breath, kept the curtain wrapped about me and peered around the edge of the window. The figure was gone. Pulling the drapes with me, I moved to look up the road. Apart from the bumper-to-bumper cars, there was nothing to be seen.

I reached for the other curtain, stepped back and pulled the two together, overlapping their edges, cutting out all the light from outside. The darkness held no comfort. There were no arms waiting in the bed to wrap around me and offer solace, no lips to whisper reassurances. No words to fill the emptiness.

And outside. Had I imagined the figure?

I didn't think so, there'd been something vaguely familiar about it.

Then it came to me... it was the woman who'd attacked me.

Babs.

Was she looking for Toby?

Perhaps I should go out, run after her, naked apart from my tears and tell her he'd moved on, tell her that they had, at last, something in common.

9

MISTY

Sleep came tantalisingly close but bounced away each time, my eyes flying open at every real or imaginary creak as my old house settled for the night. Daylight brought its own set of sounds, the pigeons landing noisily in the gutter outside the window, the early risers starting their car engines, leaving them to idle and pump out noxious gases as the drivers faffed with rear-view mirrors and seat belts.

By that stage, I'd given up any attempt to sleep and lay with my arm resting over my eyes listening to the sound of the world waking. Normality. My new normal.

I thought about the figure I'd seen outside in the early morning darkness. Had I imagined it... was it a figment conjured by the guilt I'd never really acknowledged, the real reason I'd not wanted to call the police following Babs' vicious assault. I'd seen the way she'd looked at Toby, the love in her eyes, the disbelief that made her clenched lips quiver, the beseeching hand she'd stretched towards him.

I'd listened to Toby's explanation – his insistence that it had been over with Babs months before and his argument that he'd done right by her. Thinking back, I couldn't remember if I'd truly believed him or not, because I hadn't really cared. All I knew was that he'd chosen me. That was what I'd deemed important. I'd been consumed by him and nothing else, nobody else mattered.

Was that what the unknown woman in Knightsbridge was thinking now? Perhaps she didn't even know about my existence. Toby, after all, had a history of keeping his previous life in the dark. He'd said he intended to tell me about Babs but would he have done if she hadn't arrived with her fists swinging that day.

I threw the duvet back and got out of bed. It was foolishly pathetic to be wasting time thinking about Toby. We'd only been together three months. A blink of an eye. Not four years.

If it had been Babs outside, she'd soon realise Toby had moved on and would leave me alone.

I picked up the kaftan I'd discarded hours before, slipped it over my head and crossed the landing to my office. The curtains were shut. I pulled them back, put the heel of my hand against the top of the lower sash window and shoved it up. It went too far – flies would come in, buzz around and drive me crazy. I lowered it until I had the optimum half-inch gap that would allow air in and deter bug intrusion. Only then did I head downstairs for the first coffee of the several I'd drink through the day.

I drank the first one in the kitchen, resting my head in my hands between sips. The mug was half empty when I heard the doorbell peal and I lifted my head with little enthusiasm. At that time of the morning, it was likely to be the post; I wasn't expecting anything but my publisher often sent gifts, as did my agent. Usually alcohol... or chocolate. They knew me too well.

It was tempting to ignore it and wait for the card slipped through my letter box to say I'd missed a delivery. But that would entail getting dressed and a journey to the post office where parking was often a nightmare. The bell pealing again made my mind up and I pushed to my feet.

The bell sounded again before I reached the door. More insistent as if someone was determined to get a response. 'Hang on,' I called as I slipped off the safety chain, thumbed down the catch and twisted the doorknob. I pulled the door open, expecting to find the usual postwoman on my doorstep, a smile of thanks waiting, a hand half-extended for whatever it was she'd not been able to fit through the letter box.

It took a few seconds to realise I was wrong, time to take in the elegantly dressed woman on the doorstep and to regret my own creased kaftan and uncombed hair. I shut the door over slightly in a vague attempt to hide my unkempt state. 'Yes?'

Unexpectedly, the woman stepped back and looked up at the house, a frown creasing her brow. 'What's going on? I don't understand...' She brought her gaze back to me and took a step forward. 'Who are you?'

'I'm the owner of the door you've been pounding on.' I wasn't in the mood for entertaining some lost female. 'You've obviously got the wrong address, so if you'll excuse me.' I stepped back, my hand on the door pushing it shut.

'No, wait.' The woman put her hand out to stop me. 'I'm looking for Toby Carter. Do you know him? Is he here?'

I stared, then I couldn't help it, I laughed. The Knightsbridge woman, it had to be. 'He's left you already! That didn't last long.' I pushed the corners of my mouth down and made a big deal about letting my eyes drift from the expensive hair to the slim stiletto shoes. 'If you think he's come running back to me, you're wrong. I wouldn't take him back.' *I would have done, oh I would have done without hesitation, without question.* The thought that I would be so foolish sent anger shooting through me and I clenched my hand on the door.

41

'He's not here?' The woman's expression morphed from aggressively demanding to pathetic desolation.

'No.' I looked at her face more closely. She was an attractive woman but older than me. 'It looks like he's moved on quickly this time. Has to be a record. Two nights.'

'No, you don't understand, he never arrived.' The woman held a hand over her mouth, red manicured nails glaringly stark against her porcelain skin.

I wanted to shut the door, wanted to close the woman and her pathetic, desolate face from my view. Pathetic and desolate, wasn't that exactly how I'd felt? With a sudden dart of understanding, I opened the door wider. 'You'd better come in.'

The woman passed in a whiff of perfume I didn't recognise but guessed it was expensive like everything else about her. I waved a hand towards the kitchen door and waited till she walked forward, her red-soled shoes click-clicking on the wooden floor.

I shut the front door, sorry I'd not followed my first instinct to ignore the doorbell. With a loud sigh I ran fingers through my hair and followed her.

She was standing in the kitchen, staring out the window, or maybe she was admiring her reflection. When I coughed to draw her attention, she turned. 'He's really not here?'

'I wouldn't take him back, believe me.' My voice was firm, my heart chuckling at the lie.

'But he did leave?'

Too little sleep, not yet enough coffee, my brain was mush. I pulled out a chair and sat. 'Yes, he left. Night before last.'

The woman turned then. She folded her arms across her chest, hands gripping the opposite upper arms, long nails digging in. It looked painful.

'That was when he said he was going to come to me but he never turned up.'

I frowned, trying to make sense of what she was saying. 'Listen, I need some more coffee. I haven't slept well. You want a cup?'

'Yes. That would be good, thank you.'

Elegant, beautiful and so damn polite. I got to my feet, boiled the kettle and made a pot of coffee. 'Sit,' I said, putting two mugs on the table. The jug of milk in the fridge had solidified, I emptied it into the sink. *Glug glug.* The nose-crinkling smell of sour milk wafted until I turned the water on to rinse it away. It was the only jug I had, I hadn't the energy to wash it, the Tetra Pak of milk would have to suffice.

The woman stood until the coffee was poured, then pulled a chair out and sat.

'What's your name?' She'd probably always be Ms Knightsbridge in my head but it was better to know who I was dealing with. The name of the woman who had stolen Toby away... who was better than me... sexier, richer. *Richer*, that was the key, that's what would have counted the most with him.

'Gwen... Gwen Marsham.'

'Well, Gwen Marsham. If Toby isn't with you, and he's definitely not with me, then where is he?'

10

MISTY

I watched dispassionately as Gwen's grey eyes filled with tears. What right had she to cry for his loss? She couldn't have known him long after all... could she? *Could she?* It was better to know. 'How long did you know him?'

Gwen's fingers were wrapped around the mug. She lifted it to her lips but put it down without drinking, staring into it. 'Two weeks.' She looked up then. 'You probably think I'm crazy asking him to move in with me after such a short time. To be honest, I thought I was myself, but...' Her sigh seemed to deflate her. 'I've never met anyone like him. I've never laughed so much or felt so carefree. He made me feel so special and the sex... well, it was incredible.' A smile quivered. 'Sorry, you probably don't want to hear that.'

I stared at her, my hands curling into fists. Was this the same emotion that had surged through Babs and driven her frenzied attack on me? I shook my head trying to dislodge the image of Toby naked with this woman... a full colour image with a surround sound of moans and his whispered words of love. My voice cracked as I said, 'Don't want to hear that my boyfriend was sleeping with another woman at the same time he was sleeping with me... seriously, would any woman want to hear that?'

Gwen had lifted the mug to her lips again but my reply seemed to startle her. She jerked, sloshing coffee in an arc of liquid that hit her chest. It stained the front of the cream shirt she wore, drops peppering the lapels of the beige jacket I'd not invited her to remove.

Putting the mug down, she jumped to her feet and stared at the mess then, helplessly, looked at me as if expecting me to do something.

I wanted to throw her out but I wasn't Babs; my anger was already fading. I stood, grabbed a roll of paper towel, tore reams off it and handed the wad over.

Gwen dabbed the spillage and took my second offering, dropping the first onto the table, pressing the fresh paper over her breasts. 'It's all ruined,' she said and dropped onto the chair. She pulled the wet silk away from her skin and flapped it uselessly. 'I'm so sorry. Toby told me he was living with his sister.'

I barked a laugh. 'His *sister*?'

'Yes. He said you were going through a bad time, that you were emotionally very fragile which is why he couldn't stay over with me any night. He'd come to my apartment, we'd make love, then after, we'd go for an early dinner before he had to go home to you.'

I had been so tied up with finishing my latest book, I remembered being relieved when Toby was late home, often not noticing. When I did, when I mentioned it, he spoke of meetings and overtime but I'd listened to his excuses without hearing them at all, my brain busy with people who didn't exist and what they were up to. I explained to him that it was always that way coming up to my deadline and that afterwards it would be better. I never for a moment suspected that he was lying. Never considered that there wouldn't be an *afterwards*. How naive I'd been.

Gwen was obviously trying to come to terms with the story she'd been told, her eyes wide, lips pressed in a tight line. 'He lied to me.' She bent her head to examine the stain on her shirt, plucking the damp material between her fingers again and shaking it back and forward in a vain and useless attempt to dry it.

I wondered about the story Toby had told me about his relationship with Babs, that it had been over a long time before he'd met me, that he'd not slept with her for months... had that, too, been a lie? Had I been as gullible as the woman who sat opposite looking as if the bottom had fallen out of her world. 'Where did you meet him?'

Gwen gave her stained shirt a final flap before taking her hand away. 'I have an art gallery on Knightsbridge high street. He came in to enquire about a painting that was on display in the window.'

It was so unexpected it dragged a reluctant laugh from me. 'Seriously?' I held my hand up. 'Don't tell me... he talked about buying it but decided it was too big, too small, too something or other.'

'Too big.'

'And you didn't persuade him to buy something else?'

Gwen reached for what was left of her coffee and took a sip. 'He came in a few minutes before we shut for lunch so he suggested I join him for something to eat so we could talk about it.'

'Very smooth.' I imagined Toby's smile, that way he had of tossing his head to send his fringe flying back, dragging your eyes to it as it fell so perfectly into place, the smile in his blue eyes, the curve of his lips. I swallowed the memories with a gulp and concentrated on the woman opposite. 'I bet he took you to an expensive restaurant and insisted on paying.'

'Yes. An Italian near the gallery.'

I saw the glimmer of a smile that flitted across her face at the memory, it made my voice harsh and cruel. 'And the dinners the following nights. Did he pay for them?'

Colour washed over Gwen's pale cheeks.

With quick sympathy, I reached a hand across the table towards her. 'I'm sorry. Don't answer that, I know how he works. He insisted on paying *again* with enough emphasis that you bridled a little and demanded that he let you pay and he gave in with extreme reluctance.'

'Almost exactly like that,' Gwen agreed. 'Then the next night, he said he didn't want to offend me by offering to pay, so I paid again.' She tilted her head. 'So how long were you two together?'

'Almost three months.' I picked up the cafetière and filled our mugs. 'Before me he was in a relationship for four years though.' I gave Gwen a brief description of Babs' visit and attack. 'He told me their relationship had come to an end months before and he was sleeping in her spare room. Like a lodger, he said. And I, like a fool, believed him.'

'Four years was a long time. Maybe he was lying about that. You know, making it out that he could commit and wasn't flitting from one woman to another.'

I smiled. 'It does seem a long time for someone with his track record but it was Babs who told me how long they'd been together, not him.'

'Babs... is that a nickname?'

'I don't know, it might be short for Barbara, I suppose. It suits her, she's plump and round-faced.' I picked up my coffee and sipped. 'Maybe that's where Toby's gone. Back to her.' I put the mug down and rested my arms on the table. 'I thought I saw her last night... outside on the road.'

'Really? Are you sure?' Gwen pressed her fingers to her eyes for a moment. 'Why would she be there? Anyway, I don't understand... if he'd planned to go back to her, why would he say he was coming to me? Why would he be that cruel?'

Anger flared again and tightened my voice. 'I don't know. I don't know anything. Up to two nights ago, I thought we were perfect. There was no warning. No nothing. I was trying to get my book finished. He came in, said he didn't love me anymore and left. Just like that.'

'And he went back to Babs.' Gwen's lips pressed into a tight line. 'Maybe that's why she was outside last night, she came to warn you off. You know... Toby's back with me, leave him alone.'

I hadn't given much thought as to why Babs had been there and it was as good a reason as any. 'If so, she must have chickened out because she never came to the door. It's a pity she didn't, I'd have told her that he'd already been cheating on me with another woman... slithering in and out of your bed.'

'She probably doesn't know about me.' Gwen shivered. 'By the sound of her, I'd prefer if it stayed that way. I'm not good at dealing with violent people, I've not had much experience really.'

Annoyed, I pushed my mug away and stood. 'It's not precisely the kind of thing I'm used to either.' Nor was I used to dealing with people quite as precious as Ms Knightsbridge. 'It appears we're both well shot of Toby. Babs is welcome to him. Now, I must get on. Deadlines to meet, you understand.'

As a hint, it wasn't subtle but Gwen didn't move. 'I'd like to ask him why.'

I laughed. The sound was loud and harsh and bounced around the room. 'I know why he left me, don't forget. He left me for you.'

'But–'

'No. No buts. He made his choice.' I let my eyes wander

slowly over her. So elegant, so damn polished. 'I don't know why he changed his mind, and I don't care. You or Babs. It's all the same to me.'

'Not to me, I need to find out why he lied. Babs... do you have an address for her?'

I pulled open a drawer, took out a notepad and pen and scrawled an address. 'Here you go.' I tore the sheet off and handed it across. 'I'd advise you to go carefully. Maybe Toby was lying about her but she seemed damn unstable when she was here beating the hell out of me.'

Gwen looked at the address and raised an eyebrow before tucking it into her handbag. She got to her feet in one smooth elegant movement. 'All I want is to know that he's okay.'

I could tell she was lying. If she found Toby at Babs' house, she'd beg him to come with her. She'd remind him of the words he'd whispered, all the promises he'd made. The hope he'd sparked in her heart, the vows of love, the future he'd painted.

All the lies he told.

11

GWEN

Gwen Marsham walked down Station Road to the centre of Hanwell. Conscious of the stains on her shirt and jacket, she clutched her handbag to her chest and walked as fast as her too-high heels would allow.

On the main street, she stopped. In Knightsbridge, she'd never wait long for a taxi. She wasn't sure if she'd be that lucky in Hanwell and pulled out her phone to ring for an Uber. Two minutes later, the car pulled up in front of her and she climbed in with a sigh.

'I need to stop in Beaufort Gardens, Knightsbridge, for a minute, then I want to go to Streatham, okay?'

'No problem.' The taxi driver indicated and pulled into the busy stream of traffic.

Gwen rested back, her head throbbing. Misty had been totally unexpected. Truth these days seemed to have become a flexible commodity.

Had desperation made Gwen so gullible that she'd fallen completely for Toby's lies? Even now, when she knew the truth, she couldn't quite believe it. She gave a snort of laughter that had the taxi driver's eyes fix her in his rear-view mirror, assessing her before looking away as if reassured by the sight of the elegant woman.

It was time to face it; she'd been taken for a fool. One of those pathetic women she read about with a sneer curling her lips at how ridiculous, how gullible, how idiotic they were. The hard-faced Misty would probably have laughed if Gwen had told her the full truth, if she'd told her about the money she'd given Toby when he mentioned a financial difficulty he'd been too ashamed of to explain in detail.

Gwen squeezed her eyes shut, embarrassment flooding her. She was an astute woman; she hadn't made a success of her art gallery by being stupid. Nobody could ever know about the five thousand pounds she'd handed over without a blink of hesitation to a man she barely knew.

Or maybe her mistake wasn't in giving it, but in asking for it back.

The thought brought tears that blurred the streets of London and the faces of the pedestrians who milled around the taxi as it stopped and started on its journey to Beaufort Gardens. Gwen hunted for a tissue in her pocket and pressed it to her eyes. She wasn't normally given to crying and certainly wasn't going to waste tears on Toby. They were tears of anger, of frustration, of disappointment. How could she have been so foolish?

The taxi pulled into Beaufort Gardens and stopped outside the building where she had an apartment on the second floor. 'I'll only be a couple of minutes,' she said, pushing the door open. She climbed out, kept her head down, and hurried to the communal front door.

Inside her apartment, she ignored the champagne that tilted sadly in the silver ice bucket and went through the lounge to her bedroom. Both her shirt and jacket were ruined, she tossed them on the floor and slid the wardrobe door back. The first shirt that came to her hand was another cream silk one, almost identical to the one she'd taken off. She slipped it on, fastening the buttons as she thought about Babs and Misty... and Toby, of course.

Her expression hardened. It would take a while to get him out of her mind.

Five minutes later, she was back in the taxi and on her way to Streatham. She couldn't remember the last time she'd crossed the river... or the last time she'd needed to... years before probably. There was a time, when she was younger – arty, bohemian and poor – she'd lived in various parts of the city, in squats, on the floor of friends, lovers, mere acquaintances. With success had come the gloss, the elegant façade, the money, and her world had condensed to the area where she now lived, worked and socialised.

Streatham looked interesting. She peered out the taxi window at the busy streets, the bustling pavements, the mix of independent shops, and the architecture – Victorian, or maybe Edwardian, she wasn't too sure. It was all far more impressive than she'd expected.

The taxi turned onto Wavertree Road and stopped in front of an imposing red-bricked building.

'Here you are.'

Gwen paid the fare and got out. It was tempting to ask the driver to wait. After all, the conversation was unlikely to be a prolonged one. But as she stood, hesitating, the taxi pulled away making the decision for her.

The apartment block stretched a distance in both directions with pillared entrances one to each side. With no idea which one to use, Gwen shrugged and turned to her left. She passed by the well-maintained borders that fronted the building, then took the six steps to the matt-black front door.

A row of doorbells was simply numbered with no names to

identify the occupant. Gwen pulled out the scrap of paper and checked before pressing her finger against the 12.

There was a sign to one side warning that CCTV was in use. Gwen was tempted to look up at the camera, smile and flutter her fingers, but she resisted and pressed the bell again. This time she had a response. A simple, *yes*. The voice was surprisingly clear as if the speaker was standing right beside her – clear enough to hear the tone and it wasn't welcoming.

Gwen would have liked to have been formal, would like to have asked to speak to Ms or even Miss, but Misty hadn't known the woman's surname so she was stuck with asking, 'Is that Babs?'

The reply was less than encouraging. 'Who wants to know?'

Gwen wasn't surprised. It would have been similar to what she'd have said if their positions had been reversed. 'My name is Gwen Marsham. We have a friend in common... Toby.' She hoped his name would be the key she needed but the reaction wasn't what she expected. Laughter pealed through the intercom. A raucous sound. It made her pull away and when the buzzer sounded allowing her access, she debated the wisdom of entering. This was, after all, the woman who'd beaten up Misty and whereas Gwen considered herself to be tougher than she looked, she wasn't interested in coming to blows with anyone.

But she'd not gone there to turn away at that point and before the buzzing stopped, she pushed open the heavy door.

The entrance lobby was an unwelcoming, nightmarish, green-and-black tiled space that hurt her eyes. A floor directory on the wall next to the lift door indicated that apartment 12 was on the fourth floor. Gwen pressed the button to call the lift and when the door slid open, stepped inside, holding her breath as it shut, feeling instantly claustrophobic in the tiny space.

On the fourth floor, the door swished open onto a quiet corridor. On the wall opposite, ornate arrows painted above a row of numbers directed her to the right. Her stiletto heels clicked loudly on the tiled floor and as if listening for a sign, a door opened halfway along the corridor and a woman stepped out, hands on her hips.

When the scowling face came into focus and brown eyes under heavy unplucked brows stared, assessing her, Gwen raised a perfectly arched eyebrow in response, refusing to wilt under their scrutiny. She was older and with age came the advantage of experience.

Babs sniffed, and waved a hand inside. 'You'd better come in, I suppose.'

Inside, a small dark hallway opened into a surprisingly spacious lounge. A pleasant room, it was obviously furnished for comfort rather than style. Gwen looked around the room and couldn't imagine Toby in such a domestic setting. Couldn't picture him slumped on the sofa, his feet up on the shabby footstool to watch the overlarge TV that dominated the room.

Gwen wasn't entirely sure what she was doing there. Was she seeking an explanation... or simply trying to put the pieces together hoping that when the last piece was in place, when she could see the whole picture, it would all make sense and she could let it go?

She walked across to the window and stared out at the street below. Closure. A much abused and overused word. But maybe, all the same, it was what she was seeking.

When she turned, Babs was sitting on the sofa, arms tight across her chest, eyes narrowed and focused on Gwen. 'I assume you're going to tell me why you're here.'

'I was hoping to talk about Toby.'

'*I was hoping to talk about Toby.*' Babs imitated her accent, her mouth twisting in a sneer. 'And what was it you wanted to talk about, eh?' She lifted an index finger, holding it up as if testing which way the wind was blowing. 'No, let me guess.' Pressing her lips together, she hummed off-key for a few seconds. 'Let me guess,' she said again, bringing her gaze back to Gwen. 'You didn't know him long so you probably haven't spent a fortune buying him new clothes, expensive dinners, exotic holidays so...' Babs tapped her finger against her lip. 'I bet you fell for some idiotic sob story and loaned him money. Am I right?' Seeing Gwen's expression, Babs grinned. 'I'm right, aren't I? Toby was nothing if not predictable.'

Gwen sank onto a small bucket chair. 'He left you for–'

'A writer called Misty Eastwood.' Babs tilted her head. 'I didn't think much of his taste there, to be honest.' She let her eyes slide over Gwen. 'You're older but at least you look as if you've a bit of style about you.'

'He lied to me; told me he was living with his sister.'

Babs waved a dismissive hand. 'That was the thing about Toby. He was gorgeous to look at, could charm the birds from the trees, but he didn't bother with things as inconvenient as the truth if a lie was necessary to get him what he wanted.'

'And that was?'

Babs shrugged. 'Money, status, excitement.'

'You were with him for four years–'

Whatever Gwen was going to ask was lost in the howl of Babs' laughter. 'Four years! Are you crazy? Toby lived here for six months. I spent a fortune on him in that time. Even if he'd wanted to, I couldn't have afforded to have him stay longer.'

'But... but... you attacked Misty for stealing him from you.'

Babs got to her feet and crossed the room. She vanished through a doorway, returning moments later with a bottle of red wine and two glasses. 'It's red or nothing,' she said. She put the glasses on the coffee table, twisted the cap and poured, filling both almost to the brim.

Flopping back onto the sofa, she reached for her wine and gulped almost quarter in one mouthful. 'Toby was an addiction.

Like any, you know it's bad for you, that you should stop, give it up, but you simply can't.' She took another drink. 'He made me feel like a better version of myself, slimmer, prettier, sexier.' Her laugh was bitter. 'He had a way of asking for money... no, not asking really, more insinuating in such a way that I'd be begging him to take it from me.'

Gwen reached for her wine and took a sip. It was cheap plonk but she drank it anyway. 'Yes, I can understand that. Like when he asked me for four thousand pounds and I ended up giving him five, to make sure he'd enough.'

'Big mistake.'

'Yes.' A bigger mistake asking for it back but Gwen didn't mention that. There was silence between the two women, the only sound the regular click of the wine glass hitting the table as Gwen put it down after each mouthful.

'More?' Babs reached for the bottle and wagged it in the space between them. She filled both glasses at Gwen's nod, then sat staring into her wine. Eventually, she looked up and sighed. 'I hadn't spoken to Toby since that time in Misty's house.' She smiled a little. 'It wasn't from want of trying but he'd blocked me and told the staff in his office not to put my calls through.' She tilted her glass, making the wine see-saw and slop over the edge. Switching hands, she shook the spillage away.

Gwen watched as red drops fell on the pale wood of the coffee table where they sat and shimmered in the sun that came through the window. Drops that fell on the cream carpet immediately soaked in. They'd leave a stain that would be there long after Toby's memory had faded. Gwen guessed that Babs hadn't noticed or if she did, she didn't care.

'I don't drink every day now,' Babs said, taking another mouthful. 'I did the first few days after he left. When I had a verbal warning at work, I knew I had to get my act together.' One further tiny sip of wine and she put it down. 'I didn't, and I'm on suspension. To be brutally honest, things are pretty much falling apart.' She sat silently for a moment before shrugging dismissively. 'Enough about me. Toby hadn't moved in with you so your addiction should be less. Count yourself lucky.'

'Lucky?' Gwen stared at the younger woman.

Babs reached for her wine before answering. 'Yes, lucky. Toby may have disappointed you but he didn't ruin you.'

No, Gwen hadn't been ruined. She could easily absorb the loss of the five thousand pounds. The dent to her self-esteem, her anger at being taken for a fool yet again would take longer to recover from, but she would, in time. She felt a smidgeon of sympathy for Babs, but when she thought of Toby, it was easy to brush it away. 'There's one thing I wanted to ask–'

'No!' Babs' free hand sliced the air. 'No questions.'

Of course, she was right. Gwen nodded, put her glass down and got to her feet. 'I'd better go. There's no reason for us to meet again.'

'There was no reason for us to meet today either.' Babs' voice was sharp, her eyes critical.

'True, I made a mistake. It won't happen again. We know where we stand with each other.' Gwen was being polite; what she really wanted to say, and what she hoped Babs understood, was that she never, ever wanted to see her again.

12

GWEN

B ack in the garishly tiled entrance hall, Gwen took out her mobile to ring for a taxi then reconsidered. Her head felt woolly after the two glasses of cheap wine, a walk in the fresh air might be a better plan.

The walk through Streatham didn't clear her head as she'd hoped, and ten minutes later she was feeling decidedly shaky. She'd pulled out her mobile again to ring for an Uber when she saw a taxi approaching, its vacant light a beacon of hope. It pulled up when she waved frantically, stepping out into the street to do so, jumping back when the irate driver of another car blasted his horn at her.

'You need to be careful, missus,' the taxi driver said as she half-climbed, half-fell onto the back seat.

'Beaufort Gardens, Knightsbridge.' She shut her eyes and rested her head back.

Traffic was heavy and it was nearly forty-five minutes later before the taxi pulled into her street. She leaned forward to address the driver. 'Anywhere here is fine.'

She paid, got out and crossed through the line of trees that separated one side of Beaufort Gardens from the other. Her side of the street suited her better. The evening sun hit the small balcony that opened from her living room where she'd sit and have a cup of tea or maybe the occasional glass of wine. It was where she'd planned to have the champagne with Toby the evening he arrived, the champagne that was still waiting sadly for a celebration that wasn't going to happen. Maybe she should pop the cork and drink it herself.

On her own.

A sad celebration of her lucky escape.

Because it had been an escape – her head knew it even if her heart lagged far behind, sulking. She understood exactly what Babs had meant... about how Toby made her feel... what was it she'd said... he'd made her feel *slimmer, prettier, sexier*? Gwen had barely known him, hadn't, as it turned out, really known him at all. But she could clearly remember how he made her feel. *Younger. Sexier. Irresistible.* He'd sent her emotions swirling, a chaos that washed away common sense. Being old enough to know better, being successful, intelligent, and experienced – none of it had stopped the rise and fall and pounding, exhilarating gallop of horses on the merry-go-round her life had become when Toby had stepped into it.

Her life now seemed to be shaded in faded, muted tones. She pushed open the front door of her apartment and dropped her bag on the hallway floor. Toby had never lived there, just an hour or two spent mostly in the bedroom, then a litany of promises as he departed to spend the night with his 'fragile sister'.

Gwen had believed every word he'd said.

Or had she? Was she still fooling herself, even now? Hadn't she been ever so slightly suspicious by his devotion to his sister? Hadn't she simply seen and believed what she'd wanted to?

She walked through to a living room that stretched across the front of the spacious apartment. A comfortable, stylish room, it was dominated on one side by huge beige sofas bracketing a large glass coffee table and on the other by a cherrywood table surrounded by six matching chairs. Bookshelves lined one wall; the others almost completely covered in art.

Three arched floor-to-ceiling windows overlooked the street, the central one set with a doorway that opened onto a small balcony. Outside, a neat table and two chairs sat in the middle of a collection of exotic leafy plants. She'd imagined sitting there with Toby to drink the champagne, hoping her neighbours would look over and see her with such a gorgeous man. She'd imagined tossing her hair and giving a seductive laugh. The thought made her smile. What the hell was a seductive laugh anyway?

She eyed the bottle of champagne and shook her head. The idea sounded great, but she'd prefer a cup of tea.

A compact kitchen was set against the opposite wall. Gwen made the tea and took it out onto the balcony. Sitting, she sighed loudly. *Foolish woman. Had she really thought that Toby was the one?*

She remembered his expression when she asked about the money she'd loaned him. The blank stare that had quickly slipped into hurt disbelief. And even as she'd reassured him that there was no hurry, hadn't she seen the sharp glint in his eyes, hadn't she known... *known*... that she was being taken for a fool. Worse, a cash cow.

Of course she had.

Toby had misjudged her. She wasn't stupid. Or perhaps, she qualified with a smile, not *that* stupid.

Finishing the tea, she left the cup on the table and went

inside. There were two bedrooms to the back of the apartment, the smaller of which was rarely used. Most of Gwen's friends lived within walking distance so there was rarely a need for them to stay over.

Once, she'd considered having the double bed removed and turning the room into an office or library. But there was adequate shelving in the living room for her books and she didn't really want to get into the habit of working from home so the idea had come to nothing and the bed had stayed.

Extraneous stuff tended to build up in any home but Gwen had resisted the temptation to turn the spare room into a dumping ground. Once a year, meticulously, she went through her belongings and discarded everything she no longer used or needed. The two cardboard boxes on the floor, therefore, were an aberration. And one her cleaner, who cleaned for several of Gwen's friends, would surely remark on.

To avoid speculation, Gwen needed to deal with the boxes. Of course, she'd already looked inside. That had been her downfall.

It had been Toby's idea for her to call around the day before he was due to leave Hanwell and pick them up.

'It will make it easier to leave,' he'd said, with a wry smile at how solicitous he was being of his sister's feelings. 'She uses headphones while she works so she won't hear if you call.'

Gwen had driven to the house on Myrtle Road, found parking immediately outside, and rang Toby's mobile to say she was there. After several minutes waiting, the front door opened and he'd come out with one box after the other. He placed them in the boot before coming to the driver's window. 'Thank you,' he said, with the smile that said he'd thank her better when they were alone. He bent then, leaned through the open window to capture her lips with his.

'Tomorrow,' he said with that way he had, that ability to infuse one word with so much meaning.

She'd reached up and laid a hand against his cheek. 'Tomorrow. I'll be waiting.'

At home, she parked in her usual space and carried the boxes into the apartment one at a time. They were cumbersome rather than heavy. Clothes, she assumed, dropping them on the floor of the spare bedroom.

The wardrobe there was almost empty with a couple of formal dresses hanging to one side. Plenty of room for Toby's clothes. Gwen had looked at the two boxes and decided to surprise him by unpacking.

She took out the suits and shirts and hung them on the wooden hangers, smoothing her hands over the fabric, feeling a rush of pleasure as she buried her nose in each garment and breathed in Toby's scent. It had been a long time since she'd felt so good. She hung the final suit and ran a hand over the material to ease out the creases.

Such fine fabric. She frowned when she felt a bump in the right-hand pocket, automatically reaching inside for the cause. A twisted piece of paper. She threw it on the bed and smoothed the pocket again. Perfect.

The following day, excitement bubbled as she readied the stage for Toby's arrival. Everything had to be perfect and she danced around the apartment, shutting curtains, switching on the numerous lamps to create the perfect ambience. The discarded paper on the bed in the spare room caught her eye, she picked it up to throw in the bin, carrying it with her as she finished her preparations.

She took the bottle of champagne from the fridge and

nestled it into the ice bucket on the balcony, then reconsidered and brought it inside. Finally satisfied it all looked the way she wanted, she sank onto the middle of the sofa where a pool of light from the lamp on each end overlapped.

The stage was set. She was smiling in anticipation, her fingers playing with the twist of paper she'd forgotten she was holding. It was disintegrating and a tiny piece fell from it to the sofa. Tutting, she picked it up and stood to put it into the kitchen bin.

She pressed her foot on the bin pedal, the lid gaping open to devour whatever rubbish she was dropping and held the screwed-up scrap over it... then took her foot away. Later, when she had all the time in the world to think about things, she remembered that moment, wondered what had made her stop and laughed at how different her life would have been if she'd simply let go.

But she didn't, she untwisted the paper, and read what was written there, the name and the phone number that had changed everything.

Gwen stared at it, a sour taste twisting her mouth. Toby's sister's name was Misty Eastwood, he'd mentioned it a couple of times. Who then was *Dee Carter*?

His mother maybe?

There was only one way to find out.

She rang the number.

'Hi,' she said when it was answered. 'Is that Mrs Carter?'

'Yes.' The voice gave nothing away.

'Toby Carter's mother?'

A laugh rang out. 'No, that old bat died years ago.'

'A sister then?'

'Who is this?'

It had been a silly idea. Gwen pressed the pedal of the bin

again, dropped the piece of paper into the yawning mouth, and let it snap shut with a bang. 'I'm sorry for bothering you.'

'Wait! Don't hang up.' The voice was urgent. 'If you're ringing about Toby you're probably another of the women who have fallen into his trap. Let me enlighten you. Toby doesn't have any sisters.

'I'm Dee Carter. Toby's long-suffering wife.'

13

BABS

Babs stood at the bay window of her Streatham apartment. The side window gave a good view of the entrance and a few minutes later she saw Gwen leave the building and hesitate before walking down to the main street, tottering in those ridiculously high heels, her butt cheeks rising and falling in that too-tight skirt.

Mutton dressed very expensively as lamb. Babs was under no illusions; it was Gwen's money that had attracted Toby's attention. And before that Misty's.

But for six incredible magical months Toby had lived with Babs. They'd been unbelievably happy and she'd thought it would be forever.

That Toby was her happy ever after.

Her job as a physiotherapist brought in a good salary but she was a long way from wealthy and the mortgage on the apartment ate up the bulk of her take-home pay. Her glamorous life with Toby has been built on a shaky foundation of credit cards. All three of them. They were maxed out and she'd not paid the minimum repayment on any of them last month, red print screaming her crime across the top of the one statement she'd foolishly opened. She'd scrunched it up and tossed it in the bin.

She ignored the letters from the bank piling up on the hall table. There was no point in opening them, she knew they'd simply tell her what she already knew, that she was in arrears with her mortgage repayments. Knowledge, in this case, wasn't power.

The thought of pulling her head from the sand to face it all terrified her... so she didn't.

Her salary from the clinic was due in a few days, but it wouldn't go anywhere towards paying off the arrears. It might cover the minimum payment for her credit cards. Might. She wasn't really sure.

She drained the end of the wine into her glass. It was the last bottle. She should have charged Gwen per glass; she looked like a woman who could afford it.

Babs had seen the sharp look in Gwen's eyes and guessed Toby had underestimated her. Rich, but not a complete pushover. Not like Babs had been. Not as foolish or incredibly, unbelievably stupid.

Babs and Toby had been good together before Misty had lured him away. She was to blame for everything that had gone wrong. Babs drained her glass and threw it across the room. She'd wanted it to smash to pieces, wanted the noise and destruction but she couldn't even do that right, the glass hitting the back of the small single-seater sofa and rolling unbroken to the floor.

With no outlet, the dart of anger simmered. Babs had always been quick-tempered. Following complaints to her employer from a member of the public a few years before, she'd been obliged to attend an anger management course. She knew all the strategies, even used them sometimes. She knew that chewing over Misty's part in Toby's desertion was adding fuel to her anger. It was irrational, she knew Toby's form, but the spinning hand on the blame game board stopped and pointed firmly at Misty every time.

Alcohol didn't help. Unless you drank enough to enter that wonderful world of oblivion. Unfortunately, there was no more wine. Gin but no mixer. With a shrug, Babs got to her feet.

Who needed mixers anyway?

14

MISTY

For a long time after Gwen left, I sat, too weary to move. Certainly too weary to switch on my computer and get to work. I'd catch up the next day or maybe, if I managed to get a few hours' sleep, later that day.

I tried to imagine the elegant Gwen facing up to Babs and shook my head. My money would be on Babs who was probably ten years younger and no stranger to violence if her attack on me was anything to go by. It had been savage; I considered myself tough and I'd been scared.

Still, it was none of my business. Toby was history. I had to keep reminding myself of that.

When my sister rang a little later, I was sitting in the same place trying to find some energy to do something... anything.

'You doing okay?' Ann's voice was suitably sombre.

To give her something else to think about apart from me, I told her about my early-morning caller.

'Oh no!' Ann's voice was suitably shocked. 'What an absolute bastard that Toby was!'

'You have to give the guy some credit, don't you? He had three different women almost eating out of his hands and desperate to keep him in a manner to which he'd become and wanted to stay accustomed.'

'It's like something you'd read about in one of your twisted stories.'

'Ann,' I said with a laugh, 'if I wrote a story this pathetic my agent would cry and my publisher reconsider offering a further contract. Who wants to read about three pathetic women making idiots of themselves?'

'Stop being hard on yourself, Misty. He's a con artist. They are skilled at what they do.'

'Yes, I know. She didn't say, but the woman who came around this morning, Gwen, I think she's lost more money than she was letting on. I think that's why she was desperate to find him.'

'Probably why he's disappeared too. He got what he wanted and scarpered.'

'Yes, you're probably right.'

'It's the last you'll see of him, I bet,' Ann said firmly. 'He's probably sunning himself in Barbados. You had a lucky escape.'

After arranging to meet for lunch later in the week, I put the phone down.

A lucky escape. I had to keep reminding myself of that.

I climbed the stairs, my hand heavy on the oak banisters, bare feet flap-flapping on the wood. It seemed too much effort to shower, almost too much to turn on my computer. I flopped onto my office chair sending it rocking and pressed my feet into the floor to keep the motion going, then, resting my head back, I let my mind wander.

Toby reached a hand towards her, his eyes imploring. It's only ever been you, Misty. All those other women, they meant nothing. I didn't mean what I said, I was overwhelmed by my feeling for you, by a love I'd never felt before.

I woke when my head fell forward, a cry of despair at the end of the dream. A cry of frustration at my snivelling stupidity. I dug my heels in, pulled my chair closer to the desk and switched on my computer.

Diving into my writing and the characters I'd brought to life would take me away from reality. This story had the type of strong female characters I liked to write about. *They'd* not put up with men like Toby.

I disappeared into my writing, taking solace from spending time with women who had more gumption than I, wondering once again why I could write them so well, so believably, when I was so weak and pathetic.

Sometime during the morning, I put on my headphones, music the final step to separate me from reality. Darkness had slipped into the room before I stopped, thirsty, hungry and tired, my eyes prickling. I looked to the corner of the screen unsurprised to see it was nearly midnight. It worked like that sometimes, the words flying from my fingertips as if desperate to escape. It was why living alone suited me, why I'd been foolish to think of sharing my home with anyone. I leaned back in the chair and stretched my arms overhead, flexing my fingers. *Toby*. That episode had been a crazy aberration.

Writing had soothed my agitation, eased my confusion, and settled me back into being who I was... a writer who was far happier with her fictional characters than with men who scuttled around as they sniffed the air for their next victim.

Too hungry and thirsty to sleep, I went downstairs and raided the fridge. Bread and jam and a glass of water filled the gap, and I retraced my steps. It was almost one before I reached to pull the curtains across the bedroom window, surprised to see it was raining heavily, drops pitter-pattering the glass. But it wasn't the rain that had me draw a noisy breath. There, across the road a figure stood silhouetted in the street light.

Light caught the shine of eyes focused in my direction. Could they see me suspended between the curtains? Slowly, I released my grip and, with my arms still raised, I moved backwards, one step at a time until I knew I was safe in the darkness of the room.

But then it came to me... I knew that hat and that ridiculously expensive Burberry raincoat. *Toby!* I rushed forward to stare through the rain to the street below.

There was nobody there.

But there had been... hadn't there?

15

MISTY

I stayed peering out the window until my eyes hurt, then crawled under the duvet and tried to sleep. But despite exhaustion, my brain was too rattled to switch off and there was no comfort behind my closed eyes. With a grunt of frustration, I threw back the duvet, blinked in the early-morning brightness and swung my feet to the floor.

Maybe my sisters were right; maybe writing these twisted tales was taking its toll. Or maybe I needed to take a break. Success was wonderful but the need to keep producing bestsellers was beginning to have the inevitable impact.

A holiday. That's what I needed.

I spent the next hour looking at options, at places I'd been and had promised to revisit and new, more exotic places. Train journeys, cruises, I looked at them all but nothing tempted me.

When the doorbell rang, my eyes flicked to the time. 9.20am. Too early to be one of my sisters looking to drag me out for coffee.

Whoever it was, they were persistent, the bell ringing again, the sound insistently loud, impossible to ignore. I pushed a hand through my greasy hair and glanced down at the wrinkled kaftan. Whoever it was, they'd have to take me as they found. I pushed the chair back and stood too quickly, feeling instantly dizzy... tiredness, stress, too little to eat and drink, any or all of the above.

My bare feet were sticky on the stairs as I made my way down to the front door. I reached it as it rang for the third time, unhooked the safety chain and yanked it open. The angry words on the tip of my tongue were swallowed when I saw two very official people holding identification forward for my attention.

A hand went to my throat, anger swamped by dread because only a catastrophe would bring the police to my doorstep. My first thought was it had to be about my parents. Happily retired to Portugal three years before, I'd not spoken to them for a few days. My eyes flicked from one to the other of the two officers trying to read the truth in their expressionless faces. 'My parents?'

The taller of the two officers looked over my shoulder. 'May we come in?'

Of course, they wouldn't give me bad news on the doorstep. I stepped back, waiting till they'd passed before I indicated the open door of the living room and followed them in.

'Tell me.' I sank onto a sofa, waving them to the other.

'I'm Detective Inspector Bev Hopper and this–' A thumb was jerked to the woman who sat beside her. '–is Detective Sergeant Linda Collins.' Hopper sat forward, resting her elbows on her knees, her clasped hands hanging between them. 'We're not here about your parents.' She held a hand up as if expecting an interruption. 'Or any of your family, in fact.'

'Whew! Sorry, it's automatic to associate the police at your door with bad news.' I smiled and added, 'Not that I'm used to a visit for any reason.'

There was no answering smile, the two officers maintaining set expressions. Both were dressed in a similar style: off-the-peg trouser suits, one dark grey, the other navy, and shirts that had possibly been white in the distant past.

DI Hopper stayed in her relaxed almost masculine pose, her clasped hands bouncing slightly. Her short hair was brushed behind her ears in a style that suggested convenience. Apart from well-defined eyebrows, she wore no make-up.

Her colleague, DS Collins, on the other hand, sat in an alert pose that indicated she liked to be ready for whatever visits such as this might throw at her. Her blonde-streaked hair was tied back in a bun so tight it pulled the skin at the side of her face. Unlike her partner, she wore heavy make-up that, mask-like, ended at her jawline; black kohl ringed her eyes and her long curling eyelashes were obviously fake.

I felt the women's eyes sliding over me and around the room, assessing, maybe judging. My initial anxiety at their arrival faded. 'I'm sure this silent treatment works wonders on the criminal fraternity but since I'm not a member, it is failing dismally.' I was trying for coolly amused but guessed I'd not succeeded when the expressions on the faces opposite remained rigidly grim.

Finally, as I was getting to the point where I wanted to reach over and see if I could peel the mask off the young officer's face, to see maybe if there was a human lurking behind it, Hopper spoke. 'Tell us about your relationship with Toby Carter.'

The question was so unexpected that I blinked. 'Toby?'

The expressionless faces opposite were starting to irritate. I stood abruptly, startling both, Hopper rearing back, Collins half-standing. 'I need coffee,' I said, flapping a hand at them. 'You can come with me, if you like, in case you think I'm going to make a run for it.'

My sarcasm didn't raise as much an eyebrow. Unresponsive two-dimensional characters. I would have deleted them from my books with a few taps on the keyboard.

I headed to the kitchen, hearing them mutter between themselves before they followed. 'Coffee?' I reached for a jar and waved it at them.

Both nodded a yes, and without waiting for an invitation, sat silently at the table.

A few minutes later I put mugs of coffee before them, adding the carton of milk and a sugar bowl. I poured milk into mine and left them to help themselves.

When I'd taken a few mouthfuls, I rested my elbows on the table, the mug clasped in my hands and told the detectives what they wanted to know.

'I met Toby at a function given by my publisher. We had an instant connection and a relationship developed quickly. After a few weeks he moved in with me.'

I stopped, waiting for a response, but their faces were inscrutable. I didn't know what they were looking for, couldn't believe they'd want to know the intimate details of my relationship with Toby so I decided to tell them about Babs' attack on me.

'A couple of weeks later, an ex-girlfriend turned up and assaulted me. Viciously. They'd been together for a few years but their relationship had ended months before and he was basically lodging at her place till he found somewhere else.' I could still remember the savage blows that had rained down on me, the anger, the *hatred* in the woman's eyes. 'Thankfully, she never returned.'

I thought about mentioning having seen her out on the street two nights before and decided against, afraid it might make me sound a little paranoid. 'Things between Toby and I were great.' *Hadn't they been, had I been completely deluded?* 'I thought so anyway but a few nights ago he told me he didn't love me anymore and was leaving.' I couldn't hide the catch in my voice as I said the words and saw the first hint of interest on the faces opposite.

'It was a surprise,' I explained and took a sip of my coffee. 'But we'd not been together that long so he didn't leave much of a hole in my life.'

'So, you wouldn't take him back?'

I would. Of course, I would. In a heartbeat. 'No, I wouldn't. He was a bit demanding, if you know what I mean.'

'No,' DI Hopper said. 'Explain *demanding*.'

I wished I'd kept my mouth shut. 'Look, why are you asking these questions? Is it that woman... Gwen? Did she report him missing, is that it?'

I could see the wheels turn in Hopper's brain as she considered whether to tell me or not. Maybe she decided she'd get more information if she gave a bit. 'Toby Carter has been reported missing but it wasn't by a woman called Gwen, who we'd like to know more about please, it was his wife, Dee.'

16

MISTY

I felt my jaw drop in a cartoonlike expression of surprise. 'Toby's wife!'

'They've been living apart for almost a year but it seems they're still close and he rings her almost every day. She was hoping he was, as she put it, "going through a phase", and would eventually go back to her.' Hopper raised an eyebrow at my *ha* but continued without comment. 'When she hadn't heard from him for a couple of days, she rang his mobile but there was no answer, and he didn't reply to the messages she left. Finally, she rang his place of work and was told he'd not been in for a few days, neither had he rung in sick which, according to his employer, was out of character.'

'But... almost a year?' I frowned, trying to fit this new piece of information into what I knew. 'His ex-girlfriend, Babs, said they'd been together for years. Four, if I remember correctly.'

'No.' Hopper frowned and reached into her jacket pocket for a small, red notebook. She flicked it open, eyes narrowing as she read. 'Mrs Carter said her husband moved in with Barbara Sanderson a little over nine months ago.'

I rubbed a hand over my mouth. 'I must have misunderstood.'

'You say Mr Carter left here a few nights ago. Can you be more specific?'

'Yes, it was Saturday night.'

Hopper looked up from her notebook. 'At what time?'

'Late.' I shrugged. 'I was writing, when I'm engrossed in my work, I don't keep track of the time.'

'Try.' One word, blunt, demanding an answer.

My mind drifted back to that night. 'When he came to tell me he was leaving, my lamp was on so it must have been dark, if that helps.'

Hopper scribbled a line in her notebook. 'Sometime after nine, then. You didn't see him during the day? For lunch or dinner maybe?'

'No.' I saw lines of disbelief crease both their foreheads and sighed. 'I'm a writer, I can lose hours if the writing is going well. I use headphones to shut out distractions. Once I have them on, I don't hear anything unless it's very loud or persistent. I saw Toby early that morning and he mentioned going to the gym but I've no idea if he went, or what time he got home if he did go. He may have been home hours or might have come in only moments before, I wouldn't have known.'

Collins looked around the kitchen. 'What about food? You must eat.'

'Toby knew the pressure I was under recently with my deadline. I'd snack while I worked and he'd get himself something to eat or pick up a takeaway. It was only for a few days, he understood and he knew not to disturb me unless it was urgent.'

'Like when he came to tell you he was dumping you.' Collins' lips curved in the first emotion I had seen her express.

Amusement or derision, I wasn't sure. Maybe it was funny. Maybe in a few days, weeks, months, I'd find it all bloody hilarious.

'And then he left?' Hopper asked.

I put my mug down and ran a hand over my head, inwardly grimacing at the greasy stickiness. Did these two hard-faced women think that I was falling apart because I'd been tossed aside? I clasped my hands together and lifted my chin. 'Then he left. I watched from my office window as he walked down the street, a holdall hanging from each hand.'

'I thought you said it was dark outside.' No smile on Collins' pinched face now.

'This is London. It's never really dark. You should know that.'

'He walked?' Hopper tapped her notebook against her hand. 'Where was he going?'

'He didn't say, I didn't ask.' I reached for my mug, took a mouthful of the tepid coffee and swallowed. 'He messaged me with his new address so I could forward any post.' I smiled in sad acknowledgement of what an idiot I'd been. 'When I heard the address, I knew he had to have moved in with a woman. He couldn't have afforded to rent there even if he were someone who spent his own money rather than...' I was rattling on too much and stopped abruptly.

But Hopper's eyes narrowed. 'Rather than?'

They may as well know the truth about him. If they were going to speak to the women in Toby's life, they'd soon understand. 'Rather than using mine or someone else's. Toby was charming, charismatic, incredibly sexy but he was a taker.'

'You gave him money?'

I shook my head. 'Not cash as such. It wasn't that clear cut. I paid for things.'

'Such as?'

It sounded petty to quantify, as if that was all our relationship had come down to. 'Things... meals when we went out, theatre tickets, weekends away, clothes when we went shopping, a new phone, new luggage...' My voice faltered. It had been the first time I'd enumerated it all. It made me sound so pathetic to have been milked for so much. What a sad, gullible creature I had been.

'I assume we're talking about expensive meals, five-star hotels when you went away etc.' For the first time Hopper's expression was sympathetic.

'Yes. Toby liked the high life especially if someone else was paying for it.'

'Okay. I think I've got the picture.' Sympathy faded, replaced by Hopper's previous set expression. 'Tell me about this woman, Gwen.'

I held my hands up. 'All I know is what she told me yesterday morning. She met Toby in an art gallery she works in.' I tilted my head. 'Actually, she didn't say she worked in it, she referred to it as *her* gallery so maybe she owns it. She certainly gave the impression of wealth.' I couldn't prevent my lips twisting in a sneer. 'The kind of wealth that would have lured Toby, no doubt.'

'Lured him away from you,' Collins said pointedly.

Hopper shot her a quelling glance before asking, 'How did Gwen know where you lived?'

'I didn't ask her. I assume the same way as Babs knew where I lived. Toby told her.'

'And she definitely said she'd been expecting him the night he left you?'

'Yes.'

'She must have been desperate to risk coming to the home of his ex.'

'Oh, I forgot to tell you the best bit.' I squeezed out a laugh.

'He told her I was his sister. His needy, fragile sister. She was a bit taken aback when I told her the truth.'

'Angry?'

'I don't know.' I tapped my fingers on the side of my empty mug. 'Stunned, shocked, disbelieving... maybe there was a glimmer of anger at being lied to.'

'You think Toby lied about where he was going?'

A shrug. 'Must have done. He left here, he didn't turn up there.'

'Yet he gave you the Knightsbridge address.' Hopper's eyes narrowed. 'He seemed to be very careful to keep everyone informed of his whereabouts, so why lie?'

I threw myself back in the chair. 'I don't know! Toby does what he wants. He could have been on his way to Gwen's and met someone better... someone richer. He could be shacked up with them now. I'll probably get a message one of these days, no apologies, no excuses, to say he's at a different address.'

Hopper sat back and folded her arms across her chest, her mouth twisting as if my words had left a bad taste. 'According to his wife, Toby was unfaithful but reliable. According to his employer, he was conscientious. It's hard to reconcile that with the man you're describing.'

There didn't seem to be any point in commenting.

Collins decided to make her presence felt again. 'The last you saw of Toby Carter was when he was walking down the street with a bag in each hand, is that what you're saying?'

'No, that isn't what I said at all.' I smiled sweetly at her.

The detectives exchanged glances.

'I said I watched him walk down the street with his bags after he left here that night. I didn't say it was the last I'd seen of him though.'

Hopper grunted in obvious frustration. 'Are you deliberately messing us around, Ms Eastwood? If you know where Toby Carter is, tell us now, please.'

I was beginning to enjoy myself. I could use this. Not in the book I was currently writing, but maybe the next. The two detectives, too, would make good characters to use although I'd need to flesh them out a bit. I'd write it up later when it was fresh in my brain.

'Ms Eastwood!'

Dragging my thoughts from the pages of my next novel, I looked across to the obviously exasperated face of DI Hopper. 'Sorry, daydreaming, an occupational hazard I'm afraid. Toby. Yes, I saw him last night, or should I say early this morning.'

'You saw him?'

'Yes. My writing was going well so I was late going to bed. I was pulling my bedroom curtains when I saw him.' I waved in the direction of the front of the house. 'Standing outside, staring up at me. To be honest, it was a bit spooky. It was dark, I was tired and my mind was whirling. You may already know, but I write psychological thrillers and sometimes writing about twisted people can be a bit challenging.' I looked at them, their set assessing faces. 'The kind of people you two meet on occasion I suppose.'

'Just tell us what happened.' Hopper's voice was tight with irritation.

I put the mug I'd been clutching down on the table. 'Happened? Nothing happened. When I looked again, he was gone.'

'He didn't knock on your door?'

'No. But he saw me looking. He probably thought I'd go down and let him in but I wasn't going to do anything so daft.'

'Why didn't he ring you instead of turning up in the middle of the night?'

'No idea. Maybe he knew I wouldn't have answered.' I was

tired, a yawn fighting to be released. I wondered, after all, whether I should mention that Babs had been outside the house the night before.

But there was a sceptical light in the detective inspector's eyes: if she didn't believe I'd seen Toby, telling her that I'd seen his violent ex-girlfriend, in more or less the same place, might convince her I was paranoid.

17

GWEN

G wen was having a satisfying morning with the sale of an expensive and hideously ugly painting to a man who had, thankfully for the gallery, more money than taste. It was a painting she'd been trying to persuade the obstinate artist to remove from the gallery for several weeks insisting it wouldn't ever sell, so she was delighted for him and for the gallery finances to be proven wrong.

'It's sublime.' The man was staring at it as Gwen was hastily writing out an invoice, wanting to get the deal completed before he changed his mind. She felt no guilt. She'd tried to lure the man towards more aesthetically pleasing work to no avail. Short of telling him that he had no taste and that the piece he was buying was terrible she couldn't have done more. Business, after all, was business. And, as she kept reminding herself, it wasn't her role to press her taste on the customers.

The man was droning on. 'It's really an amazing piece, isn't it? It aims at a void that seems to signify precisely the non-being of what it represents.' He must have taken Gwen's blank expression as acquiescence. 'It subverts the aesthetic norm, doesn't it?'

Looking across to where the picture stood on a dais, Gwen smiled, pleased to be able to sincerely agree with this final comment. 'Yes, it does that extremely well.'

She slid the invoice across the desk, two fingers of her other hand crossed under it. But he barely glanced at it before he shoved it into his pocket and reached inside his jacket for his wallet.

Gwen took the proffered credit card and started the process, handing the card reader over for him to input his PIN number. A tinkle as the gallery door opened drew her attention to the two official types who entered. Her eyes flicked from them to the man... was this it? He'd escaped from somewhere. An institute of some sort? It explained everything. She sighed, expecting the credit card to be declined, surprised when it went through without delay.

He took his card back and continued to extoll the artistic merits of the painting he'd bought. She answered monosyllabically as her eyes flicked restlessly to the two people who'd moved to stand in a corner. It was second nature to assess each customer, to gauge whether they were serious buyers, browsers, or simply time-wasters. The two women didn't sit comfortably in any of these categories. An odd couple: the taller of the two looked faded and worn next to the over- and badly made-up woman who stood inches away. Their trouser suits lacked style and the taller woman looked as if she cut her own hair but it was their hard cold expressions that singled them out as not being her usual visitors.

It took a few minutes to wrap the painting, the new owner fussing over it as he ensured his purchase would be safe during the transfer. Finally, it was done to his satisfaction and he stood back. It wasn't heavy, but it was awkward and cumbersome, and after lifting and putting it down several times he agreed to do what Gwen had suggested from the start and have it delivered.

Another five minutes of paperwork and the customer was heading out the door with a satisfied smile.

Gwen moved the wrapped painting to a back room before crossing the gallery floor. The grim, fixed expressions on the two women didn't alter as she approached.

Used to dealing with the public, in all their many guises, Gwen was able to hold her smile in the face of their rather intimidating stares. 'Can I help you?' Her smile faded when the older of the two held identification forward.

'I'm Detective Inspector Hopper, and this–' She indicated the heavily made-up woman beside her. '–is DS Collins. Is there somewhere we can talk?'

Gwen swallowed. The police. It had to be Toby. She pointed to the front door. 'I'll put the closed sign up and we can talk here.'

The sign was changed and the catch on the door released, Gwen's fingers fumbling as she did both, conscious of the eyes that followed her. She turned and waved to the desk at the back of the gallery. 'Let's sit and you can tell me what this is all about.'

Gwen sat behind the desk, her forearms resting on the arms of the chair, manicured fingers dangling. Relaxed, professional, efficient: it was the impression she liked to give her customers to convince them she was reliable, that she'd only ever tell the truth.

'Toby Carter,' DI Hopper said without elaborating.

Gwen wondered what reaction the detectives expected. Surprise? Shock? Was she supposed to wail? She did nothing but sit and wait, her eyes unwavering.

'His wife has reported him missing.'

'His wife?' Gwen concentrated on keeping her pose relaxed, spreading her fingers to stop them curling into fists. 'I didn't realise he was married.'

'Neither did his other girlfriend.'

'It seems Toby was rather selective with the truth.'

Hopper raised an eyebrow. 'We spoke to Misty Eastwood earlier. I'd say Toby Carter was a whopping liar myself.'

'It's deemed poor form to speak ill of–' Gwen stopped abruptly and her hands gripped the edges of the armrests.

'Of the dead? Was that what you were going to say?' Hopper leaned over the desk, reducing the distance between them. 'Now why would you say that?'

Gwen released her grip and took a breath. She needed to be careful. 'You've been speaking to Misty Eastwood so you'll know that he was leaving her to be with me on Saturday but he never turned up. It's a sad but logical conclusion that something happened to prevent his arrival. This is London... bad things happen to people all the time. Misty hasn't heard from him, I've not heard from him, ergo my remark.'

Hopper sat back but her expression said clearly that she wasn't convinced. 'Tell us about your relationship with Mr Carter.'

Gwen blew a noisy exclamation of frustration. 'As I'm sure you already know from Ms Eastwood, my relationship with Toby was built on a foundation of lies. He'd told me he was living with his sister, pah!' That was all she needed to tell them.

But it wasn't enough for the detective inspector who leaned forward again, her eyes fixed on Gwen's face. 'Mr Carter has history of being... let's call it high maintenance... was that your experience?'

'He liked nice restaurants, expensive wine.' Gwen shrugged. 'I've plenty of money, it didn't bother me paying for things.'

'For everything?' Hopper pushed.

Gwen forced a laugh. 'Toby and I were only together for a little more than two weeks, detective inspector, there was only so much I could pay for in that period, especially since I believed he was rushing home to be with his unstable sister.'

'You must have been upset when he didn't turn up as promised,' DS Collins said.

Gwen turned to look at the younger detective who up to then had sat quietly. *Really someone should tell her not to wear so much make-up or at least advise her how to use it correctly and blend that unseemly line along her jaw.* 'But you know nothing about me do you?' She held the detective's gaze for a second before looking back to the inspector. 'I don't invite men to move in with me on a whim. I'd given it some thought. I thought he had too.'

'You knew him such a short time.' Hopper held her hands up as if in apology. 'That sounds very much like a whim to me.'

Gwen lifted her chin and met the detective's gaze without wavering. 'Well, it wasn't, it was a considered risk.' She tilted her head a little. 'One, as it happens, that didn't work out. To be trite, that's life.'

'You seem very philosophic about it yet you went to Ms Eastwood's house trying to find him.'

'What? Did you think I'd gone to throw myself at his feet and beg him to come with me? I'm forty, not twenty, inspector. At heart, I'm a businesswoman. I'd obviously miscalculated and I was interested in knowing why, that's all. I'd do the same in any business deal.' Gwen waved a hand around the gallery. 'If a sale falls through or a customer changes their mind, I investigate to see why, learn from the experience and move on.'

She sounded good. Cool. In control. Nobody need ever know how stupid she'd been. She'd get rid of his belongings and it would be as if Toby had never existed.

18

GWEN

When DI Hopper said she'd no further questions and got to her feet, Gwen struggled to hide her relief. Her fingers gripped the edge of the desk as the two detectives crossed the gallery to the exit. Even after they'd departed, she maintained a cool, confident façade and stayed where she was, afraid they'd come back, knowing if they did, she would fall apart and let it all out.

Hoping that no customer would come in while she locked the storeroom and grabbed her bag, she put the alarm on and left the building. The gallery was only a ten-minute walk from her apartment. Normally, she took her time, enjoying the walk through an area she loved but today her feet sped along the path, her focus on getting home.

The police had never mentioned calling to her apartment but she couldn't take a risk that they would. She'd brought one of the boxes of clothes to the recycling area the previous night, she needed to get rid of the other.

She stopped in her apartment only long enough to change from her gallery-appropriate clothes to casual trousers, a T-shirt, and flat shoes. The second box was a little heavier than the previous one. She balanced it against her chest with a grunt and wondered about taking the car, deciding it was quicker to walk the short distance than to negotiate the one-way streets and London traffic.

It was rare to see anyone coming in or out of her building and that day was no exception. The road outside was quiet, too, and she hurried along, shifting the bulky box in her arms as she walked.

She was puffing by the time she reached the recycling bin in the grounds of a local supermarket, her arms ached and she regretted her decision not to have taken the car. The bin was situated to the back of the car park. Often packed to overflowing, Gwen was in luck and there weren't bags of clothes oozing from it. Had there been, she'd have had no compunction, she'd have pulled them out to make space for Toby's clothes. She put the box on the ground and tore away the tape she'd used to fasten it. The hatch of the recycling bin, heavy and stiff, was a two-hand job. She gripped and pulled it open, emptied half the contents of the box into it, slammed it shut to empty it and opened it again. The second go finished the job and she slammed the hatch shut with a satisfied grunt.

The recycling bin for cardboard was full. With a glance around, she flattened the box, laid it on top, then dusted her hands and walked away.

Physically and emotionally lighter, she headed home convinced that her part was done and she could put it all behind her.

Gwen was always good at fooling herself. She'd had a lot of practice.

Plus, unfortunately, a lot of experience in dealing with men who let her down.

19

BABS

Babs was watching TV when her doorbell buzzed. She didn't move. People frequently rang the wrong bell by accident or sometimes kids, thinking it was hilarious to disturb people, would press all the bells and run away giggling their silly heads off.

She didn't move when it rang the second time either, this time because she simply couldn't be bothered.

It wasn't until the third buzz that she got to her feet and crossed to the intercom. 'Yes?'

'It's the police, Ms Sanderson, DI Hopper and DS Collins. We'd like to have a word with you about Toby Carter.'

Babs' ragged breath fogged the stainless-steel surround of the intercom. *The police*. Why had she answered the buzzer? Too late now. Refusing them entry would simply make them suspicious. 'Come on up, fourth floor. Apartment twelve.' They'd rung her bell, so they already knew this. How much more did they know about her? That she was off work... but did they know why?

She hovered at the apartment door, waiting for the sound of their footsteps on the tiled floor of the corridor outside. It would take them a few minutes, the lift was old and slow. She took deep relaxing breaths, slowing her heartbeat down, easing some of the tension.

What would they think when they saw her? She brushed her fringe back in what she knew was a vain attempt to hide the dark track line along the parting of her dyed blonde hair. They were looking for Toby... had they met his other women: his wife, that writer woman, the elegant Gwen? Would they wonder at his poor taste when it came to Babs? All the money she'd spent on turning herself from a plain plump woman to a woman someone like him would be interested in... the expensive haircuts, designer clothes, carefully applied make-up... it had been worth it but she couldn't keep it up.

She'd sold the designer clothes for less than a tenth of what she'd paid for them. It stopped her electricity being cut off. It hadn't paid for a hairdresser. There wasn't even enough for a supermarket colour, not if she wanted to eat.

A loud knock shook her out of the spiral of self-pity she so easily slipped into and with a neutral expression in place, she opened the apartment door.

'I'm Detective Inspector Hopper.' The detective held identification forward. 'And this is Detective Sergeant Collins. May we come in?'

Babs gave their cards a cursory glance. 'Sure, why not.' She stood to one side and waved them in. 'D'you want a drink? Water or tea. No coffee, I'm afraid. I'm out.' Out and she couldn't afford to buy more.

She flopped back onto the seat in front of the TV, reaching for the remote to freeze the programme. She hoped they'd see it as a hint that she didn't expect them to stay long. 'You can sit, if you like.'

Hopper sat on the sofa Babs indicated, Collins deciding to remain standing.

'Toby Carter appears to have gone missing,' Hopper said. 'Do you know his whereabouts?'

'Missing?'

'Yes. He's not been to work for a few days and they've not been able to contact him.'

'Did they report him missing?'

'No, his wife did.' When Babs didn't comment, Hopper added, 'You knew he was married?'

'Of course. He didn't keep secrets from me. But it was over between them years ago.'

'And you and Mr Carter were together for how long?'

'Six months.'

'Six months? We were told you were together for longer, for four years.'

'Really?' Babs raised an eyebrow. 'I don't know who you've been speaking to, detective inspector, but I think I should know, don't you?'

DI Hopper's lips tightened. 'Right, six months, then he left you for another woman.'

Babs couldn't prevent her face twisting into lines of anger. 'That woman! Sells herself as a successful writer. Ha, she's nothing but a slut who writes trash and uses slippery words to lure a man away. Women like her...' Babs shook her head as if to say that said it all.

'Not men like him?' Collins said with heavy sarcasm.

Hopper darted a *shut-up* look at her but Babs wasn't letting it go. 'You've made up your mind about him, have you, and you've never even met him. You've made up your mind that Toby Carter was a gigolo, a leech, a blood-sucking monster who would always find one more vulnerable woman to prey on. You have no idea.'

Hopper shuffled in her seat drawing Babs' attention back to her. 'Our job is to find Mr Carter, not criticise him or condemn his morals. We're interviewing the people who knew him, trying to get a sense of who he was in the hope it might lead us to find out what happened to him. You seem to be critical of Ms Eastwood and I'd like to know why.'

Babs looked at Hopper. The older detective appeared more sympathetic or was that what she was supposed to think. Was this a version of the good cop/bad cop routine beloved of the traditional detective series she'd been binge-watching for the last few days? How could she explain her obsession to these two strong women? Once, Babs had been as strong. Her forehead creased in a frown as she tried to remember when that had changed, the very moment when everything altered...

20

BABS

B abs hadn't lied to the police, she'd only been with Toby for six months; she'd not lied to that writer slut, Misty Eastwood, either. Babs had known Toby for four years. He hadn't, however, known her for the same length of time.

Three and a half years before they'd officially met, Babs had gone into the waiting room of the private clinic where she worked as a physiotherapist. She was looking for coffee, she found something better.

Toby Carter was sitting staring into space, a folded newspaper in one hand, the other tapping on the arm of the chair in time to music he was listening to on headphones. His head, too, was gently bobbing along to the unheard beat and a lock of hair had fallen across his forehead. The sleeves of his plain white shirt were rolled up to show off glowing, tanned, muscular arms, dark, curling chest hair visible at the v of the open neck. He glanced her way, vivid blue eyes sliding over her before returning to stare at the ceiling.

That one sight was enough to start a fixation that had led her to where she was now. She'd left the waiting room without her coffee and gone to the reception desk. It wasn't unusual for her to check the list of clients due in over the day so it caused no raised eyebrows as she flicked down the page. There was no male client expected until later that day so the man had to be waiting for someone.

Reaching for a piece of scrap paper, she scribbled down the names of the clients who were currently having treatment and returned to her office where she switched on her computer. It took only a few minutes, quickly ruling out three out of the four on her list. Dee Carter was having minor surgery. Her next of kin was listed as Toby Carter. Babs wrote down their home address and tucked it into her pocket.

Over the next few hours she was busy with clients. 'Excuse me for a moment,' Babs said several times during each consultation. Sometimes there were more important things than clients' aches and pains. She slipped out and down the corridor to reception where she peered through the glass door of the waiting room.

Toby Carter. It looked as if he hadn't moved from one of her visits to the next. Wondering how much longer he'd be waiting, Babs went to the minor surgery room where his wife was having her procedure.

Babs nudged the door of the anaesthetic room open a crack. It was empty apart from a nurse she didn't know who was tidying away equipment. Babs pushed open the door fully with a smile. 'I'm out of micropore tape, do you have a roll to spare?'

'Sure.' The nurse pulled open a drawer, took out a roll and handed it over.

'Great, thanks.' Babs tilted her head to the operating room. 'A long case?'

'No, nearly done, thank goodness. I could do with a break.'

'Good.' Babs waved the roll of tape. 'Thanks for this.'

She'd left her latest client having treatment for shoulder pain using transcutaneous electrical nerve stimulation. The sound of the machine beeping to say the programme was complete came to her as she approached the door of the room and she swore under her breath. 'Sorry,' she said, pushing through the door with a frown of professional concentration on her face. 'A complicated case came in.' It sounded good but she could see by the tight lips of the client that she was neither fooled nor impressed.

The client remained silent as the two electrodes were peeled from her shoulder and left without a word or glance in Babs' direction. She waited ten minutes to make sure the client had left the building before going back to the waiting room, desperate to catch a sight of Toby again.

Unfortunately, the client was in reception. Worse, she was in conversation with the physiotherapy department manager and neither of them looked happy.

Babs ducked back out of sight, swearing under her breath again, her eyes darting between the obviously irate client and the door to the waiting room.

Only a minute later, the nurse she'd spoken to earlier came along the corridor, a short, weedy, pale woman at her side.

This is Dee Carter? Babs sniffed, muttered a hello to the nurse and walked a few steps away, turning when she heard her name called, her hands curling into tight fists when she saw the furious expression on her manager's face.

The manager was too professional to deal with the issue in the corridor and requested Babs' attendance at a meeting in her office the following day. Unfortunately, Babs was only half-listening, too busy looking over the woman's shoulder to where Toby and his weedy wife were nodding and smiling at the nurse.

'At 2pm, if that's not too much trouble.'

The acid sarcasm brought Babs' attention reluctantly back. 'Sorry, what?'

'Have you been listening to a word I said?'

'Of course,' Babs said, trying to infuse her words with sincerity. 'I'm sorry, it's been a stressful day.'

The manager's downturned mouth didn't indicate sympathy and her next words were staccato sharp. 'Tomorrow. At 2pm. My office.' She gave Babs a scathing look and walked away.

As soon as she'd gone, the following day's meeting was forgotten. Babs hurried to the floor-to-ceiling windows at the front of the reception area to scan the car park, her eyes narrowing against the glare of the sun as she searched for one more glimpse of Toby.

Over the next few weeks, Babs found out as much as she could about Toby Carter. It wasn't hard, it simply took persistence and dedication. She used some of her precious annual leave to hang around outside his house in Croydon, followed him when he left for work, then hung around there gathering more information.

She found him on Facebook, drooled over the few photographs that were public. Unsurprisingly, her friend request was denied so she made do with what she had and copied and printed out the few photographs available. Cutting his wife and friends from them, she had them blown up to poster size and hung them on her wall, adding other photos over the years – the ones she snapped with her mobile phone when he wasn't looking.

Her obsession became her passion but, eventually, looking at him from a distance wasn't sufficient. She wanted much more.

It required weeks of careful preparation and planning to arrange an accidental meeting. She knew where he worked, which gym he visited, the shops he liked to frequent, the café near his office where he liked to stop for coffee.

The café seemed the most suitable venue for her plan. Sometimes Toby stopped for coffee on his way to work in the morning, sometimes he'd call in for one mid-morning or at lunchtime or, very occasionally, later in the afternoon. But it was a rare day when he didn't go in at some stage.

Years of observing him had given her an advantage; she knew he liked the finer things in life and in preparation for their meeting, spent a fortune on herself. It was, she decided, an investment in her future.

When the day she'd planned for came, she arrived at the café early. She sat with her Armani jacket hanging over the back of a spare chair, her Gucci handbag on the tabletop beside her and her legs crossed, one foot swinging to show off the red sole of her Louboutin shoes. Her mousy brown hair had been cut and expertly dyed, shades of blonde shining in the overhead lights.

The stage was set. She had her Kindle with her and was willing to wait the whole day, reading book after book, if that was what it took for the meeting she knew would change her life.

When Toby walked through the doors of the café mid-morning, she took his early arrival as a good omen and struggled to keep a smile of pleasure from curving her lips. Her eyes flicked from the book she wasn't reading to where he stood in the queue. He'd order a macchiato. He always did.

She waited until he'd taken a seat on the other side of the busy café before getting to her feet, and with her Gucci bag over her arm she weaved around the tables to the exit. She stopped to slip on her jacket, turning as she did so to let her eyes drift around the room. Then she gave a loud gasp, lifted a hand in greeting and rushed over to his table. 'Peter!' Her voice was pitched husky *sexy* as she bent down to press a kiss against his cheek and her breasts against his shoulder. 'It's been so long.' She pulled back then and let a look of horror appear, open mouth, wide eyes. 'Oh my goodness, I'm so sorry. Gosh, please forgive me, you are so like an old college friend of mine.' She held both hands over her chest, careful to emphasise the Gucci logo on her bag.

'Lucky friend,' Toby said with relaxed gallantry.

'I'm so embarrassed.' Babs flapped a hand before her face. 'Do you mind if I sit a moment?'

Of course, he hadn't minded and offered to get her a drink.

Babs, who'd drunk enough coffee that morning to last a lifetime, nodded. 'That's so kind of you. A macchiato would be lovely, thank you.'

And that was the start of what she had hoped would be the rest of her life. She didn't give the skinny whippet of a wife a second thought. If she couldn't hang on to Toby, someone else would and that would be Babs. She'd hang on to him and keep him so happy he'd never want to leave.

When, after only a few weeks, Toby left his wife and moved in with Babs, she'd thought, *this was it. Happy ever after*. Her life became a whirl of dinners in fancy restaurants, weekends away, shopping trips to top up her, and his, expensive wardrobes, nights wrapped in his arms, days when her face ached from smiling.

Her life, so dull and lifeless before, sizzled.

Then Misty had slithered in and stolen Toby away.

21

BABS

'Ms Sanderson?' DI Hopper's voice dragged Babs back to her Streatham apartment. 'I asked you... was that why you called around to confront Misty Eastwood? You held her responsible for Mr Carter leaving you?'

'We were happy together until he met her, so what do you think? That day–' Babs remembered the absolute pleasure she'd felt as her clenched fist had connected with the writer's cheek. '– I was having a bad day, had a bit to drink and lost my temper.' There was no point in telling the police that she'd spent hours outside the house in Hanwell hoping to catch a glimpse of Toby and even more time staring up at the window where Misty sat, hating her with a fury that had finally driven Babs to act. There was no point in telling the police that she still went every day.

'Sounds like you have a nasty temper, you were lucky Ms Eastwood didn't call the police.'

'She was lucky I didn't kill her.' Babs grinned as if to indicate she was joking, but she wasn't sure she was. She'd often wondered, if Toby hadn't returned, would she have stopped, or kept going until she'd beaten the bitch to a pulp.

Hopper didn't look amused. She made a note in her

notebook and sat back. 'According to Ms Eastwood, Mr Carter was leaving her for someone else. How did that make you feel?'

Babs stared at the detective for a moment before releasing a sigh. 'I didn't know about that until that woman called here yesterday looking for him. Gwen something or other... glamorous but old. Anyway, in the last few weeks, I've come to my senses, you know. Faced reality.'

'Reality?' Hopper queried when the silence stretched.

'That I'm broke. Behind in my mortgage. Maxed out on my credit cards.' Babs ran a hand over her hair. 'I can't even afford to go to the hairdresser.'

'You gave him money?'

'Fifty quid now and then, when he'd–' She made inverted commas in the air. '–forgotten his wallet. But that wasn't the problem really, it was all the other expenses. Toby liked the good life. Expensive restaurants, fine wine, a whisky to finish off a meal. He liked to get gifts too...' Babs' voice faded. 'He was very amorous and attentive afterward, the more costly the gift, the more amorous he became. Plus there were the weekends away in posh hotels where everyone wore designer clothes. Every trip meant shopping beforehand to buy new clothes for us both.'

Babs had tried to keep Toby so happy that he wouldn't want to leave her. Unfortunately, his happiness was directly proportionate to how much money she spent on him and the money ran out. And now here she was... broke. She'd no illusions about the job either. For the moment she was on suspension but she'd a feeling one of those letters she was refusing to open was from the human resources manager of the clinic. Babs was ignoring it the same way she was ignoring the final demands and the letters from the bank.

'Did he force you to pay for everything?' Hopper's voice was suddenly gentle as if she wasn't sure what she was dealing with here and was making an effort to tread carefully.

Babs brought her thoughts back from her money woes and looked at the detective with wide eyes before snorting a laugh. 'What, you think I was gaslighted or something? You don't understand.' She laughed again but this time the sound held thick layers of sadness. 'Toby is charisma personified. He has the ability to make you feel like you're something special, something amazing.' She held her arms out. 'I mean look at me, I'm not exactly a beauty.' Her voice dropped to a whisper. 'But when I was with him, I felt gorgeous and charming, everything I ever wanted to be but wasn't. I would have spent every penny to hold on to that.' She slumped back with a loud sigh. 'I *did* spend every penny: all my savings, all my salary every month.'

'I'm sorry.'

The sympathy on the older detective's face looked genuine. Babs nodded in acknowledgement and decided to ignore what she took to be an expression of derision on the painted face of the younger detective. Babs pressed her lips together to hold back the tears she felt building. 'Do you know what the saddest thing is, Detective Inspector Hopper? It's that despite this reality, despite waking up to my situation, I'd take him back tomorrow and sell my soul to keep him.'

22

DEE

Dee Carter lived in a small, terraced Victorian house on Cedar Road in Croydon. A black-and-terracotta tiled path led from a wrought-iron gate to an unattractive uPVC front door but the windows, one down and two above, were original wooden sashes. The area between the front wall and the house would no doubt at one time have been a pretty garden but necessity had caused it to be concreted in; now all that bloomed in it were a proliferation of recycling bins.

Dee had been waiting anxiously for someone to call with news since she'd reported her husband missing early that morning. Mug after mug of tea was downed as she sat on the sofa in the living room with the phone beside her, afraid to turn on the TV in case she missed something.

Fine voile curtains at the windows gave a soft-focus view of the road outside. But the fabric didn't soften the edges of the two women who arrived and stood at the gate staring at the house. *Police*. Panic jolted Dee to her feet. Wasn't it only bad news that was delivered in person?

She heard them mumbling outside before they pressed the

doorbell. Maybe they were practising the words they were going to use to impart the news.

Dee swallowed a sob and before the echoing chime of the doorbell faded, she wrenched the door open. A petite woman, she was immediately intimidated by the tall officers who stood shoulder to shoulder on the doorstep. She glanced blankly at the proffered identification, stood back and waved them into the narrow entrance hall.

Their grim, set faces increased her nervous anxiety. She wanted to bark out *tell me* but she was a woman used to waiting and convinced as she was that the news was bad, she wanted contrarily to put the words off as long as she could, to live in ignorance a little longer, to pretend that everything was going to end happily ever after as she had for so many years.

She wondered if they found her silence odd or if they were used to people's varying reactions to bad news. *Bad news. Toby, my love.*

She finally found words to use. 'Please, go in.' She pointed to the doorway of the living room. 'Have a seat. Can I get you coffee, tea or something?' She saw them look around, their eyes assessing.

She'd done her best with the small space. When they'd bought the house almost fifteen years before, there had been shelving to both sides of the chimney breast. She had it removed from one side to fit one of the two sofas they'd brought with them from their previous home but they still overpowered the room. Between them, a low coffee table almost covered the remainder of the polished wooden floor.

The two detectives sat and looked up to where she hovered in the doorway. 'Coffee would be good,' Hopper said. 'Both black, thank you.'

Dee returned minutes later and set a tray down on the table.

'Here you go, coffee and biscuits. You can't have a cuppa without something to eat, can you?' Her forced cheerfulness sounded wrong even to her ears and she wondered what they thought of her.

She waited until they'd picked up their mugs before she sat on the other sofa. A mug of tea was held clasped to her chest. She wanted to draw the heat from it in hope it would stop the shivers that had been sweeping over her since she'd realised Toby wasn't coming back.

Hopper's stubby fingers curled through the handle of the mug. She lifted it and sipped, her eyes never leaving Babs' face. 'You went into Croydon Police Station this morning to report your husband missing, Mrs Carter.'

'Dee, please.' A nervous smile fluttered and died.

'Dee, you reported your husband missing.'

'That's right.'

'You haven't heard from him.'

'No. No, that's why I reported him missing.'

'He might have contacted you since, is what I mean.'

They thought she was stupid. She could see it in their eyes, in the derisive smile on the younger officer's bright-red lips. 'Ah, sorry, I'm sorry.' Dee shook her head, annoyed with herself for apologising, with them for making her feel a fool, with Toby for leaving her... again. Maybe they were right, maybe she was stupid. 'I get you. No, he didn't, I haven't heard from him.'

'Right.' Hopper reached into her pocket for her notebook, flipped it open and searched in her other pocket for a pen. 'You told the station you haven't seen your husband since last week but he normally rang you every day.'

'That's right.'

Hopper looked at the notes, squinting to read. Despite the window, there was little light in the room. 'You last heard from him three days ago.'

'Yes, that's right.'

'What did you talk about?'

'Nothing special,' Dee said. 'He asked how my job was, I asked him how his was, and that was about it.'

'He didn't say anything about the woman he was living with?'

'No.' One curt word. Dee could have told them that he never did speak about them... these women he dallied with, the bits of fluff he picked up and dropped as quickly, the ones he lingered with for a night, a week, longer, all the women there had been over the years. He never spoke about his women but she knew about them. Sometimes she'd follow him, weighing up and assessing her opponent in a fight she won in her head every time.

When Hopper waved a hand to get her attention she wondered how long she'd been lost in her memories. 'Sorry,' she said again. 'It's all a bit stressful.'

'I was asking if you knew where he was living?'

Dee's expression stayed grim. 'With some tart called Babs, in Streatham.'

'You didn't know he'd moved from Streatham to Hanwell and was, in fact, planning a move to Knightsbridge.'

Dee's mouth twisted. 'The tart came into money, did she? He'd have liked that.'

'No.' Hopper sat forward. 'You didn't know he'd left Babs and moved in with another woman in Hanwell?'

Dee's fingers tightened on the mug she was holding until she felt she might crush it. 'No, I didn't know that but Toby's fallen on his feet if they're moving to Knightsbridge.'

'*They* weren't moving to Knightsbridge. No, he was leaving the woman in Hanwell and moving in with someone else.'

Dee's mouth fell open, then she put the mug she was holding down on the table and laughed. A hysterical belly laugh that rolled on and on, the sound growing louder, wilder. The look of helplessness on the older detective's face made Dee laugh harder.

'You're supposed to wallop her across the face,' DS Collins said, lifting the mug of coffee to her mouth and taking a noisy slurp.

'And get arrested for assault. No, thanks.' Instead, Hopper moved to sit on the sofa beside Dee's heaving body and put a hand lightly on the other woman's arm. 'Stop, you'll make yourself sick.'

Dee put her hands over her mouth but the laughter continued to sputter from behind them. It was another minute before it died with a final hiccup. 'I'm sorry,' she said, wiping her sleeve across her face.

'There's no need to apologise. You've had a bit of a shock.'

Dee shook her head emphatically. 'It wasn't a shock, nor a surprise. I don't even know why I was laughing... maybe for the months of waiting for him to come back... for fooling myself for years before that. All the years when he promised to be faithful, until the next woman he couldn't resist.'

Hopper's hand still rested on Dee's arm. 'How long have you been married?'

'Twenty years.' Dee managed a smile at the look on the detective's face. 'Surprised? We were both eighteen. Young and in love. And for the first year, it was perfect.'

'Why did you stay with him?' Collins leaned forward and met Dee's eyes.

Not a shred of sympathy warmed the younger officer's face, her heavily kohled eyes regarding Dee as if she were some form of alien.

She didn't think there was any point in trying to explain. A woman like Collins couldn't begin to understand. Dee felt the heavy weight of the older detective's hand on her arm and turned to her. There was so much understanding in her eyes that Dee felt tears well and her voice was thick when she said, 'Because I couldn't live without him... I *can't* live without him. And he always comes back. At least he always did till now.'

'There have been three women since he left you,' Hopper said quietly. 'None of them know where he is.'

'Three...' Dee swallowed. She'd only known about the Streatham woman. She'd assumed when Toby got tired of her, he'd come home. He always had done before. 'He always comes back to me. I'm sure he will again but it's so unlike him to be out of communication. I've rung his mobile several times, left several messages.' She picked up the mobile that sat on the sofa beside her. 'It's newish, with a new number. Toby called around last Wednesday.' The memory brought a smile. 'He did now and then.' She didn't say that her heart leapt every time, hoping that this time he was going to stay, feeling the plummeting disappointment when he'd say he was simply calling for a chat.

'I remember he laughed when I told him I hadn't figured out how to use it yet.' She shook the memory away. 'He wanted to take it from me and get it going but I said I had to start doing these things for myself. I'd written the number down and I gave it to him.'

He'd laughed when he read what I'd written on the scrap of paper. 'You've put your name on it, did you think I'd forgotten?' I wanted to ask if he had. If he'd forgotten me and how much I loved him. I'd wanted to beg him to come home.

'Mrs Carter?'

Dee blinked and shook her head again. 'Sorry. Anyway, he put my number into his phone straight away so I know he has it.' She put the phone down on the sofa beside her. 'I messaged him later that day to say I'd succeeded in getting it working.'

'We're trying to trace his mobile but so far we've not had much success.'

'He's never without it... ever.'

Hopper took a card from her pocket and handed it over. 'We'll keep in touch, Dee, but if you hear from Toby, let me know. You can get me on this number whenever you want.'

Dee put the card beside her phone without looking at it.

These police officers might think she was stupid, and perhaps she was, but she was smart enough to know she was never going to need it.

23

GWEN

S elf-pity and anger vied for the upper hand as Gwen tried to put every memory of Toby from her head, her heart, her life.

When she was younger, she wouldn't have been so gullible. Was she becoming too needy... too desperate... was that why she'd been so foolish the last few years?

The last few years. Her thoughts drifted back to the first man who'd tried to con her. It should have been impossible to catch her out, she read the newspapers, knew about the millions of pounds women were conned out of every year and the appalling statistics regarding internet romance scams. She'd shaken her head when she read about catfishing, that wonderful name for the heinous practice of faking an identity with the sole aim of conning some poor unfortunate out of money, sex, their self-esteem.

Gwen knew it all. What she didn't know, what she hadn't read about was that the emotional toll was often as bad as the financial. That she learned from personal experience.

Sam Burke.

Gwen had been lulled by his absolute ordinariness. He was a

chubby, medium-height man with a receding hairline and a stutter she'd found endearing when she'd met him in a café near her home.

Looking back, she could see how it had been the perfect setup. It had been a year since her previous relationship had ended and she'd been alone, maybe she'd looked lonely, even sad. Sunday mornings often made her feel melancholy as she read the newspaper surrounded by families, by couples sharing the various sections of the paper, passing them across the table automatically with time-learned intimacy and knowledge of the likes and dislikes of their partner.

It was an intimacy that Gwen missed. That Sunday, she'd been nursing her cup of coffee, the café newspaper sitting folded on the edge of the table.

'Excuse m-m-me.'

She'd turned automatically with a frown that faded quickly. 'Yes?'

'Are you f-f-finished with the n-n-newspaper?'

'Sure.' She handed it over. He'd fumbled as he reached for it and it had fallen, spreading its pages as it hit the floor in an untidy mess. Later, she realised it was a well-rehearsed manoeuvre that had instantly built a connection between them.

She had laughed and insisted it was her fault that the paper had fallen. Between them they'd picked it up and by the time it was back in order, they were chatting in a friendly manner... so friendly that when he'd haltingly asked if he could join her, she hesitated only a second before agreeing.

Coffee had led to a midweek dinner. Gwen had used the intervening days to check Sam was as ordinary as he'd appeared. His social networking presence was a Facebook page he rarely used and a Twitter account he'd used once. That was it.

Over dinner on the Wednesday, he mentioned he was a self-employed finance consultant. 'It sounds as boring as it is.' His laugh was warm, self-deprecatory. 'Really, it's all about telling people what they should do with their money. Sometimes people even listen to me.'

He'd been impressed by her job, his eyes widening appreciatively. 'You own an art gallery in Knightsbridge, wow!'

Later, she wondered if behind his soft brown eyes, dollar signs hadn't lined up in a row, ready for the big payout. But then, his appreciation had warmed her. The evening had been enjoyable and at the end Sam had insisted on paying. 'After all, I invited you.'

And they'd arranged to meet again, and the next time, he'd gone back to hers for coffee and stayed. The sex had been comfortable, almost cosy rather than exciting. Pleasant, Gwen had decided, trying to convince herself.

She'd no misgivings about their relationship as it quickly developed. They were both old enough not to have to play games.

Three weeks later, Sam mentioned a finance deal he'd been invited to invest in. 'It sounds great. What people would call a sure thing. It's a shame it's come at the wrong time for me, my money is tied up for another few weeks in another deal.'

Gwen's eyes, shut for three weeks, snapped open. Sam was careful. He didn't ask her for the money or suggest she should invest for herself. Instead, he was unusually quiet for the rest of the evening, looking into the distance, answering her absently until finally, she followed the script he'd written for her and asked, 'What's wrong?'

He smiled, shook his head, and reached for her hand. 'Sorry, sorry. I'm fed up missing that deal, you know. Such a great opportunity I'm letting slip away.'

'How much money are we talking about?' She felt the slight tightening of his hand and kept her expression carefully neutral.

'There's a minimum twenty-five k investment,' he said. Then

with a flick of his other hand, added, 'It'll make five k in a month.'

Gwen had frowned as if she was seriously considering the offer. 'If I could get it for you, I'd get five k back on top of my investment?'

He laughed. 'Well, really it should be less my commission but since it's you I'll forgo that.' He squeezed her hand tightly. 'Gosh, are you serious, would you want to invest that much money?'

'You said it's a sure thing. Five k for a month sounds tempting.'

'I'm sorry that my money is tied up but it's great that you can avail of it.' He leaned close and kissed her on the cheek. 'I'm pleased for you.'

He sounded so sincere, his gaze was steady, his smile so warm. An Oscar-winning performance.

'The offer is closed tomorrow,' he said. 'We need to be quick; I'd hate you to miss this opportunity.' He took a pen from his pocket and wrote his bank details on the back of a business card. 'You could transfer it as soon as you get home, then I could process it tonight.'

'Sure.' Gwen took the card and looked at it. 'In fact, I have fifty thousand in my savings account. It's every penny I have, but if I invested that, would I get ten k back?'

Sam couldn't prevent his eyes widening or his hand tightening further as if to grasp this wondrous offer. 'Oh yes, absolutely. You'd have sixty k in a month.'

She'd sat there, her hand in his, feeling bitterness twisting her mouth and a heaviness in her belly. And she thought of the sex and wanted to throw up. Then the arrogance of the bastard, that he'd think so little of her, made her pull her hand away and get to her feet. While he was still trying to understand the change in temperature, she drew her arm back and hit him squarely across the face. The loud clap as flesh connected with flesh was loud enough to halt conversation in the restaurant as every face turned to stare.

She left, managing to walk from the restaurant with her head high, stumbling up the street, unable to see for the tears that clouded her eyes. Tears of anger mixed with those of self-pity and loss.

The next day, regretting she'd let him get away with it, she tried to contact him but his number had been disconnected. Although she knew where he lived, she'd never been to his home; he'd always stayed at hers and she couldn't remember if that had been his choice or hers. She realised why, when determined to have it out with him, she called to his address to discover he didn't live there, and the people who did had never heard of him.

Perhaps she should have reported it, admitted to her stupidity, to being as much of an idiot as those women she and her friends had laughed at for being so gullible. She didn't; afraid it would slip out. She didn't want to face the derision, to listen to the smart remarks, the pitying looks. Anyway, she'd lost no money... just her self-respect.

For weeks afterwards, she'd looked for him in every café, every pub and every public area. She read her newspaper with more care, checked the news on the internet, checked references of fraud or catfishing, every mention of someone being conned out of money. And each time, she remembered how close she'd come. So close she spoke to a financial advisor in her local bank and had her savings locked away in a special account where she couldn't access it for at least five years.

She swore she'd never be taken for a fool again.

And then she met George.

24

GWEN

I t was over a year after her close call with Sam Burke that Gwen met George at a party given by mutual friends. She was careful, took her time before getting involved, determined this time to get it right.

He was divorced, his ex-wife living with a polo player in Argentina. 'We wanted different things,' he told Gwen when their relationship entered its second month and they started talking about past relationships.

There was no bitterness in his voice when he spoke of his marriage, no sense of hostility towards his ex-wife. Gwen let herself fall a little further in love with him.

In return for his relationship disclosures, she made him laugh with stories of past lovers. But she left out the story about Sam.

They married a year after they met. It was another six months after she'd walked down the aisle of a pretty country church before Gwen realised exactly what he'd meant by he and his ex-wife *wanting different things*. She, like Gwen, had probably wanted and expected fidelity whereas George considered it to be a ridiculous concept.

She came to understand that her husband needed a string of foolish, cheap women to feel powerful. Gwen was too much: too strong, successful, rich. Her fault, too, that she owned the apartment in Knightsbridge and the successful art gallery. She, as George told her many times when he'd had a few drinks, *emasculated him.*

Every new affair had diminished her a little, had taken small painful bites out of her self-worth. George probably thought he was being discreet but she always knew... he'd wear that certain smile he only wore after one of his assignations... and she'd know he was off again and wondered if this time, this woman was the one that would finish their marriage.

In the end, she stopped asking and condemning but she'd never stopped loving the lying, cheating bastard. Only his death had solved that heartache.

Two years before, he was killed during a burglary while she was away at an art conference. Stabbed, dead before he hit the floor according to the investigating officer. Gwen had been shocked, devastated... and almost relieved.

'He was supposed to come to the conference with me,' she told the officer. 'But he wasn't feeling well during the afternoon so decided to stay home.'

'You're well known in the art world, Ms Marsham. Someone knew your apartment was supposed to be empty. By the time they realised their intel was wrong, it was too late.'

And that was it, it was deemed to be a robbery gone wrong. The investigation tapered off after a few weeks and although it was still an open case, Gwen didn't think they'd ever discover what happened that night.

She'd sworn off men after George and over the last two years she'd come to accept that she was better single.

Then Toby had walked into the gallery and she knew she'd been lying to herself.

25

GWEN

G wen was feeling grubby after getting rid of the last of Toby's belongings. She had a long shower, used her favourite scented moisturiser, and pulled a cotton robe on to encase the scent. She breathed it in, feeling automatically more relaxed. It was over.

A glass of wine seemed in order. A mini celebration.

Gwen grabbed a chair cushion and went onto the balcony with her icy cold glass of Sémillon. The unseasonal rain that had battered the city for the last couple of days had stopped and the evening was warm with none of the humidity that could make summer in London uncomfortable. She tilted a chair to drain the rainwater, dropped the cushion on it and sat.

The chair faced the end of the road. It was a quieter, prettier aspect than the opposite and one she normally chose. If she'd been facing the other direction, she'd have seen a car stop halfway along the street and the two detectives who'd visited her earlier at the gallery get out and walk towards her apartment. If she'd seen them, she could have slipped back inside before they saw her, could have ignored the doorbell.

But she didn't and when it shattered the quiet she jumped

and dropped her wine glass. It hit the ground and smashed, dumping the cold wine she'd barely touched in a puddle that immediately inched on the slight slope towards the apartment.

The entrance door of the building was recessed so she knew it was pointless to lean over the balcony to see who was calling. She got to her feet, stepped over the mess of glass and wine and went inside. An intercom screen was set to one side of the front door. With one press of a button, she could see who was outside. Two figures. Gwen wondered if they'd pressed her bell in error... or maybe she hoped. She was still hoping when one of the figures moved closer to press the bell again, the painted face instantly recognisable. It was those blasted detectives. Gwen could ignore them. They didn't know she was here, did they? Or had they looked up and seen her?

Her question was answered when the intercom buzzed again and, this time, they pressed the button to speak. 'We know you're there, Ms Marsham, we'd appreciate it if we could have a moment of your time.'

She didn't bother answering but pushed the buzzer to release the entrance door. Her apartment door was locked, a safety chain in place. Trembling fingers undid the chain with less than usual dexterity and by the time she pulled the door open with a grunt of frustration, the two detectives were standing outside.

'I'm sorry,' Gwen said. 'I always put the lock and chain on when I come home, they can be fiddly to remove.' She was babbling, showing her unease. Usually, she was good at reading expressions, but theirs were granite. 'Come in, please.' She took a step backwards waiting till they'd gone into the living room before shutting the door, using the time to get a grip on her churning emotions.

She followed them and waved towards the sofas. 'Sit, please.'

She crossed the room to shut the balcony door and hide the broken glass from view. 'It's getting a little cool.'

The detectives sat beside one another, leaving the other sofa for her. She eyed it but instead of sitting she pushed the corners of her lips up in what she hoped would pass for a normal, relaxed smile and said, 'May I get you some refreshments? Tea or coffee, perhaps?'

Hopper shook her head. 'We're good, thanks. We won't keep you long.'

Gwen sat then and pulled her robe tightly around her. She leaned back, trying to give the appearance of being at ease.

'We're still attempting to locate Toby Carter and in the course of our investigation we spoke to Barbara Sanderson.' The detective watched Gwen's face carefully. 'You didn't tell us you'd been to see her.'

Gwen lifted a hand and pushed loose hair behind her ear. 'I didn't see it was necessary. As I told you earlier, I like to know why arrangements fall apart and thought Ms Sanderson might have had the answer.'

'An awful lot of trouble for a man you barely know.'

'Yes.' Gwen shrugged slightly. 'Foolish of me, I suppose.'

'You've had bad luck with men in the last few years.'

Gwen's expression hardened and bitterness flavoured every word when she spoke. 'Is that how the police are classifying the stabbing to death of my husband, detective inspector? As bad luck? Perhaps that's why they've had no success in charging anyone with his murder.'

Hopper held her hands up. 'I'm sorry, that was an unfortunate choice of words.'

'Certainly inappropriate.'

'My apologies.' Hopper waited a moment before continuing. 'You were away at a conference when your husband was killed. It must have been an awful shock.'

Gwen glared at her. 'My husband was stabbed to death in our home. I was shocked, horrified and devastated.'

'There was some talk at the time, that your husband may have been unfaithful, inviting women here when you were away.'

'I'm a wealthy, successful woman, detective. There's always talk. I let it go over my head.'

But Hopper wasn't letting it go. 'So there was no truth to the rumours?'

'George thought fidelity was something thought up by women to control men,' Gwen said with little inflection. 'By the time he was killed, I'd stopped caring.'

'It must have reminded you of it when you discovered Toby Carter was equally promiscuous. Must have hurt.'

'Must it?'

Hopper sat forward. 'Yes, I think it must have done. You're a glamorous, successful woman and yet men don't think you're enough for them, always having to have other women.'

Gwen laughed. 'You make me sound like such a pathetic cow!' She pushed her fingers through her hair, lifting it and dropping it so it fell in waves around her face. 'You know little about me. Believe me, I'm nobody's victim.' She got to her feet in one smooth, elegant movement. 'Now, if that's all.'

'One more question, Ms Marsham,' Hopper said, holding up a hand. 'This conference you were at the night your husband was murdered... it was held in a hotel in Canary Wharf, wasn't it? A forty-minute taxi drive away. You mentioned your husband being unwell, I'm surprised you didn't come home when the conference ended.'

'You've obviously no idea what these art conferences are like. I have a vague idea I got to bed around 5am and was certainly in no state to travel anywhere at that stage.' She put hands that were trembling slightly into the pockets of her robe. 'Now, if that's all, I've had a tiring day.'

'Thank you for your time,' DI Hopper said but she stopped at the door and turned with a final word. 'We may have more questions, Ms Marsham.'

Gwen resisted the temptation to slam the door behind them.

26

MISTY

I spent a few hours tidying the house and removing every hint that Toby Carter had ever lived there. He'd taken most of his belongings but there were still a few things... a single sock in the laundry basket, a pair of boxer shorts in the airing cupboard that I picked up and held to my face for a ridiculously long period of time, tears trickling to dampen the cotton.

Then there were the items of food I'd bought because he liked them. The expensive olives, epicurean cheeses, salami that stunk the fridge out and tainted the milk, pâté in jars that were more trouble to open than they were worth. I pulled a rubbish bag from a roll and dumped the lot, taking pleasure in the crash of jars and packets, pushing the clothing items in on top and tying the top of the bag in a knot before throwing it outside.

Only one thing remained, a bottle of wine I'd bought recently, spending far more than I usually did because he'd mentioned it was a wine he liked. 'Fifty quid,' I muttered, picking it up to look at the label. I wasn't going to waste it but I wanted it gone. I pulled open a drawer to search among the chaos inside for an opener.

The cork came out with a satisfying pop. I poured the rich

red wine into a glass and slurped a mouthful. It was nice, but hardly fifty quid nice. I guessed it had been the price that had appealed to Toby rather than any knowledge of the wine. Easy to like expensive things when someone else was forking out the money.

I wasn't going to go there. Wasn't going to enumerate all I'd spent on the cheating toerag. It was over.

It was important that I pull myself together. The book I was working on for one reason, it wasn't going to write itself. My schedule was tight; I couldn't afford to waste any more time. Tomorrow, I'd pull myself together. Right now, it was time to drown my sorrows and finish the wine.

There was pizza in the freezer. I threw it into the oven and when it was done, took it and the wine into the living room.

A candy-floss movie on the TV, pizza, and wine. It had been my idea of a perfect night before I met Toby, it would be again. But maybe not that night. Tears ran down my face as one glass of wine followed the other until the bottle was empty. I'd barely finished a slice of the pizza and had no idea what the movie had been about.

It was galling... cringeworthy... to admit what a foolish woman I'd been. Those weeks with Toby had been an aberration, a fantasy I'd spent a fortune trying to keep from dissolving in the harsh reality of truth. I couldn't have written a story so awful.

It was almost midnight before I switched off the TV and got shakily to my feet. I'd regret leaving the pizza where it was. In the morning, the room would stink of stale pepperoni. But the knowledge didn't make me change my mind and I left everything where it was and headed upstairs.

Toby's particular scent still lingered in the bedroom. It brought memories tumbling around me as I climbed under the covers in the same kaftan I'd worn all day. The wine had been stronger than usual, or maybe I'd drunk too much and eaten too little. Whatever the reason, my head spun under the onslaught of remembered whispers and my skin quivered under ghostly fingers. I shut my eyes and pleaded for sleep to blot everything out.

But sleep was a traitor and abandoned me. By dawn I was exhausted from twisting and turning and frustrated by the blow to the morning I'd planned. Being sleep-deprived wasn't going to be a good start.

Curling on my side, I stared at the curtains I'd pulled shut hours before. Was that why I couldn't sleep? Was I wondering if Toby was outside? And if he were, if he regretted leaving and wanted to return. Knowing what I did about him now, would I be strong enough to tell him to stay away from me?

I simply wasn't sure. But once the idea that he might be outside had wormed its way into my head, it kept creeping around, developing stinging tentacles. With an exasperated grunt, I flung the sheets back and got to my feet. I reached for the curtains to pull them back, but rather than jerking them fully open as planned, I opened them a crack and stepped closer to peer through. All I could see was a tiny section directly in front of the house. It was deserted. Slowly, I increased the gap until the curtains were wide open and I could see both ways. There was nobody to be seen. Although I'd known the idea was crazy, I felt a weight float from me.

I slipped back into bed and within a few minutes had fallen asleep.

Noise outside woke me mid-morning. I stretched and opened my eyes, relieved to be feeling better. Determined to get my life back to something remotely resembling normality, I swung out of bed. The sight of the grubby, wrinkled kaftan I wore made me grimace. I pulled it off and threw it to the floor. It was followed seconds later by the bed linen.

After a long shower where I scrubbed my body and washed my hair I still wasn't singing but, despite a hangover headache, I was feeling better than I'd done in a while. I dressed, then shoved the laundry into the washing machine and switched it on. I cleared away the abandoned pizza and opened the window for a few minutes to dispel the stink of pepperoni. Normal things. They felt good.

Needing fresh milk, I decided to walk to the local shop for a few necessities. It was raining again, light summer rain that looked harmless but I knew better, it was sneaky and would quickly soak through my T-shirt. I grabbed a raincoat and pulled it on.

It was a ten-minute walk but it felt good to be outside despite the rain. The small convenience store was on the opposite side of the busy Uxbridge Road. Too lazy to walk further to where a pedestrian crossing blinked brightly, I stood and waited for a gap in the traffic, looking quickly both ways. It was only then that I saw a figure I thought I recognised. I ran across the road then, causing cars to break and blast their horns, running until I was inside the store, turning to look through the window, my eyes wide as I looked to where I'd seen him, craning as far as I could. But if Toby had been there, he wasn't there now.

I was being foolish. It had been a trick of the light. A mirage. Light refracted in the rain.

It wasn't until one of the assistants came over to ask if I was okay that I pushed away from the window. 'Yes, sorry. I thought I saw someone I was trying to avoid.'

The assistant smiled uncertainly. 'Do you need help?'

I shook my head. 'No, thank you. I'm being silly. I'll just get what I came for.'

Still unsettled, I grabbed the milk I knew I needed and left the store with the hood of my raincoat pulled down over my forehead. I was almost amused at my childish *if I can't see him, he can't see me* thinking as I speed-walked home. My dash across the busy road earned me more horn blasts, one driver rolling down his window to shout obscenities at me as he passed.

Back on the quieter Myrtle Road, I walked even faster, breaking into a run for the last few metres. Safe inside the house, I locked the front door and slipped the safety chain into place. Leaving the milk in the hall, I went upstairs and pulled the curtains shut before peering through a crack. At that time of the day, there were plenty of people walking to and fro but none were wearing Toby's distinctive hat or Burberry raincoat. My hands clenched on the fold of the curtains I held and I rested my head against them.

I was tired. That's all it was. Nothing more than that.

I couldn't have seen Toby.

27

GWEN

G wen opened the gallery at ten the next morning as she always did, Tuesday to Saturday. It was important to be seen to be in control, to be business as usual. Especially if the police decided to visit her again.

There was no reason they should but there'd been no reason for them to have come the day before either and yet they had. Or maybe she was being naive. Toby, after all, was supposed to have gone to her apartment the night he went missing. He hadn't, of course, but it was the police's job to be suspicious.

That they seemed to be suspicious of George's death worried her. There had never been any indication that the police had suspected her of having a hand in her husband's death at the time. Or had she simply refused to see it?

Gwen sat at the desk and rested her head in her hand. She'd been taking a leaf from George's well-thumbed book when she started the affair with Toby and had expected great sex and the handsome man's companionship to be enough. She hadn't expected him to fill a hole she'd not known existed, hadn't planned for happiness to put a bounce in her step or to suddenly be aware of possibilities... or a future with such a devastatingly gorgeous man.

The gallery door opened. Gwen lifted her face and pasted on her professional smile. It faded quickly when she saw who it was. 'What are you doing here?'

Misty shook her head as she crossed the gallery floor. 'I needed to talk to someone and strangely, you're the only one who would understand.'

'You look wretched,' Gwen said, getting to her feet. 'Sit, I'll get you a glass of water.' She took two glasses from the small kitchenette at the back of the gallery and filled them from a bottle in the fridge. 'Here you go.'

Misty took the glass and gulped a mouthful. 'Thank you.' She took another drink, put the glass down and wiped her mouth with her hand. 'I went to my local convenience store this morning and I saw Toby. I was crossing the road and looked back and there he was.'

The glass Gwen was holding shook. She put it down carefully. 'Are you sure?'

'I don't know. It looked like him. He was wearing a Burberry raincoat and that tweed flat cap he likes... you know, the one he thinks makes him look *country*.'

'Lots of men wear those hats thanks to David Beckham. You look pale. You said you'd not been sleeping well; I'd guess your already vivid imagination is running in overdrive.'

'Maybe.'

'You miss him but are refusing to admit it so different ideas in your brain are warring with one another.' Gwen smiled, hoping she looked suitably sympathetic. 'You didn't see Toby. It's those books you write. I've read a couple; you've written some seriously creepy characters. Maybe your tired brain is simply projecting?'

'Toby hasn't turned up though, the police are still looking for him.'

Gwen reached across and rested her hand on Misty's arm. 'He'll turn up.' When tears filled the woman's eyes, Gwen reached for a business card, picked up a pen and scrawled a number on the back. 'Here,' she said. 'You can ring me if you want, okay? Anytime.'

'Thank you, that's very kind.' Misty put the card in her bag, then pulled a tissue from her pocket, dabbed her eyes, and blew her nose. 'It's been the stress of it all. I'll be fine.' She stood, straightened her jacket, and lifted her chin with a pathetic attempt of strength that might have succeeded if it weren't for the downturned mouth and the slumped shoulders that seem to droop further as she walked to the exit.

Gwen groaned. How had she got herself into this mess? *Toby.* When she looked back over the years, every time things went wrong there was a blasted man somehow involved.

28

DEE

Dee Carter slept on and off, half-expecting the phone to ring or the doorbell to chime. Once, years before... she smiled as she remembered...Toby threw stones up at their bedroom window when she'd slept through the doorbell ringing. She'd opened the window and seen him there smiling in the moonlight and her aching heart had, once again, forgiven him for straying.

So many times. Twenty years of forgiving. Twenty years of defending her husband, defending her decision to stay with him.

Friends advised her to leave him. And Dee listened to them, listened to their words, saw their happy, solid marriages, their lovely husbands... their dull, boring, faithful husbands. It had been a toss-up then – stay with her errant, straying husband, drown in the magic when things were going well and soak up every last bewitching drop in the hope it would sustain her when he got bored and drifted – or leave him and be alone. Alone, because how could she ever replace Toby with a mere mortal.

Ava, their nineteen-year-old daughter, had left home as soon as she was old enough, sick of the constant dramatics, tired of her mother's tears and her father's promises. She was living in Aberdeen and rarely came home.

Maybe Dee would go and visit her. Tell her it was finished between her and Toby at last.

She rolled over in the bed and buried her face in her pillow. She couldn't leave Croydon. Not yet. It would take time for reality to sink into the brain she'd coated in platinum years before.

Reality. She'd never been too good at facing it. Now she didn't have to. Now she didn't have to face the truth that Toby wasn't coming home to her. She thought he'd get tired of that Streatham woman, Babs, and it seems he had. Only he'd not returned to her, he'd moved on to richer pickings, then on again when a better opportunity presented itself.

Moved on to someone more suitable than his dull wife.

Someone more exciting, maybe someone dangerous.

Dangerous. The police appeared to have no idea what had happened to Toby but Dee was convinced of two things.

Toby was dead. He had to be, because in all the years of his philandering he'd never been out of contact for more than a day.

And if she was right, Dee was convinced that one of the women he'd been involved with had something to do with it.

Dee had worked for the same company for fifteen years so when she rang that morning to say there was a family emergency she wasn't surprised to be told to take as much time as she needed.

As much time as she needed to find out what had happened to the man she loved.

And which of the women Toby had found so fascinating was to blame.

29

MISTY

Outside Gwen's art gallery, too weary to negotiate the underground, I hailed a taxi to take me home.

Gwen was right, of course. I should do what she was doing, put Toby out of my head and concentrate on getting back to normal. Business as usual. I needed to meet that deadline and keep my publisher happy.

Back home, I looked warily up and down the street before clambering out of the taxi and hurrying the few feet to my front door, the key ready in my hand to stab into the keyhole. Then I was inside. I slid the safety chain in place and locked the catch.

Determined on that return to some semblance of normality, I changed into a clean kaftan. This one a swirl of turquoise and yellow silk that normally brought a smile to my face. But it was hard to find anything to smile about that day.

I sat at my desk, switched on my computer and opened the book I was working on. It was the tale of two women who shared a secret and were being stalked by a man from their past. It was a common trope in psychological thrillers but I was hoping my spin on it would be something new.

I reread what I'd written the last time, getting back into the story and the characters. The stalker was a suitably creepy middle-aged man that I hoped would make readers look around fearfully. I stopped with my hands on the keyboard as I read over his description and laughed uncertainly. I'd thought Gwen had been spouting psychobabble with her idea that I was projecting my characters into reality but maybe she was right. Had I planned for the stalker to wear a raincoat and flat cap? I rifled through the sheaf of handwritten notes for his character profile. Middle-aged, grey-haired. Neat dresser. Suits and ties. No mention of a raincoat or any kind of hat.

Had I seen Toby outside and subconsciously written aspects of him into my character or had I written memories of Toby into my character's profile, then allowed my imagination to take over, picturing him where he wouldn't be?

I stared at the screen, the words blurring. Had Toby's desertion affected me that badly? I felt lost... fearful for my sanity. Did I really miss him that much?

He was a lying, cheating bastard. I dug deep for the anger that seemed to be a healthier reaction. Anger at him, at my foolishness. I hit the keys with more vigour than was required and deleted any reference to a flat cap and raincoat from my work, doing a word search to make sure. Simmering emotions kept me focused and that afternoon I wrote more than I'd written for over a week. Enough to bring me back on schedule. It was late before I saved my work and switched off with a sense of satisfaction that succeeded in washing the last of the anger away.

For the first time in days, I felt hungry. A quick search of the cupboards and I found enough packets and jars to put together a pasta dish. Pasta carbonara and a glass of white wine. Couldn't get much better than that. I took them through to the living room, curled up on the sofa and switched on the TV.

There was a movie I'd not seen before. It was good enough to take my mind off things for a while but not good enough to prevent thoughts of Toby from edging their way back in when I dropped my guard.

I looked back on our time together as if it were a dream. Or maybe, more honestly, a fantasy. And it had been that, hadn't it? My sisters had been right, I'd changed and not for the better. The expensive clothes, the ridiculously expensive handbags and shoes, weekends away, dinners, wine. I'd been so stupid. What had I been trying to prove?

That I was successful both professionally and personally. Was that it?

I loved my sisters, their husbands and children and their comfortable lives, and it used to annoy me when they'd enquire about my moribund love life, but hadn't it been even more depressing when they'd stopped asking as if they'd given up hope for me.

Was that why I'd foolishly rushed into a relationship with Toby, ignoring the truth that he wasn't suitable at all. And all the money I threw at him was never going to change that.

I'd been almost blinded by his superficial attractions but only almost – deep down, I'd known we weren't suited. Was that why it had come as such a shock that he was dumping me? Had I expected to be the one to do the dumping?

I remember the tide of anger that had swept over me making me scream a litany of abuse at him.

Then he was gone.

I remember slipping the headphones back in place and increasing the volume of the music to the maximum so I couldn't hear myself continue to scream obscenities.

I'd lied to the detectives; I hadn't watched him walk out of my house and down the street with a holdall hanging from each hand.

No, I'd deleted and rewritten the script to make myself out to have been less distraught, less maniacal, than I had been.

It didn't matter whether I had calmly watched as Toby walked away from me, and from the life I'd fantasised we'd live, or screamed my disbelief in words only the most odious of the characters I'd ever written would have used... the truth was he had left.

He *had* left.

30

DEE

There was no point in wasting time. Despite her reluctance to speak to Babs, Dee knew that it was the fastest way to find out the name of the woman who had lured Toby away from Streatham.

Thanks to Toby's consideration, Dee had Babs' phone number. 'In case of emergencies,' he'd said when he'd scribbled it under the address. 'No other reason, okay?'

What other reason would there be? To ring and beg Babs to leave Toby alone. Or perhaps to ring and sing 'Jolene' down the line. To be utterly pathetic.

Dee dialled the number, hoping Babs would be there, relieved when the phone was answered on the first ring with a bored, 'Hello.'

It would have been satisfying to have spit anger down the line, but she drew a steadying breath instead. Playing nice would get her the information she wanted. 'It's Toby's wife, Dee,' she said, placing heavy emphasis on the word *wife*. 'You know Toby is missing. The police were here. I know they've spoken to you and they said you don't know where he is.' Dee took a deep breath. 'Will you tell me the name of the woman he went to after he left you?'

She hoped Babs wouldn't ask her why she wanted to know, unwilling to put the truth she knew in her heart into words. To take that final step and say aloud, *Toby is dead*. She recognised her reluctance as being a foolish glimmer of hope that she was wrong. But she knew she wasn't wrong about those women... they had to know something. She held the phone tightly to her ear and waited for an answer.

The cackle that came down the line was what she'd expected from the plump woman with the dyed blonde hair who had lured Toby away.

'You mean the *women* he went to after me,' Babs said. 'His boredom threshold is getting lower, he's moving on quickly now.'

Dee's hand tightened on the phone. Babs was one in a long line of women Toby had strayed with. She was nothing special. *But how did she know so much?* 'Do you know their names?'

The cackle sounded again. 'Oh yes, I do. The next was a crazy writer woman called Misty Eastwood. And after her there was a rather glamorous woman, Gwen Marsham.'

'Misty Eastwood and Gwen Marsham,' Dee repeated. 'Okay.' Then, reluctantly, she added, 'Thank you.'

'Wait, I have more. Since you're interested, you might like to know where they live.'

Of course, Dee did, but her unwillingness to be under a compliment to the woman made her curt *yes* simmer with hostility.

'Since you ask so nicely,' Babs said with heavy sarcasm. 'The Eastwood woman lives in Hanwell, Myrtle Road. And glamourpuss lives in Knightsbridge. Beaufort Gardens. Very upmarket. Our Toby was going places.'

Our Toby. It was the final nail in the coffin of Dee's patience.

'He was never *your* Toby.' She cut the connection and threw her mobile across the room.

But she'd got what she needed. Misty Eastwood and Gwen Marsham.

One of them knew what happened to Toby.

Dee was sure of it.

31

GWEN

G wen shut the gallery a little before five. It had been a quiet day with only one sale among the several browsers who had asked questions, one of them humming and hawing about the colour and size of a painting as if the subject itself held no weight.

Some days, and that day was one of them, Gwen wondered if she should sell the gallery and retire. Maybe rent out her apartment and live abroad for a while. She thought about it as she walked, weighing up Italy versus the south of France, the only two countries she'd seriously consider.

Or perhaps, she should get a manager for the gallery, do a trip across Europe by car and seek out some new and exciting artists. It was something to think about.

There was an exhibition she'd promised a friend to attend that evening but she couldn't find sufficient interest to drag herself out and rang her friend with a vague but suitably impressive excuse that she knew wasn't believed.

'You owe me,' the friend said, ringing off.

Gwen ordered food from a local restaurant and poured a glass of wine while she waited for it to come. She opened the door of the balcony, stopping with a tsk of annoyance when she saw the glass she'd dropped still strewn in shards across it. It would have taken a moment to clear away but she couldn't rustle up any enthusiasm for the job. She shut the door and was twisting the lock when her eye was caught by a figure at the corner of the road. The street was well lit, the figure standing in a ring of light.

Gwen gasped and pulled back. *Toby!*

Impossible. Misty's nonsense had remained in Gwen's head. That was all it was. Opening the door again, she avoided the glass and stepped out onto the balcony. With her chin in the air, she turned to face the direction she imagined she'd seen her erstwhile lover. Of course, there was nobody there. Of course, she couldn't have seen Toby.

He was dead.

32

MISTY

My fingers were flying across the keyboard, my forehead furrowed in concentration as the headphones played a classical music selection that helped without distracting. I'd tried country music but so many songs had stories worth listening to – stories that distracted me from the one I was writing – that I'd given up and switched to music without words.

Only very loud repetitive noises made it through the music to disturb me. Noises like someone hammering on the front door.

I unhooked the headphones to listen. Then it came again, someone slamming the knocker down, metal hitting metal.

With a grunt of annoyance, I saved my work, rolled my chair back and got to my feet. With my arms stretched over my head to release the knots that were an occupational hazard, I peered out the window and felt the instant acid burn of anxiety in my belly when I recognised the two women outside.

It was tempting to stay hidden, to ignore their knocking. *But they'd be back.*

I gathered the folds of the kaftan I was wearing that day – the dark floral pattern suiting my mood – and went slowly down the stairs, one step at a time, half-hoping they'd give up and leave before I got there.

I guessed my hopes were in vain when they hammered again, ringing the bell simultaneously. The resultant cacophony was jarring enough to wake the dead.

The safety chain was in place, I took my time unhooking it and pulled the door open. 'Hi,' I said with what I hoped sounded like casual coolness mixed with surprise. 'Have you been knocking long? I'm afraid once I have my headphones on, it takes a lot to get through to me.' I made no move to invite them in, I didn't want them inside. They could say what they wanted on the step.

But it seemed the detectives had other ideas. 'Is it okay if we come in?'

I wanted to tell them I was too busy, had deadlines to meet, had nothing more to tell them in any case. Instead, I raised my eyes to the ceiling and huffed a sigh of impatience. 'I suppose so.' I stood back and waved them into the living room.

The heavily made-up detective whose name I couldn't remember, sat without invitation.

'Do you mind if we sit?'

I thought I saw sympathy in the older detective's eyes and wondered why. 'No, of course, please sit. Can I get you something to drink?'

'No, thanks.'

'What can I do for you, detective...?' I shrugged, sending a ripple down the silk of my kaftan. 'Sorry, I've forgotten your names.'

'I'm Detective Inspector Hopper.' A jerk of her thumb indicated her partner. 'And DS Collins.'

'Thank you.' I stayed on my feet. This wasn't a social occasion, I wanted them gone. 'So what can I do for you today?'

'You haven't heard from Mr Carter, I assume?'

'Had I done so I'd have contacted you.' I resisted the temptation to fold my arms across my chest. It was a classic defensive movement. I had my fictional characters do it often enough and the fictional police officers always commented on it afterwards. Instead, I tucked my hands into the deep pockets of the kaftan.

'And you haven't seen him hanging around outside again?'

'No.' There was no point in telling them that I'd been mistaken, that I no longer believed I'd seen Toby. Certainly, I wasn't going to offer Gwen's theory that I was projecting characters from the book I was writing into my reality, nor was I going to admit that the fictional stalker in the book I was working on, despite everything, still bore an uncanny resemblance to Toby. I wasn't going to admit any of that... it made me sound crazy.

I made an issue out of plumping up a cushion on the sofa before sitting. It gave me time to rearrange my features into a carefully benign expression. 'Was that all you wanted to ask me?'

'You mentioned that Barbara Sanderson told you that she'd been with Mr Carter for four years. It was, you'd said, one of the reasons you didn't report her attack on you. You said you felt sorry for her having been with him for that long.'

I wondered where she was going with this. 'Yes, that's right.'

Hopper tilted her head. 'That's where there's a problem. Ms Sanderson, you see, laughed when we mentioned her being with him for four years. She said she couldn't have afforded to have been with him that long. The six months she was with him, she says, has left her pretty much broke.'

'I'm sure...' I shook my head and frowned.

'She had attacked you; you were probably in shock.'

'Probably.' I agreed for convenience but I clearly remembered Babs mentioning she'd been with Toby for four years. Four years, not six months. At that stage, I had been with him for only two weeks... still in the honeymoon phase of our relationship.

Wondering why Babs had lied, it was a few seconds before I realised the detective was speaking and I held my hand up. 'Sorry, what did you say?'

'I was asking why you switched from writing romance to the rather dark novels you write now.'

I looked from one detective to the other. Was this a trick question? 'What has that to do with your investigation into Toby's disappearance?'

DI Hopper smiled slightly. 'I like to build a rounded picture of all the characters involved in a case. I haven't read your books–' She indicated her partner with a wave of her hand. '– Collins here has. She says they're quite dark.'

'I said very dark actually,' Collins corrected her, her sharp eyes never leaving my face.

'Very dark then,' Hopper said. 'I wondered if maybe something had happened two years ago to make you change direction.'

My clenched hands relaxed. Some questions were easily answered. 'Writing is a business like any other. I love what I do but I have to be mindful of the market, what's hot and what's not. Sales of my romances were dropping so when I sent a proposal for a psychological novel to my agent, she jumped at it. The market for this genre is huge and the move has been professionally and financially successful for me.'

'Interesting,' Hopper said. 'Thank you.' She jigged a knee, her heel tapping the wooden floor underneath with a rhythmic thud. 'Getting back to Mr Carter. You said he left, taking everything.'

Deep breath in, let it out slowly before answering. 'That's right.'

'Everything he owned in two holdalls.' Hopper felt in her handbag for her notebook and pulled it out.

I stared as the detective flicked through the pages. It was an affectation. She knew exactly what she was going to ask and I waited, my breath catching.

'You mentioned going clothes shopping with Mr Carter. So, in fact, did Ms Sanderson. Mr Carter, it appears, liked to look well.'

'Yes.' *One word: don't elaborate. Listen carefully.*

Hopper flicked to a page and peered at what was written on it before looking up to catch my fixed gaze. 'This is where I have a slight problem. It took two holdalls and two large cardboard boxes to move his belongings from Ms Sanderson's home in Streatham to here. She remembers clearly because he had to make three trips to the lift with his belongings.' Hopper flicked the notebook shut and put it back into her pocket with unhurried actions. 'Yet, although he bought more clothes when he was living with you, he managed to fit all his belongings, according to you, into only two bags.'

33

MISTY

I kept my eyes on the detective as I searched my brain for a reasonable explanation and couldn't think of one. With all that had happened, I'd never given Toby's belongings any thought. He'd had the bags with him. But what had happened to the boxes?

When Toby had moved in, I remember him unpacking his clothes into the drawers and wardrobe I'd readied for him. The empty boxes had been folded flat. I'd suggested putting them into the recycling bin but he'd demurred, saying they might come in handy someday. *Someday.* I almost laughed aloud at how foolish I'd been, I was thinking of *forever* when he'd obviously been thinking of *for the time being* or possibly *until someone richer comes along.*

The empty boxes had been put up in the attic. As far as I knew they were still there.

'I only know what I saw,' I said. 'He had two bags when he left here, one in each hand. Nothing else.'

'Did he leave stuff behind, maybe with the intention of coming back to get it. Perhaps that was why you saw him outside the following night.'

'N-no.' I stumbled over the word. 'He didn't leave anything.' I managed a quick laugh. 'Unless you count a friendless sock and a pair of boxer shorts.'

'Odd though.' Hopper looked at her partner. 'Don't you think?'

The painted woman's mouth turned down. 'Very. To be honest, two holdalls and two boxes seems little enough belongings for a man who liked his clothes. Two holdalls alone doesn't seem likely to me.'

They both looked back to me, staring intently as if waiting for me to say something that would somehow explain everything. The problem was, I'd no idea. *Say nothing.* It seemed to work. Hopper looked as if my response was as expected and shuffled to her feet.

'That's it for the moment, Ms Eastwood. Thanks for your time.'

I saw them out and watched as they walked the short distance to where their car was parked. They didn't move off straight away. Talking about me. I shut the door with a snap. That's what I'd have my police characters doing; they'd sit in their car and wonder about the person they'd been interrogating. They'd be sitting there trying to take me apart to see what made me tick, what I knew.

I reached for the safety chain and put it in place.

Upstairs, I looked at the attic door and frowned. Had Toby opened it, taken the boxes down and packed while I was working on my book, while I was cocooned from reality thanks to my headphones?

There was only one way to find out. The rod for opening the hatch and releasing the pull-down stairway was kept in the airing cupboard. It was there, where it always was.

It was easy to hook the ring on the hatch and pull, the stairway unfolding with a clunk. I'd not been in the attic for a long time. It had been Toby who'd put the boxes there. Only part of the attic was floored. If the boxes were still there it would be easy to see them.

The stairway was solid enough but still swayed alarmingly as I climbed. Heights made me anxious. I took one step at a time, holding my kaftan bunched in one hand. As soon as my head was inside the attic space, I felt for the switch and the small area flooded with light.

There were old suitcases, some pictures I'd brought from my previous home and couldn't find a place for, an old fake Xmas tree and some other paraphernalia that had gathered there over the years. But there were no flat cardboard boxes. Wanting to be certain, I crawled inside and looked behind the suitcases. I was momentarily distracted by a box of old LPs I'd forgotten were there and flicked through them wondering why I'd kept them. Then the memories of some made me smile and I knew why, and why I'd keep them despite no longer owning a player.

I backed out, down the stairway and stood on the landing. Okay, so Toby had gone up and brought his holdalls and the boxes down. What had happened to the boxes? The detective was right; all Toby's belongings wouldn't have fitted into the bags. We'd gone shopping only a couple of weeks before. I'd bought a few things, he'd bought far more, adding them to my credit card without compunction. No, two bags wouldn't have been sufficient.

My mobile was beside my computer. The card Gwen had given me was pinned to the board behind, I took it down, flipped it over and rang the number on the back, shuffling from foot to foot while I waited. 'C'mon, answer.'

'Hello?'

'Gwen, it's me, Misty. The police have been here again.' I waited for a comment and when one didn't come, asked, 'Did Toby bring any stuff around to yours?'

'Stuff?'

'Boxes, Gwen. The police know he brought his belongings here in two holdalls and two boxes and wanted to know how he could have left with only the bags. The boxes had been flattened and put in the attic. They're gone.'

'How odd. No, of course he didn't bring them here.'

I walked to the window with the phone pressed to my ear. 'So where are they? You don't think...'

'That he had someone else?' A laugh tinkled down the line. 'Who knows with Toby.'

I squeezed my eyes shut. 'But he was supposed to be going to you that night, wasn't he?'

'He was supposed to be.'

I heard the coolness in Gwen's voice and opened my eyes. 'Listen, I'm sorry for ringing. That police detective, Hopper, she worries me. She's a bit like a dog with a bone, and now she has those damn boxes between her teeth.'

'But you don't know anything about the boxes, do you? Toby left your house and that's all you know. The police are simply trying to find out what happened to him. They can't make you say things you don't know. Just stick to your story.'

'Okay. Thank you. I won't bother you again.' I cut the connection and stood staring out the window, tapping the mobile against my hand.

Stick to your story.

I frowned. Didn't that infer it was a lie? Did Gwen believe I'd something to do with Toby's disappearance?

34

MISTY

I tried to settle back to work after speaking to Gwen but the words wouldn't come, my fingers staying frozen on the keys. *Stick to your story.* The words kept flashing before my eyes. I'd told the truth. It wasn't a *story*.

Was that what the police thought?

I was the last person to see Toby, I suppose it was understandable that they were taking a close look at me. A smile flitted when I remembered Hopper's question about switching from romance to thrillers. I wondered what she'd hoped to hear – that I'd had a life-changing event that sent me off the rails. Something so awful that it had brought deeply hidden psychopathic tendencies to the surface and sent me running around, killing anyone that crossed me.

The deaths in my books were painstakingly planned. I was careful to ensure there were no plot holes to annoy readers. If I were writing this story – the story of Toby's disappearance – who would be the guilty party?

In a book, it would have to be one of the characters that had already been written into the story. In real life, it could be anyone. A completely random person. Toby might have met someone he knew on his way to Knightsbridge and gone with them. He might have met another woman on the way – someone richer than Gwen Marsham.

After all, as I knew only too well, there were lots of women out there waiting to fall for his charms.

The way I had.

Gullible, my sisters called me and I supposed they were right. I took people at face value, assumed an honesty that wasn't always there. *Gullible*. My sisters were right.

I'd not been completely honest with the police. The financial implication was certainly one of the reasons I'd switched from writing romance to writing thrillers. But the main reason was that I was sick of writing lovey-dovey stories about happy-ever-after land.

It took me a while to find my feet in this new-to-me genre. The theme, characters, words were contrary to everything I'd written before. I'd needed to tap into the seedier side of life and connect to my dark side. Instead of looking for love and romance, I was searching for the lies people told, the secrets they kept hidden, the depths they'd go to for success, love, revenge. I'd done internet searches that had opened my eyes to the depravity that was freely available and to the seedy, sordid side of life that I'd either ignored or didn't realise existed.

I'd come to believe we were all born with a dark, violent streak and it was only specific circumstances that brought it oozing or erupting to the surface where it resulted in anger, hatred and vile deeds that defied explanation.

Sometimes, when I'd spent too many hours with the more wicked of my characters, it took me a while to pull back. To an extent, my sisters were right. Writing books that dwelled on twisted and immoral characters had changed me. Apart from my kaftans which were mostly all glaringly multicoloured, I'd noticed that recently I was opting for darker, more subdued clothes. And I'd become more cynical, more suspicious.

Or was that Toby's doing?

I'd known, very quickly, that I'd made a mistake with him. That the charming, charismatic man who'd bowled me over was a character straight from my romance books – only more two-dimensional and superficial than any I could write. I'd known, but I was lying to myself if I ever really believed I'd have finished with him. No, I'd have held on to the fantasy... and probably would have kept holding on if he'd not decided to leave.

The round glass paperweight my publisher had sent me as a gift the previous year was back on the desk where it belonged. Within touching distance. Within grabbing distance.

I picked it up and slid my hands over its curves. So solid.

So deadly.

35

DEE

Dee sat back with the names and addresses of the women Toby had preferred to her. There had been so many women over the years. Young, old, fat, skinny. It never mattered to him. All that mattered was that they had something to give him.

Sex and riches. Toby was a basic creature when it came down to it. Basic, but blessed with good looks and an innate charm that he used to full effect when he needed to. When he didn't need to – when he wasn't trying to charm someone out of something, or into doing something he wanted – he could be as petulant as a child.

But up to then, he'd always come back to her.

He wouldn't come back now. She felt the emptiness. The world had tilted on its axis and nothing would ever be the same again.

The police were clueless. Perhaps they thought someone had him locked away, chained to a wall. A sex slave. It happened. She'd read about it somewhere. For a time, years before, when he'd gone wandering yet again she'd considered it as an option. She'd even searched for suitable properties in which to keep him. It had entertained her for weeks, kept her from wondering what he was doing. And who he was doing it with.

But of course, she'd never really considered going through with her plan. Well, not for long anyway. A few weeks later, he came strolling back as if he'd simply left for work that morning, wearing a smart suit she'd not seen before. And without a word... without explanation... he fitted back into her life like the essential jigsaw piece needed to complete the picture.

Maybe she should have known the Streatham woman was going to be different when the weeks became months. Maybe she should have understood that this time, he wasn't going to come home.

Dee had followed Babs for a while, had found out where she worked, her eyebrow rising when she realised it had been a clinic where she'd had minor surgery years before. She found out the cafés Babs frequented, sometimes sitting at a table nearby, her eyes fixed on the plain, slightly overweight woman. Most painfully, she'd watched as Babs had strolled arm in arm, hand in hand, with Toby. Jealousy had twisted her gut, bitterness a burning pain she suffered when he was away.

Her mantra of *he'll come back to me* began to sound stale even to her.

She was sure he'd come back to her when he tired of Babs. And he would have done... *would have done...* if he hadn't been lured away first by the Eastwood woman, then further away by the other woman.

Lured by their money.

And one of them had killed him and finished her marriage for good.

36

DEE

Misty Eastwood's house in Hanwell was probably bigger than Dee's, the area a little better, the nearby shops and restaurants a little more upmarket. She strolled past the house as she checked out the neat front garden, the original wooden front door and sash windows, the side passage that elevated it above its terraced neighbours.

Her eyes swept over the upstairs windows. She wondered if the writer had a home office behind one of them. If she was there right now hammering on the keys as Dee walked by. She'd bought two of her recent books: they were too violent, grim and depressing for Dee's liking and she'd taken the time to write an anonymous, scathing one-star review for each.

She walked to the end of the short street, turned and came back along the other side. It would have been simple to knock on the door and feign a mistake of some sort when it was answered. She was sure she could have carried off the deceit but it wasn't her way. It was much preferable to watch the woman, to follow her and find what made her tick. What made her special? What had made Toby want her more than his wife of twenty years?

The arrival of a van an hour later gave Dee her first glimpse of the writer. A delivery person, in a multicoloured jumpsuit and hat that made it impossible to determine gender, stood on Misty's doorstep with a large parcel. Obviously a regular, they rang the doorbell and waited for far longer than was usual. But their persistence paid off when the door was finally opened.

It was only a glimpse but Dee soaked up the few details: the pixie haircut, the wildly colourful flowing garment she wore. Trying so hard to be arty. Trying too hard. It was a glimpse that told Dee a lot.

Back at home, she found the writer through the social media links that were conveniently listed at the end of her books. The prolific Misty Eastwood was everywhere. Dee joined any Facebook groups she was linked to, followed her there and on Instagram and Twitter.

In a couple of the Facebook groups, there were live author interviews on file and Dee searched through until she found one where Misty spoke about her books and her writing. It was in watching these that Dee saw what had attracted Toby. Misty was undeniably a good-looking woman but when she spoke about the stories she wrote, it transformed her into something more akin to stunning. Her hands waved about, her eyes sparkled and she spoke with infectious enthusiasm that was appealing. Dee's lips curled as she listened. Misty would no doubt be that enthusiastic during sex too... and Toby would have enjoyed that.

But Dee had no illusions. It was the money that would have been the real temptation for Toby who valued purchasing power more than anything else. It didn't take her long to discover that Misty was a remarkably successful author with several books in the top ten. Add in foreign rights from the numerous translations, and the movie and TV series that were in the offing, and Misty Eastwood would have been very wealthy indeed.

She seemed ideal. Beautiful and rich. So why had he decided to move on?

More importantly, had Misty been angry when he said he was leaving? Dee thought about the violence in the books she'd read. Had the writer directed that anger towards Toby? He wouldn't have expected it, certainly wouldn't have retaliated. Toby had many faults, but violence wasn't one of them.

She stared at the upstairs window where she could see Misty's seated figure.

Was she the one to blame for Dee's loss?

Dee wanted to hammer on the door and beg Misty to tell her the truth. Instead, with a sigh she turned for home.

She put her suspicions of Misty to one side, turned on her computer and typed Gwen Marsham into the search bar. Her eyes widened at the information that was available. Much more than she expected. Juicy stuff too. Details about the bungled burglary two years before that had led to the murder of Gwen's husband, George.

Dee read everything there was to find and discovered that Gwen had been away for a night at a conference when the burglary had taken place. The police, according to the papers, speculated that the burglar knew about the conference and thought the apartment would be empty. There were articles that hinted at George's frequent infidelities, and a thinly veiled rumour in a society column that his death wasn't an accident but had been orchestrated by his long-suffering wife.

Dee searched various sites using several keywords but it

appeared that nobody had ever been charged with the burglary and murder.

'Interesting,' Dee murmured. She reached for her tea, frowned to find it cold and got up to make another. She kept it in her hand, sipping as she read about Gwen's successful art gallery in Knightsbridge, reviews and praise from artists whose works she sold.

On Google Maps, Dee found Beaufort Gardens and used the street view to have a look at the apartment where Gwen still lived despite the burglary and murder of her husband. From the outside, the apartment was stunning and Dee felt a quiver of envy.

Gwen, by any and every account, was seriously wealthy. Dee brought up her photographs, enlarged them and examined every feature, every line; Gwen was older than Dee had expected but she had a certain elegance that might have appealed.

Dee snorted a laugh. She knew exactly what had attracted Toby and it was nothing to do with the woman's age or style.

Switching off her laptop, she sat back and finished her tea. Reading about Gwen was something, but nothing could beat seeing someone in the flesh. She looked down at the rather scruffy chinos and T-shirt she was wearing. Not Knightsbridge clobber.

Two hours later, a light raspberry-coloured trench open over black trousers and T-shirt, Dee walked down Knightsbridge high street and pushed open the door of the gallery. She'd little interest in art and her eyebrows rose at the paintings that hung from the walls. No prices, she noticed.

'Is there anything I can help you with?'

Dee turned to the woman she knew to be Gwen Marsham.

In the flesh, she looked older, ... closer perhaps to fifty than forty. Lines radiated from the corners of her eyes, two deeper creases between them making Dee wonder why the woman had not, with all her money, tried Botox.

'Yes, I'm looking for something for my apartment.' Dee walked over to a large colourful canvas and tilted her head in what she hoped was an appropriate pose. 'But I'm not sure what would suit.'

Gwen's smile was sweet and encouraging. Chatting pleasantly, she led Dee from one painting to the other, discussing the artist, the composition. No mention of the price.

She guessed that the people who bought artwork in the gallery weren't the sort that needed to count the cost. 'I like this one.' She stepped back to one that really did appeal to her. It might have been a seascape, she wasn't sure, but the colours were vivid and captivating.

'A good choice. Scott Naismith is one of our most popular artists.'

'The colours are mesmerising.' Dee stepped closer. It really was very beautiful. She'd never thought about purchasing a painting but decided she wanted this one. Maybe it would fill the gap that Toby had left. Something entrancing to feast her eyes on. 'How much is it?'

Gwen told her, following the price with an obviously rehearsed speech about how art was an investment, especially art as charismatic as this.

Charismatic. Like Toby. 'I'll take it.' It was a change to spend money on herself. Thankful for her generous overdraft limit, Dee hesitated only a second before handing across her credit card. Her hesitation, worry that Gwen would comment on the surname, was unnecessary. The card was barely glanced at before it was slid into the card reader to be processed.

Gwen chatted away as she wrapped the painting,

congratulating Dee on her purchase as she did. 'You'll have years of pleasure from it, I have no doubt.'

'I'm sure I will.' The neatly wrapped painting was small enough to take with her. Gwen opened the door and Dee left the gallery with the package clasped to her chest.

She would hang it in her lounge where it would stay.

It wouldn't wander off... wouldn't find a better wall to hang on, or a more admiring viewer to stand and stare at it.

It wouldn't disappear and leave her sad and bereft.

37

MISTY

I sat in front of my computer, switched it on, brought up the book I was writing and tried to focus on getting the words down. The optimistic daily word count I aimed for was four thousand. I didn't always get there, and recently not even close, but it was something to work towards.

Only a few words later I stopped, my fingers poised over the keys. The sun shone through the window, light bouncing off the glass paperweight that sat nearby.

It had become a habit to curl my fingers around it when I was struggling for a word or drowning in a plot hole and my hand crept over it now, sliding over the slippery cold surface. The chill from it slithered up my arm, a strange darkness sweeping in its wake. I wanted to take my hand away but, instead, my fingers squeezed the glass, tighter and tighter. I pictured it exploding, sending vicious shards of glass like arrows to pierce my skin. With a gasp, I finally pulled my hand away.

It was minutes before the strange sensations faded. I laughed, stopping abruptly when I heard the edge of hysteria in the sound.

What was wrong with me?

Strangely afraid to touch the paperweight again, I used a sheaf of paper to push it to the back of my desk, moving catalogues that were waiting to be read some day out of the way to make room for it, piling them on top then to hide it from my sight.

It was another few minutes before I returned to my work. My fingers were once more on the keyboard, tapping out the secrets and lies of my characters. Sometimes it was that easy. The words would come, the story unfolding with each sentence.

A few minutes later I stopped. My eyes flicked back over what I'd written and I pushed away from the desk with a cry of horror. The wheels of the chair caught in the rug behind and with another cry I spun round and jumped to my feet. I had to get away and staggered across to the door to wrench it open and run.

Only when I had the door open, when my escape was assured, did I look back to my computer screen, a hand creeping over my trembling mouth.

How could I have written that? It wasn't true.

I shut the door behind me with a bang, tempted to reach inside for the key and lock the door from the outside. But that was being ridiculous... crazy.

I wiped my face with the sleeve of my kaftan. Maybe I was hungry. I couldn't remember eating that day and wasn't sure I'd eaten the day before. Hunger, that was it. Probably a low blood sugar as a result. That was all. It was making me hallucinate.

A shiver of relief at the simple solution loosened the band of tension that had wrapped around me.

Downstairs, I opened a tin of mushroom soup, poured it into a bowl and put it into the microwave spinning the time control randomly.

A search of the freezer for bread to go with the soup was in vain. It might be a good idea to do an online food order that afternoon. But that would mean going back to my computer. It would mean looking at what I'd written, reading those terrible words.

Only three words... but repeated over and over for several lines.

I killed Toby.

The ping from the microwave distracted my thoughts. I opened the door, groaning when I saw the mess. The soup had been in for too long: it had boiled over, filling the microwave tray with volcanically hot liquid.

Too hot to clear up. I shut the door with a bang and turned away, wringing my hands.

The glass paperweight. That was the key. Hadn't I lifted it that night? My memory was hazy. Toby's rejection had been so shocking it had thrown me off track, I simply couldn't remember what had happened.

But I did remember picking the paperweight up from the floor the following day. How had it got there?

Had I thrown it at him?

Was it possible that what I'd written was true? That I had killed him?

My head was spinning. I dropped onto a chair and put my hands over my face. I wasn't a violent person, was I?

All those evil, murderous creatures I was so easily able to conjure up – where did they come from?

I remember I'd screeched at Toby with words I'd researched for the worst of my characters to use. Words I'd never spoken aloud. Angry, ugly words.

Had they been enough, or had I resorted to action?

38

MISTY

I couldn't get my thoughts straight... one moment convinced I must have had something to do with Toby's disappearance, the next that I was suffering from delusions brought about by hunger and stress. Dealing with the hunger situation seemed to be a sensible step.

But before I could leave the house, I needed to delete those shocking words. I returned to my office and looked at the computer. The cursor was blinking at the end of the lines of the repeated '*I killed Tobys*' that filled the lower quarter of the screen. I put my finger on the backspace key and held it there, deleting those words and more. I didn't care. The rest saved, I shut down the programme and left the room.

The day was hot and clammy but I still wasn't brave enough to leave the house in my kaftan. I didn't want to get a reputation as *that crazy eccentric writer lady*. I pulled on chinos and a T-shirt, slipped my bare feet into flat shoes and ran a comb over my hair.

At the front door I hesitated, suddenly wary. The figure I thought I'd seen, it had simply been my imagination, hadn't it?

It couldn't have been Toby. *Toby was dead*. The thought

popped into my head unbidden, unwanted. I shook it away and opened the door.

There was nobody to be seen but the wariness lingered. I was sure I hadn't imagined it when I'd seen Babs lurking outside. Perhaps she blamed me for Toby's disappearance? *Was I to blame?*

The thought that I was somehow responsible seemed to have dug its tentacles into my brain. I was mixing fact and fiction, that was all. Tiredness, overwork and stress were enabling the twisted characters from my pages to take possession of my thoughts. *Of my actions?*

I wish I could remember what happened that night after Toby left. But all I could remember was the sound of my shrieking before I buried my head in my headphones and lost hours.

Hours.

Had I really stayed at my computer for all that time or had I got up to do something?

Like get rid of a body?

I tried to laugh it off. What, was I superwoman? Toby wasn't a big man, maybe five nine but it would have required enormous strength to move his body. And if I had found that superhuman strength, what would I have done with it... drag his body down the stairs, out into the garden, dig a grave and bury him.

Maybe I would have found the thought amusing if I weren't slightly worried that I was wondering if it was possible.

Maybe I'd have found it bloody hilarious if I weren't still standing on my doorstep with my head spinning. I had to concentrate on what might be a real threat. Babs had launched a violent, terrifying attack on me for "stealing" Toby from her. What would she be capable of if she thought I was somehow involved in his disappearance?

I stepped out of the house and stood on the doorstep for

several minutes. There wasn't a heavy footfall on the street. There were more direct ways from the nearby train station to the centre of Hanwell and only the occasional stranger passed my house. I waved to a neighbour from a few doors up. I didn't know her name, had never done more than say hello. People kept to themselves. It suited me. The house next door, separated from me by a passageway, was empty for most of the year, the owners spending long stretches of time in what they described as their *villa in Spain*.

The house to the other side was occupied by a quiet elderly couple who rarely left their home. I couldn't remember the last time I'd seen them, only the regular opening and shutting of their drapes told me they were still alive.

Normally, the quiet semi-isolation suited me, but that day I wished for helpful, even nosy neighbours, ones who would answer if I called for help.

I pushed my hand into my pocket and closed fingers around my mobile phone. My sisters would come if I called. It gave me some reassurance. I shut the door, then grunted with annoyance and opened it again. From the cupboard under the stairs, I pulled out two carrier bags and tucked them under my arm.

This time, I settled for a glance up and down the road before stepping out and walking briskly along the street. It wasn't far. The day was sunny. An occasional car passed in each direction. A man on the other side of the street, walking faster than me, sped by and was around the corner before I'd gone halfway. It was all so normal.

What wasn't was my convulsive grip on the phone, my need to look behind me every few steps, my indrawn breath when I saw the man across the street, my fixation on him until he'd passed, until he was out of sight. What wasn't normal was my heightened perception of the individual noises. My footsteps seemed strangely loud, so did the man's. There was only a slight breeze but it whistled in the leaves of the trees as I passed. My breath rasped as I picked up speed, a demented percussionist pounding in my chest.

The contrast of the quiet inside the shop was even more startling. It was a popular convenience store and it was unusual to be the only customer. The silence was almost as disconcerting as the noise had been. I stood without moving, waiting for something to happen.

When it did it was almost bizarrely normal.

The young assistant popped up from behind the cash register, looked across and smiled. 'Hi,' she said, piling paper bags on the counter beside her. 'A lovely sunny day, isn't it?'

I rang a desiccated tongue around my even drier mouth and managed to emit a squeaky, 'Yes.'

The assistant's normality did something to restore calm. I was being silly and allowing my imagination to overpower common sense.

I pried a basket from the stack that was piled to one side of the door and walked up and down the aisles picking up items in a haphazard manner. My basket was full to overflowing when I put it on the cashier's desk.

A heavy bag hanging from each hand seemed to ground me on the walk home and I reached my front door without a return of the earlier panic. I dismissed it as simply the result of hunger and thirst. I might even use it all in a book one day. With that thought putting a smile on my face, I unpacked my bags and decided that scrambled eggs on toast would make a healthy breakfast.

It was much needed, very satisfying and I finished the lot then sat back with my mug of coffee feeling better than I had in days. That was all I'd needed. A decent meal.

The back of the house faced west and the afternoon sun flooded the small garden with light. Previous owners had extended, converting the original galley-kitchen into a kitchen/diner with French doors opening to the garden.

I rarely sat at the dining table to eat, hadn't done so since Toby left, instead taking my meals through to the living room to eat as I watched TV.

When Toby lived with me, it had been different. We rarely ate in – he preferred restaurants and eating out on my credit card – but on the rare time when we stayed home he insisted that the ambiance was part of the eating experience. I'd laughed and spent money on several candle holders and non-drip candles. I'd light them and position them around the room where they'd be reflected in the darkened glass of the doors. We'd sit, chat, eat the meal I'd cooked and drink the expensive wine he'd chosen and I'd paid for.

I sipped my coffee to wash away the sour taste of tainted memories. What a fool I had been. With a sigh, I looked through the glass doors to the garden. When I moved in I'd planned to fill the small patio area outside with pots of flowers that would bloom all summer. But I'd never managed to find the time, always too busy with the next book.

It had been Toby's idea to redesign the garden. 'You could make so much more of it,' he'd said, waving his hands around dramatically. He grabbed a sheet of paper and pen and with a few strokes drew his idea of how it could look.

'See. Raised beds on either side of a grassy area – AstroTurf, not real grass. And brick raised beds, none of your sleepers that need work to maintain. So this–' He tapped his hastily drawn plan. '–is the formal part. Then here, a pathway through wide beds planted with wild flowers would give amazing colour in the summer.'

I had smiled at his enthusiasm. 'What about the shed?' The garden was long, ending in a narrow v at the bottom. Previous owners had plonked a wooden shed at the end cutting off a few feet of ground behind that they'd used for a compost area.

'I'd keep it,' Toby had suggested. 'But paint it to make it a feature rather than something practical.'

Probably nothing would have come of his idea if a leaflet promoting *Seb's Garden Services* hadn't come through the letterbox the following morning.

'Kismet!' Toby had laughingly insisted.

I'd agreed and phoned the number on the leaflet and that was it. Seb took a look at the plan, asked a few questions, and a week later started work.

He'd done a wonderful job and the fuchsia he'd planted in the raised beds were already filling out and flowering.

Perhaps I'd buy pots and plants and ask him to organise them for me too. Some colour, even this late, would brighten the area outside the door and lift my spirits. I got to my feet and stood at the door picturing pots filled with flowering plants. Maybe more fuchsia? The ones in the beds were so pretty. I looked across to the shrubs in question, then tilted my head and frowned.

Turning, I put my nearly empty mug on the table. The French doors were uPVC, locked with a key that sat in a bowl on the counter. I reached for it, inserted it into the lock and pushed up the handle to open the door.

It was a hot day. The sun was working its way around the sky and would soon fill the garden. I stepped outside with my attention fixed on the far bed. The day after Seb had finished, I'd come out to assess his work, more than pleased at the care he'd taken, the well-built raised beds, the small patch of real grass I had chosen over the AstroTurf Toby had wanted.

Seb had suggested laying grass turf between the beds rather than seed and I'd agreed, delighted with the immediate impact of lush grass.

Grass that was now flattened for a stretch of several feet in front of the far bed.

And the fuchsia... I'd laughingly asked Seb if he'd used a measuring tape to get them so evenly spaced. Now, no matter which way I looked at it, it was clear that the shrubs were out of alignment.

I walked backwards and stumbled when I got to the tiled patio, losing my balance as I stepped into the dining room. Flailing, I reached for the back of the chair, knocked it over and tumbled on top of it, banging my chin on the seat. I lay there unable to move.

My lost hours.

Maybe it hadn't been my imagination... maybe I *had* killed Toby.

And buried him in the garden.

39

MISTY

I barely slept. How could I with thoughts galloping through my head like those scythed chariots in *Ben Hur* slicing their way through any attempt at making sense of it all.

I lay tossing and turning, reluctant to get up and face another day. When I did finally struggle from the bed to head downstairs, the peal of the doorbell startled me to an instant halt, one foot hovering in the air. I peered down to the front door with eyes that were gritty from lack of sleep. Was it my imagination, or was the door moving? My breath caught as I waited for the explosion and I half turned to run away. Then the doorbell pealed again, a prosaic ding-dong that served to make me blink away my flight of fancy.

Down in the hallway, I checked the safety chain was in place before I opened the door and looked around the edge. If there'd been any colour in my face... and I knew there wasn't, I'd seen my vampire-pale face in the bathroom mirror and had wondered about applying concealer to the dark shadows under my eyes before deciding not to bother... but if there had been any, it would have leeched away at the sight of the detectives standing on the doorstep.

'May we come in.'

I tried to get some sense of what they wanted, but although the older detective had kinder eyes, it was impossible to gauge from either of their expressions whether they were there with bad news or good. 'Do I have a choice?' I didn't wait for an answer. Closing the door over, I slid the safety chain off and opened the door wide. 'Come in then.'

I wasn't going to invite them further. I wrapped my arms across my chest and stuck my chin out.

'If you don't mind me saying so,' DI Hopper said quietly, 'You look like you could do with a cuppa.' She shrugged. 'To be honest, we've had an early start and coffee wouldn't go amiss.'

I hesitated but being rude didn't come naturally to me. 'Coffee. Right, yes, of course.' I walked ahead of them into the kitchen and busied myself making drinks while they stood looking on. I put the mugs on the breakfast bar rather than inviting them to sit at the table in what I hope they'd see as a subtle hint to drink their coffee and leave.

'Have you heard from Toby?' Hopper asked.

My mouth was dry, my brain stalled. I blew on my coffee and slurped a mouthful, hoping it would both lubricate and jump-start. I could feel the two sets of sharp, assessing eyes weighing me up and tried to channel some of the tough veneer I gave to my fictional characters, raising an eyebrow before I answered. 'No, I haven't. But I didn't expect to, really. We were done, there wouldn't have been much point.'

'You thought he might send you a forwarding address for wherever he did end up, didn't you?'

'Yes, but he hasn't.'

Hopper frowned thoughtfully. 'Maybe because he's dead?'

If the detective was hoping for a reaction from me, she was disappointed. I kept my eyes down and refused to comment.

'I think you know he is, don't you, Ms Eastwood?'

I put my mug down on the counter with a snap, the coffee I'd barely touched slopping over the rim. 'I know he's dead to me, detective. Toby Carter milked me for everything he could get, then when he found a richer source to mine, he moved on. You've no idea how that made me feel.'

'Angry, I'd guess.'

'Yes,' I agreed. 'But at myself for being such a gullible fool.' My eyes were fixed on DI Hopper's face so I was surprised when DS Collins spoke.

'Nice little garden you have there.'

I turned to see that the younger detective had moved to the French doors and was craning her neck to see the total area of the garden. 'Looks like you've had some work done.'

'Yes.' I moved to a drawer, pulled it open and rummaged inside. 'Here you go.' I held a business card out. 'If you're so interested, here's the gardener's card.'

Hopper took it. 'Always worth knowing, thank you. Was it done recently?'

'A few weeks ago.' I indicated the door with a tilt of my head. 'Now, much as I'd love to stand here all day and talk about gardening, I really do have things to do.'

I saw frustration in Collins' eyes and knew she wanted to say more but Hopper put her mug down and nodded. 'We'll be off. Thanks for your time, Ms Eastwood.'

I didn't walk them out. When I heard the clunk of the front door, my shoulders slumped. I moved to stand where Collins stood and stared out over the garden.

From there, the fuchsia looked to be in line.

But I knew they weren't. Someone... me... had moved them.

40

DEE

Dee had no plan when she arrived outside Misty Eastwood's home early that day. It was a bright sunny morning, too warm for the jacket she'd hurriedly pulled on. She took it off and carried it over one arm as she walked aimlessly up and down Myrtle Road. So far, she'd been unable to come up with a suitable plan to enact revenge on the woman she was convinced was responsible for Toby's disappearance.

She'd never considered the various women through the years as serious competitors for Toby. Not even Babs, despite the longer time he'd stayed with her. Six months. It had almost broken Dee but she knew it would end, that he would come back to her.

It was the way he was. Fidelity wasn't something he understood. A weak man, easily swayed by the shine and sparkle that came with money, but the novelty had always worn off and he'd come back to his true love. To the only woman he'd married, his wife, the mother of his child.

Always, until Misty Eastwood. It didn't matter that it appeared he'd decided to move on from her, it was she who had broken the strings that bound Toby to Dee despite everything.

The writer had probably talked him into it using silky words to spin a new life for them both, lavishing money on him, always something more twinkly and shiny to keep his attention.

It was almost amusing that she'd taught him too well, that he'd moved on when he found someone who could provide even more glitter.

Bored with staring at Misty's house, Dee sat on a garden wall to rest. Unable to think of any riveting plan, she was about to leave when she saw two people she recognised walk up the street. It was instinct to duck behind a pillar, eyes narrowing as she watched them approach Misty's front door.

They were persistent, ringing the doorbell for far longer than was polite. One, the detective with the painted face, was more impatient and strode off to the side entrance, returning a moment later and gesticulating to the other detective.

Dee cocked her ear in a vain attempt to hear what they were saying. She guessed the younger detective had wanted to go around the back, but the older one – Hopper, Dee remembered her name because it was unusual – she shook her head.

They rang the doorbell again and their persistence paid off, the front door opened and they vanished inside.

They must be there to talk about Toby. Dee felt a quiver of irritation that she was left out of the conversation. Toby was her husband. *Hers.*

Irritation made her brave. After a glance up and down the street, she sidled up to Misty's front door, then scooted down to peer over the ledge of the front-room window. But Dee was out of luck. It was empty.

With another glance up and down the street, and a moment's delay to allow a car to pass, she bent down and carefully pushed open the letterbox. She could see straight ahead to where a door opened into a back room. Twisting her head, she held her ear to the opening and listened to the faint murmur of voices that drifted towards her, holding her breath to try to catch the words.

Unable to hear anything, she pulled back and walked to the side of the house as the detective had done. There was nothing to be seen except the wooden gate that shut the garden from view. Giving up, Dee retreated across the street to the same pillar she'd stood behind earlier and waited.

It wasn't a long wait. The front door opened and the two detectives came out, their expressions giving nothing away.

There was no sign of Misty.

Myrtle Road wasn't wide and the pillar was almost directly opposite. Had Dee stepped out, the detectives would have seen her immediately.

They had no reason to believe anyone was watching... and listening. Hopper's voice was quiet, inaudible, but the other, her voice was gratingly harsh, satisfyingly loud, her words shocking. *'I'm telling you, Bev, I feel it in my gut. Toby Carter is dead and Eastwood had a hand in it.'*

Dee swayed and grabbed onto the pillar with one hand as she shoved the side of the other into her mouth, biting down hard to prevent the cry of anguish escaping.

41

MISTY

I stood staring out at the garden.

The older detective had seemed sympathetic and I'd been within a hair's breadth of telling her the worrying thoughts that were running through my head, was actually framing the words to say when I realised I was falling for the oldest trick in the book... the old good cop/bad cop routine beloved of every crime show I'd ever seen. I'd used it myself in my books, for goodness' sake, and I'd almost fallen for it.

Gullible. My sisters were so right. I was so damn gullible. I'd fallen for Toby's blatant charms and now here I was falling for the detectives' less than subtle attempt to force me to confess.

Confess.

I was locked in a cycle of doubt about what had happened, what I'd done. Had I really thrown the heavy glass paperweight at Toby and killed him?

His words had seared me, unexpected and devastating. Had they been enough to drive me to a violent act that was against everything I believed myself to be. And having done such a deed, was I then capable of following it through?

Was there a darkness inside that I'd never acknowledged

except to dip into for the sick, twisted, wicked characters I wrote in my books? Maybe there was, maybe it was why readers said these characters were so scary, so *real*.

I unlocked the French doors and stepped outside. There was one sure way of finding out if I had done such a terrible thing. If I'd really dragged his body down the stairs and buried him.

I could dig.

The thought sent shivers through me that sent me stumbling back into the house, shutting and locking the door and flinging the key across the room.

I sat at the table and rested my head on my crossed arms. Exhaustion pressed me down and I might have fallen into a desperately needed sleep if the doorbell hadn't rung, followed by a hammering of the knocker.

Those blasted detectives had obviously thought of something else to ask me. Well, to hell with them, I wasn't moving.

But the hammering and ringing continued. This time, I decided as I got to my feet, they weren't coming inside.

The safety chain hadn't been replaced but I wasn't expecting a problem and opened the door. It was immediately pushed in with a force that shocked me. I squealed in fright when instead of the two detectives I'd expected, I saw teeth bared in a rictus of anger. There was no time to see more, no time to speak, I was grabbed, slapped, punched and my hair yanked by a force that growled and muttered.

I fell to the floor under the onslaught. *This couldn't be happening to me again.* I tried to fight back, tried to push the other woman off so I could get away, but once again, anger fuelled my attacker. 'Stop, please stop,' I shrieked, trying to get through to her. There was no let up. Desperation curled me into a ball, my hands wrapping over my head.

Last time, Toby had come to my rescue. He wouldn't be coming now.

The pummelling increased in strength; each blow accompanied by a single guttural, 'Murderer.'

Another blow.

'Murderer.'

Then several blows in quick succession. 'You murdered my husband, my Toby.'

'No,' I cried out. 'I didn't, I didn't, it was an accident, I never meant to kill him.' I curled tighter as the blows continued. 'It was an accident.' I said it repeatedly even when the blows had stopped. And when I dared uncurl a little, I said it again. 'I didn't mean to kill him; it was an accident.'

I uncurled completely on the last word and looked straight into DI Hopper's eyes.

42

MISTY

I could feel blood oozing from my split lip and pain everywhere the crazy woman's tight fist had jabbed.

'Can you stand?' Hopper asked and when I nodded, she indicated the open door to the living room. 'Get yourself inside.'

I struggled to my feet and stumbled past as the two detectives tried to restrain the still-snarling woman.

'She murdered Toby.' A foot connected with my thigh making me wince and move faster to the safety of the room where I collapsed onto the sofa.

'If she did, we'll get her for it, okay?' Hopper said. 'Meanwhile, you're under arrest for assault. Calm down, Dee, or I'll add resisting arrest to that.'

Whether it was Hopper's words, or exhaustion from the attack, the woman... and I suddenly realised she must be Toby's wife... stopped shouting. It seemed unbelievable that I should have been beaten up on two separate occasions by ex-lovers of my ex-boyfriend. It was the stuff of bad movies, or dreadful novels. I dabbed at my cut lip with the edge of my kaftan and eyed the bloody marks on the material as if they were medals of honour for surviving the attack.

I rested my head back and listened to what was going on in the hallway, feeling distant from it all. Shock, I supposed.

DS Collins read the woman her rights, then Hopper's firm voice said: 'Here's what's going to happen. We're going to ring for a squad car to take you into the station where you'll be charged. Get yourself a good solicitor and you'll probably be out on bail in a few hours.'

I couldn't hear the murmured reply.

'Meanwhile, if Ms Eastwood is up to it after your attack, we'll see what she has to say about Toby's disappearance.'

This time, I could hear every word Toby's wife said. 'Murder. You heard her saying she killed him. She said it. She's a murderer.'

The final word was barely audible as if anger had given way to a sorrowful acceptance of loss. Acceptance was ahead of me now.

I was a murderer.

43

MISTY

Everything hurt. I pressed my fingers gently against my cheekbone. I didn't think it was broken but it was already starting to swell. I hoped they'd good doctors in prison.

Prison.

All my doubts had faded. I still couldn't remember what happened that evening when Toby left but it seemed clear now that I had killed him.

I'd done research for a book I was writing years before about a character who'd experienced a fugue state – that pathological state of altered consciousness where a person can do something but have no recollection of it after the event. It could be caused, I remember reading, by a traumatic event.

Did being dumped without notice by a man you were living with classify as a traumatic event?

Was that what had happened?

The only evidence I had to support it was the glass paperweight being on the floor instead of where it should have been, some fuchsia bushes out of alignment, and my confused, twisted thoughts.

I wondered about ringing my sisters. They'd come, of course, with eyes full of compassion and hearts filled with love. That was who they were. Solid, decent people. What would they think about their sister now.

Their sister the murderer.

I held my hand over my mouth. I'd go to prison. Lose everything I had, everything I was, destroy my life, my sisters' lives, everyone would be affected by a period of madness I couldn't recollect.

Other voices came from outside. The wife... what had that detective called her? Dee? She'd be taken away, charged with something or other. I wouldn't have to face her again. Wouldn't have to see her sorrow and know I was to blame.

More voices drifted through, deeper male voices this time, followed by the front door shutting. Then the living-room door opened and the two detectives came in, their faces set into grim lines.

'Are you okay?' the older woman asked. She was more sympathetic than her partner, with eyes that said she understood.

Maybe she did. 'Bruised, sore, a bit shocked but nothing is broken.'

They sat opposite and stared at me with a certain amount of fascination, as if I'd performed a party trick and they wondered if I was going to do it again.

'DS Collins is going to read you your rights before you say anything, okay?'

I nodded and listened, muttering *yes* when asked if I understood.

'You have the right to have a solicitor present, if you'd prefer to wait,' Hopper said.

'No, that's all right.' I was weary. There was time enough for talking to solicitors. After the reality had sunk in, after I'd accepted I was a murderer.

'Will you tell us what happened?'

I was almost tempted to say I'd opened the front door and the woman had attacked me but I didn't have the energy for games. 'I was writing, Toby came in, he had his bags with him and he said...' I could still remember how handsome he'd looked standing in the doorway, how my heart had leapt at the sight of him. And the words. 'He said he didn't love me anymore and was leaving.'

That was the bit I could remember. 'Then I must have thrown a glass paperweight at him–'

Hopper held up her hand to interrupt. 'You must have? What do you mean *you must have*?'

I felt a bubble of blood build up on my cut lip and lifted the sleeve of my kaftan to dab at it again. But it was serous fluid this time. Already my body was responding the way it should, a healing process that only death could stop.

'I don't remember anything after what he said really–'

This time it was Collins who lifted her hand. 'You said you watched him walk down the street, a bag in each hand.'

'I lied. I didn't want to appear completely pathetic and say I'd fallen to pieces when he'd gone.'

'Okay, tell us what you do remember,' Hopper said.

'I remember finishing the book I was writing. It was much later than I'd expected but often I get lost when I'm writing so I didn't think much of it. The glass paperweight is usually beside my computer but next day it was on the floor near the door. I don't remember how it got there but now–' I lifted my hands and dropped them helplessly into my lap. '–I think I might have thrown it at him.

'Then, yesterday, I had the oddest thought.' I looked from one detective to the other. 'I thought that I'd killed Toby and buried him in the garden. The psychological thrillers I write are full of twists and turns, and the seedy, wicked side of people, and I thought I was simply projecting my stories into my life – you know, blurring the lines between fact and fiction.'

I stopped, slumping back on the sofa. 'Now I know it's true. I murdered him.'

'You told Dee that you'd accidently killed him,' Hopper said. 'If you had thrown the paperweight in your distress and it hit and killed him, that would absolutely have been an accident.'

I took a gulping breath.

'What happened then?'

'Then?' I wiped a hand over my face and brushed away tears. 'I don't know. I really don't remember.'

'But you think you buried him in the garden?'

'The fuchsia...' It all made sense to me now. 'They're out of alignment.'

44

MISTY

I sat back, suddenly overwhelmed by what I'd done... by what I'd become.

Hopper and Collins exchanged glances, eyebrows rising. 'Ms Eastwood, I'm sorry,' DI Hopper said, 'but that doesn't make much sense to us. Can you explain?'

'Explain?' I wanted to laugh. How could I when none of it made any sense. I dabbed my lip with the sleeve of my kaftan again, pleased when it came away dry. I dropped the sleeve, conscious of the detectives' eyes on me as they patiently waited for me to say something. 'I didn't lie about the gardener. His name is Seb and he's the kind of worker who takes incredible pride in his work. It took him two weeks to build those raised flower beds because he wanted them perfect. I swear he faffed with a spirit level with almost every brick.

'But when he was finished, I had to admit it all looked lovely.' The memory brought a smile that faded quickly. 'Yesterday, with the odd thought going through my head that I had killed Toby and buried him in one of the raised beds, I went outside to look.'

Hopper's puzzled expression cleared as enlightenment

dawned. 'Are you saying that Seb planted those fuchsia plants in a row, and now they're out of line.'

'Exactly. I must have taken them out, emptied the brick container of soil, put Toby inside, then put everything back.'

Deep lines cut across Hopper's forehead again. 'We're going to need to dig out that bed, Ms Eastwood. And you're going to need to come to the station with us.'

'Yes. I know how it works.'

'You write about it, Ms Eastwood. I'm sure you write very well, too, but you might find the reality a bit tougher.' Hopper indicated my kaftan. 'For starters, I think you'd better change into something else. DS Collins will go with you in case you need a hand while I make some phone calls.'

I accepted this without argument. In fact, I needed help to get up from the sofa and grimaced when Collins gripped my bruised arm roughly.

She walked behind me as I went up the stairs. I wasn't sure if she would support me if I fell backwards or simply let me fall. The doubt made me cling to the banisters with both hands as I ascended, one slow step after the other.

She stayed watching as I opened the wardrobe and searched for appropriate clothing, settling for jeans and a long-sleeved T-shirt. I thought she might turn away while I changed, instead, she propped a shoulder against the wall and kept her eyes on me as I slid the kaftan over my head. Everything was out in the open now, even my naked body was exposed to critical eyes.

I wrote about crime, but my characters were left in the police station, their stories ending with them being taken away. I'd never researched further and everything I knew of what happened afterwards was learned from TV shows. Nothing I'd seen gave me any confidence in my future.

With no idea what I'd be allowed to bring, and unwilling to

ask the unsympathetic detective, I grabbed a holdall and packed some spare underwear, another T-shirt, and basic toiletries.

I didn't think I'd been more than a couple of minutes but when I went downstairs two uniformed police officers were waiting. Hopper introduced them, the names dissipating as soon as said, my sad, confused brain no longer able to process something as simple as names.

I went with them without question or comment.

45

MISTY

When we arrived at the police station, I was taken to an interview room that bore little resemblance to the fictional ones in my books. There, they were grim, odorous places with sticky floors and scarred tables. This room, on the other hand, could have been a conference room. The table was clean, the chairs comfortable, walls painted a relaxing sage green. The air-conditioning was set too low, however, and the room was so cold I shivered.

I had phoned my agent, Theodora, on the way and given her a brief account of my position. She'd been understandably stunned and unusually lost for words.

'I don't know what to say,' she'd finally said, 'but I know what to do... get you a good solicitor. I'll contact the legal team the agency uses, see if they can recommend someone. Okay? Meanwhile, hang tight.'

Hang tight was an expression I never used, had never really understood what it meant. Now, perhaps I did. I was hanging tight to what was left of my sanity.

The solicitor arrived a little over an hour later. A tall, thin, pale woman with an incongruous thick mop of ginger hair, she introduced herself and demanded a comprehensive account of what the police were accusing me of to which she listened in silence. There were none of the encouraging words or empathetic nods I'd have had my fictional solicitor give to someone in my situation.

A page of an A4 pad was covered in her neat, tidy writing by the time I'd finished my story. She queried a few specific details and clicked her pen shut. 'Okay, let's wait to see what the police say.'

She pulled a neat laptop from her briefcase, opened it, and proceeded to ignore me.

I sat with my hands clasped on the table in front of me, my fingers interlaced. It was a strange moment to be aware of how ragged my nails were. Everything was strange. It was almost a relief to see the familiar detectives coming through the door.

They sat opposite, their serious faces set into grim lines, and I knew what they were going to say before they said it. 'You found him.'

DI Hopper nodded slowly. 'They've found the body of a man we assume to be Toby Carter buried in the bottom of that raised brick bed exactly where you indicated it might be.'

Bizarrely, it was almost a relief to know the truth.

'Ms Eastwood, you couldn't defend yourself against Dee Carter who must be three inches shorter and several pounds lighter than you. Yet you had the strength to get Mr Carter's body down the stairs, through the house and into the garden, then more strength to lift him up and put him in the bottom of that raised bed.' Hopper shook her head. 'Something doesn't add up.'

I felt her eyes boring into me. What did she want me to say? Hadn't I confessed, wasn't that enough for her?

'Leaving that aside for the moment, there were also two holdalls beside the body. Are they the ones you mentioned Toby having that night?'

I frowned. I'd dragged his body out, put him in the raised bed, then calmly went back for his bags before putting all the soil back on top of him. What kind of a monster was I that I could do such a thing? 'He had two so I suppose that makes sense.' My attempt at sounding rational was spoiled by the distinct quiver in my voice as panic increased its hold on me.

'But you don't remember putting them in beside him?'

I shut my eyes briefly. Did they hope if they asked often enough, the lost memories would come tumbling back? I wished they would, wished there weren't this horrible, scary blank, this dreadful space where a part of me I didn't recognise was capable of such horror.

'Ms Eastwood?'

'I told you. I don't recall anything about what happened.'

'Okay. What about the rest of his belongings?'

'The rest...' Hadn't I wondered the same thing? 'I don't know. He'd put the empty boxes up into the attic, I checked and they were gone so he must have taken them down and put the remainder of his stuff into them.'

'Then where are they? Did someone come and pick them up?'

'Not that I know of.' I felt so weary, so numb. I'd killed Toby, what more did they need to know? I wished they'd stop asking questions and simply lock me away. My eyelids felt heavy, I was thinking about shutting them when Hopper's insistent voice came again.

'Mr Carter was supposed to be moving in with Gwen Marsham that evening, could she have come around and collected the boxes without you knowing?'

I'd almost forgotten about the solicitor sitting to my right but at this, she held a hand up. 'If it was done without my client's knowledge, she could hardly be aware now, could she?'

I was almost amused at the solicitor's pedantry. I knew exactly what the detective was asking but I sat back and waited for her to rephrase the question.

'Let me ask another way then,' Hopper said with a tight smile. 'Could someone have called to your house, Ms Eastwood, rung your doorbell and be given those boxes by Mr Carter without you being aware that such an action was taking place?'

I had come to that conclusion myself as being the only option. 'If I was working, with my headphones on, yes, they could have done.'

The interview room door opened and a uniformed constable appeared in the gap. 'Sorry to interrupt,' she said, 'but it's urgent.'

I sighed and slumped down in the chair assuming the interruption would bring the interview to an end. When Hopper announced for the recording that it was being suspended I looked to my solicitor for... something, anything. I felt like a child wanting someone to say everything would be all right. When the solicitor merely raised a ginger eyebrow in response, as if this was all perfectly normal, I turned away.

The other detective, her with the painted face whose name I had once again forgotten, had stayed behind and sat staring at me. Meeting her gaze, I refused to look away until I saw amusement creep into her eyes.

Amusement. Over the next few days, I supposed I'd have to get used to being greeted by a variety of emotions. My sisters would be shocked, devastated and would probably refuse to believe I'd killed Toby until faced with the proof; my agent and editor would be horrified; various friends would be stunned. It was all ahead of me, and their reactions would be out of my control but here, for the moment, I still had some power. I looked back at the detective, her name coming to me in time. 'Perhaps you could tell me, and my solicitor, Detective Sergeant Collins, why you find the current situation so intensely amusing?'

I was pleased to see her expression change to a more suitable grim one and was about to make a further comment when the door opened and DI Hopper returned looking even more inscrutable than usual.

She sat and shuffled in her chair before announcing the resumption of the interview.

'Ms Eastwood, I know you've told us you have no recollection of what occurred that night.' Hopper hesitated and appeared to be searching for the right words. 'You don't remember throwing the glass paperweight at Mr Carter but you found it on the floor of your office the next day so you're assuming you did. Is that correct?'

'Yes.'

'You assume this blow was responsible for killing Mr Carter and in your panic you chose not to ring for an ambulance or the police, but instead dragged his dead weight down the stairs, through the house and across the garden to the raised flower bed and managed to get him inside.'

I waited for my solicitor to say that I'd told them, several times, I couldn't remember. When she remained silent, I shook my head in frustration. 'I keep telling you, I don't know what I did. But since you've found Toby's body where I told you, it must have happened that way.'

'I think you might have rung someone for help.' Hopper leaned forward, her arms sliding on the table so that her clasped hands were almost touching mine. 'Which is why we've asked to see your phone records.'

The solicitor who'd been listening carefully suddenly shuffled in her seat. 'Methinks you've had some news, Detective Inspector Hopper.' She smiled. 'You've found fingerprints that don't match those of my client, haven't you?'

'Someone else was there?' I was stunned. 'Who?'

Hopper sat back. 'That's what we're going to find out.'

46

GWEN

Two hours later, in another interview room in the same police station, Gwen Marsham sat drumming her nails on the table. She'd been given little choice by the two uniformed constables who had arrived at the gallery. Luckily, it had been empty, nobody to witness the embarrassment.

She got to her feet when the door opened and the two detectives she was sick of seeing walked through. Agitation made her voice tremble. 'I do not appreciate having uniformed officers descend upon my gallery,' she snapped. 'I have worked hard to build up my business, anything with a whiff of scandal can do it irreparable damage.'

'Unfortunately, circumstances necessitated that we acted quickly, Ms Marsham.' DI Hopper took the seat opposite, Collins the seat beside her. 'Toby Carter's body has been found. His wife formally identified him a few minutes ago.'

Gwen sank back onto the chair. She tried to get her thoughts in order, tried to fix her expression into one resembling horror, shock, sorrow – aiming for Edvard Munch's *The Scream* or maybe the Face Screaming in Fear emoji. She wondered if she should put her hands to her face to make it clear how she felt.

Because she was horrified, of course she was. They'd found Toby's body.

When she saw Hopper's lips tighten, she wasn't sure she'd managed to convey the correct emotion and dropped her eyes to her clasped hands.

'Mrs Carter was understandably upset, so much so, in fact, that she needed medical attention. Despite his infidelity, she referred to Toby Carter as being–' Hopper crooked her index fingers in the air. '–the love of her life.' She rested her forearms on the table, her fingers interlinked. 'To be honest, Ms Marsham, I'm sorry not to have met the man. I find it staggering that he could behave as he did and still garner so much devotion.'

Gwen kept her eyes down and twisted her hands together. 'As you say, detective, you never met him so you couldn't possibly understand.'

'No, obviously not.' Hopper sat back, her hands flat on the table, the pads of her fingers tapping, a dull thud beating in rhythm to some unheard music. She stopped, linked her fingers together again and slid them forward, bringing her closer to Gwen. 'You didn't ask where we found him, Ms Marsham.'

Gwen opened her mouth, then shut it again. She'd seen cats toying with mice they'd caught, the almost bored pat with a paw that sent the mouse flying, the quick grab again, the pressure of sharp teeth, then the drop and the mouse's attempt to escape. Did the poor mouse know that whatever he did the outcome was going to be the same? But as the mouse did, Gwen decided to try to escape.

'No, I didn't.' Let the detective make of that answer whatever she wanted.

'Mr Carter was buried in Misty Eastwood's back garden. As a result, Ms Eastwood is in custody helping us with our enquiries.'

'Poor Toby, what a sad end.' At least with these words she

could be sincere. How Toby would have hated being given such an undignified resting place. 'I am, of course, pleased to have an answer to the mystery of why he didn't arrive as he'd promised, but I'm puzzled as to why you thought it necessary to bring me here.'

She saw a sweep of satisfaction cross both detectives' faces, a subtle shade of it on the older detective, a gleeful waft of it across the painted face of the younger. She knew in that second that the mouse had been caught.

'You were arrested and charged with a drugs offence when you were twenty-two,' DI Hopper said. 'For which you received a suspended sentence.'

Gwen opened her eyes wide and raised one perfectly plucked eyebrow. 'My one and only foray into recreational drugs and it's still being brought up! That's simply ridiculous and can't possibly have anything to do with what I'm doing here. If you're thinking Toby was into drugs I can tell you you're totally wrong.'

'We're not looking at a drugs connection. At least,' Hopper shrugged, 'we've not considered one yet. No, what we have been looking at is your fingerprints and thanks to your arrest, they're on the system. But before we go any further, we need to caution you–' Hopper tilted her head toward Collins. '–my colleague will do the honours.'

The strands of tension that had been wrapping themselves around Gwen since the uniformed police had arrived at the gallery suddenly jerked tightly cutting off her breath. She hid her gasp in a grating, 'What?'

Collins made no effort to hide her satisfaction and rolled off the words. '*You do not have to say anything. But it may harm your defence if you do not mention now something which you later rely on in court. Anything you do say may be given in evidence.* Do you understand this caution, Ms Marsham?'

She suddenly understood everything. *Her damn fingerprints.* She licked her lips. 'Yes, I understand.'

'You might prefer to have a solicitor with you before we go any further.'

Gwen almost smiled as she imagined the stunned expression on the face of the petite, delicate solicitor who handled the legal affairs of the gallery. She'd have to ring her eventually, but not yet, not until she found out exactly what the police knew. 'No, I'd like to get whatever this is over with.'

Hopper opened the slim file that sat on the desk in front of her and withdrew an A4 colour photograph. 'For the record, I'm showing Ms Marsham a photograph of two holdalls.' She slid it across the desk. 'Do you recognise these?'

Gwen felt the colour slide down her face and vanish. Of course, she recognised them and worse, she knew they were going to be her undoing.

'You need to answer for the record, Ms Marsham.'

Instead of answering, Gwen lifted her hands, palms up, and rubbed her thumbs over her fingertips. 'My prints are on them so there's no point in my lying, is there?'

'These holdalls–' Hopper tapped her index finger on the photo. '–were found buried alongside Toby Carter's body. Did you help Misty Eastwood bury him?'

Gwen was still rubbing her fingertips but she looked up at that and met Hopper's gaze. 'Help Misty bury him...' She shook her head. 'No, you've got it all wrong.'

Collins muttered something unintelligible and Hopper let out a grunt of frustration. 'Perhaps then you'll tell us what did happen.'

47

GWEN

Perhaps Gwen had always known it would come to this. She'd been so stupid. Doubly so, she should never have fallen for Toby's charms.

A heavy sigh seemed to deflate her in the chair. 'I'll tell you everything.' She shuffled as if to make herself comfortable for the story she was about to relate. She'd have liked to ask for coffee but didn't want to delay. 'The day before he died, Toby rang me and asked if I'd call to the house on Myrtle Road and pick up a couple of boxes. I did as he asked. When I arrived, I rang his mobile and he came out and put them into the boot of my car.'

'You didn't see Misty Eastwood?'

'No. I didn't know about her. Toby had told me he was living with his sister.' Gwen sniffed. 'I was a gullible idiot. Anyway, I brought the boxes back, carried them one by one into my apartment. Then, because I wanted to make Toby feel at home when he arrived, I decided to surprise him by unpacking.' Once again she wondered what would have happened if she'd not done so, if she'd never found that phone number and discovered what an idiot she'd been.

'I found a piece of paper screwed up in one of his pockets with a name and phone number written on it.' Gwen shrugged. 'Maybe deep down, I knew I was being a fool so, anyway, I rang it and discovered that not only was Toby incredibly sexy, charismatic and charming but he was also married and a compulsive liar.'

She thought back to that moment of clarity... the stinging pain of realising she'd been made a fool of again, that she'd fallen for another George. That old adage had come slamming into her with force. *Fool me once, shame on you... fool me twice, shame on me.*

With anger fizzing through her veins, she'd pulled all his clothes from the hangers where she'd carefully hung them, from the drawers and cupboards where they'd been lovingly placed and she'd rammed them higgledy-piggledy back into the two boxes.

She would have liked to have been dramatic, tear them into strips and fling them from the balcony, stand waiting till he arrived then lean over and spit in his eye.

It was tempting, but if she had stooped that low she'd have had to put up with the neighbours' quizzical looks and raised eyebrows for weeks, and some of them knew people who came to her gallery. The word would spread faster than mould on week-old bread.

Instead, she sealed the boxes up and left them on the bedroom floor. But having no outlet, the anger still fizzed. It was that that had made her decide to go to Myrtle Road. A decision she would have lots of time to regret.

'May I have a glass of water, or better, a coffee,' she said. She'd need one or the other. It was a long story.

A few minutes later, her hands were wrapped around a disposable cup of murky coffee. She took a sip. They hadn't asked how she wanted it, and it was sickly sweet. She put it down and sighed. 'Okay.'

Gwen would have smiled at the suddenly intent expressions on the two detectives if there had been anything amusing in her situation. Instead, she took another mouthful of the sweet coffee. 'Let me tell you a crazy story.'

48

GWEN

When Gwen had discovered Toby's deceit, she had waited until her anger had faded to a low simmer before deciding what to do. It was self-directed anger. How could she have been so stupid... again!

At first, she was going to wait until Toby arrived but quickly dismissed the idea. He was too charming, too cunning, she might succumb to his lies. And there was the deep-seated fear that if Toby came to the apartment... where they'd made love in every room and on the balcony as rain peppered their naked bodies with every cold drop on overheated skin an erotic charge... she might, probably would have, forgiven him. Because she was a fool when it came to men. Sam, George, Toby and a host of others.

Better that she should stop him before he left the house in Hanwell. Whoever he was living with... not a sister.... she could keep him.

Too agitated to drive, at first she tried for a taxi but was told it would be thirty minutes. 'No, that's okay,' she said, hanging up. Determined on immediate action and fuelled with anger, she changed into flat shoes and took a Tube.

It took longer than she expected and she was afraid she might have missed Toby but when she got to Myrtle Road, she saw him up ahead coming out of the house, a bag in each hand. She hurried along to meet him, mentally rehearsing the words she was going to say.

'Gwen, how lovely,' he said, reaching forward to plant a kiss on her cheek. 'I didn't know you were coming to pick me up.' He looked behind her. 'Where's your car?' He was smiling, his eyes soft and appreciative as they looked at her and she'd found herself weakening.

'We need to talk,' she said. 'Can we go inside?'

For the first time she saw him look shifty. 'It's not a good idea.' He dropped the bags at his feet, reached out and gripped her shoulders. Then he looked straight into her eyes and with a sincerity that was unbelievably convincing, said, 'My sister was a little upset at my leaving.'

'Your sister.' Gwen threw her head back and laughed, cackling loudly when she saw his look of total confusion. Toby, she guessed, wasn't used to his plans going awry.

'Listen,' he said, reaching for her arm, grabbing hold as she tried to pull away. 'Come over here and we'll talk.'

The end-of-terrace house had a side passage that led to the back garden. With the house on one side and a high wall on the other, it was a narrow, dank area with a wooden gateway at the garden end.

Toby kept hold of her arm and pulled her round the edge of the house, down toward the end of the passage where the shimmering glow from the street lights made little impact. 'What's the problem, you getting cold feet?'

Gwen looked at him. Words churning in her head were desperate to get out and tell this conniving, deceiving bastard exactly what she thought of him. She'd opened her mouth ready for the words to spill forth in all their justified glory when suddenly, like a domino, Toby fell backwards.

Gwen struggled to understand what had happened. The thud as Toby hit the ground was loud. She knew him to be a liar, but surely even he couldn't lie this well.

'Toby?' She nudged his body with the toe of her shoe. When there was no answer, she bent to look closer, moving her hands up his body, feeling the warmth of him with a quick erotic charge. Was this what he wanted? Dangerous sex in an almost public place. She laughed, feeling her way to his face. 'You're crazy!'

But there was no answer, no mutual exploration. She felt his face, ran her fingers over his lips, tapped his cheek, gently at first, then with more force. 'Toby... Toby!'

It was a minute before she faced the truth.

He was dead.

49

GWEN

Gwen straddled Toby's body, her hand on his face. What was she going to do? Stunned, she got to her feet. She jerked around when she heard footsteps approaching to see a figure thrown into silhouette by the street lights. Still in shock, she said the first thing that came to her. 'I think he's dead.'

'Dead!' The woman hurried forward, pushed her out of her way and bent over Toby.

'I was speaking to him, next thing he keeled over. I didn't do anything, I swear!'

'A heart attack or stroke or something, I suppose,' the woman said.

'You're Misty?' Gwen took the silence as confirmation. 'He told me you were his sister and I believed him. He was supposed to be moving in with me tonight but I discovered his lie.'

The woman lifted Toby's hand, pushed back his sleeve and felt for a pulse.

She looked as if she knew what she was doing and Gwen held her breath. Maybe she was wrong and he'd only fainted. She let her breath out in ragged sobs as Misty put her hand on his chest and reached to lay a hand against his neck.

'He is dead, isn't he?' Gwen asked.

Misty's fingers were pressed to Toby's neck. Instead of answering, she asked, 'He was moving in with you?'

'Yes. He said he loved me and that you were his sister. But you're not, are you?'

'No, I was his girlfriend, his lover. I thought we'd be together forever. Toby, unfortunately, had a problem with fidelity and the truth.'

Gwen heard the sorrow in the other woman's voice but she'd none to share. The double shock of Toby's treachery and death had left her numb. She hovered uncertainly, then asked again, 'He is dead, isn't he?'

Misty pushed to her feet. 'Yes, I'm afraid he is.'

'I'd better ring the police.'

'The police? I think we should get him into the garden in case someone passes by and sees us. We'll be able to decide what to do then.'

'What?' Gwen twisted her hands together. 'Shouldn't we leave him where he is?'

The sound of the gate latch being lifted was loud. 'No. Grab him under an arm. Let's get him inside.'

Gwen looked at Toby's body, horrified. 'Grab him?'

'I can't do it by myself, come on.'

Perhaps it was shock that made Gwen move forward and when Misty grabbed Toby under one arm, Gwen took the other. Between them they dragged the dead weight of the body through the gate, Toby's heels dragging on the ground.

A wave of nausea hit Gwen. She dropped the arm and backed away.

'Come on, we have to move further in, we need to get the gate shut.'

'I can't.' Gwen took another step away, she couldn't touch his body again.

'You have to. I know you're distressed but I can't do this alone. Come on, one more move.'

When it didn't appear she had any choice, Gwen moved back and slid her hand under Toby's arm again. Another heave, and he was in the garden bracketed by the two women.

'My name's Gwen.' She looked at the woman who was staring into the garden behind. 'I'm sorry, Misty. I foolishly believed him.'

'Toby treated truth like an optional extra.'

The remark brought a brief smile to Gwen's face. 'I didn't know him long enough, I suppose. Two weeks,' she added before there was a need to ask.

'Two weeks. Quick work. I didn't realise he was in such a hurry to move on.'

Gwen heard the bitterness in the voice and shuffled nervously. 'So now what? We should ring the police, shouldn't we?'

'There'll be questions asked. Like why you were talking to him in the side passage of a house neither of you own. The police and the press will put their own spin on it, of course. It'll probably involve seedy, scurrilous headlines.'

Gwen's hand crept over her mouth. Of course they would, and they would dig into her past.

'The post-mortem will show how he died, but that will take a few days. So as long as you can ride out the gossip and the poking into every corner of your life until then, you'll be okay.'

Gwen saw a slight smile appear on Misty's face as if she knew that Gwen had things to hide, things she didn't want the police poking into.

'Nobody saw what happened. I think we should get rid of him.'

Gwen looked at her and laughed uncertainly. 'We're not talking about a bad smell!'

Misty shut the gate, then stepped back into the darkness of the garden behind. 'Wait here.'

Gwen could see an indistinct solid shape at the end of the garden. A shed, she guessed. A moment later she heard the squeak of a door being opened. Perhaps she should go and help Misty do whatever it was she was doing, but instead, she stayed, staring down at the body of a man she'd laid naked with only two days before. She looked up as Misty returned holding a spade that she swung almost carelessly.

'Right, do you have your mobile?'

Gwen tapped her pocket. 'Yes.'

Misty pointed to a raised flower bed. 'Bring up the torch and direct it there.'

'What?'

'We're going to bury him.'

50

GWEN

Gwen's heart hammered painfully as the words hit home. They were going to bury Toby? Her mouth was hanging open, she shut it with a painful snap and shook her head. 'This is crazy.'

'What's crazy is that Toby is lying there dead and two women he'd been sleeping with, two women that he'd lied to, are standing over his body worrying about doing the wrong thing.'

'But...' Gwen stepped over the body and peered into the garden. Her eyes were adjusting to the darkness and now she could see the two raised brick beds that bordered an area of grass. They were both planted with small shrubs. 'It looks as if it's been recently done.'

'It has, only a couple of weeks ago. It's designed to be low maintenance. The brick beds are filled with soil. We can take the plants out of one, remove the soil, put the body in the bottom and fill it back in. Any extra soil, we can scatter over the wild flower bed or put it in the compost heap behind the shed. It won't be noticed. Nobody will ever know.'

'We'll know.' Gwen gasped when fingers tightened painfully on her arm.

'We'll do this,' Misty said, 'and never speak of it again. *Ever*. Not a word, not a hint. We'll never acknowledge what we've done, never tell a soul. Eventually, it will fade as if all of this had been a dream.

A dream? A nightmare. Was that it? Was this all a horrible nightmare, Gwen would wake up any moment and be stunned at how real it all felt. The fingers pressing into her arm told her otherwise. 'It won't work. Anyway, what if they find out, it'll make it all so much worse, won't it, if they find we've buried him.'

'There's no reason they should find out if we're careful. We get rid of all the evidence. Carry on as if this night had never happened.' She lifted the spade she'd taken from the shed. 'We're lucky, the soil will be soft and easy to dig. It won't take long and nobody will ever know.'

'And we'll never speak of it?' Was Gwen really going to agree to this? But the alternative... the police looking into her life... the press digging and speculating. Her beloved art gallery would suffer. Artists mightn't be too concerned at her involvement with Toby's death, but they wouldn't want their work to be associated with the sordid, scurrilous slant the press would put on his death and the pathetic truth that Toby had been a gigolo.

They'd laugh. And withdraw their work.

She glanced back to where Toby's body lay. It would already be starting to decay cell by cell. No longer the charming, charismatic man who had obsessed her. He was dead; nothing she could do now was going to change that. 'Okay, I'll do it.'

'Right.' The spade was dug into the soil. 'No time to waste.'

Gwen looked up to the houses on either side. Both were in darkness. 'What about the neighbours? Won't they hear and come out to investigate what we're up to?'

'No. There's a very deaf couple on one side, and the family on the other side is away.'

Gwen shivered. The stage was theirs to perform their creepy play. 'Come on. Switch on your phone's torch. I need light.'

There seemed to be no reason to delay. Gwen reached for her mobile, switched on the torch app and shone it over the top of the nearest raised bed, holding it steady as Misty dug out the first of the shrubs. Soon they were piled up together.

Misty climbed up onto the flat edging stone of the bed. 'It'll be easier to dig it out from here.' She began to move the soft soil out, dropping it to the grassy area in front, the mound quickly growing.

Despite the cool night air, and Gwen's easy role in simply focusing the light on the surface of the soil, perspiration ran in a rivulet between her breasts and dampened under her arms. The scent of fear came from her in wafts.

She was impressed with Misty's steady work: she only stopped now and then to wipe her sweat-slippery hands on her belly. As the level of the soil inside lowered, it was harder work to lift the spade up and empty it over the side. 'Almost done,' she said after ten minutes.

Gwen shone the torch inside. 'No, it needs to be down to the bottom.' She was committed to this now. It needed to be foolproof.

'Then you get down here and dig for a change.'

'This was your idea, don't forget! I wanted to call the police from the very beginning.' Gwen should have done. She still could. Her mobile was in her hand. Wouldn't it be better?

'Okay, okay, I'll go a bit deeper. God forbid you should wreck your precious nails.'

Gwen swallowed the retort she wanted to make and held the mobile's torch light steady.

Five minutes later, the spade was thrown to one side. 'That's it.' Misty climbed out and stood looking down. 'It's perfect.'

Gwen joined her. 'Yes, I think so.' She looked at Toby's body. 'What a sad end.'

'Yes, he'd have preferred something much more elegant and expensive than a raised flower bed in the garden of a former lover.'

Gwen was staring into the brick coffin. Could she do it? She gritted her teeth. Yes. It was the best way. She turned, shone the light over the body and saw Misty's form hunkered over it. 'What are you doing?'

'Checking for a pulse, to make sure, but there's nothing.' She dropped the wrist she was holding and got to her feet. 'Okay, this isn't going to be easy. It'll take both of us. Put your phone down somewhere where it will give us a bit of light.'

There was a plant pot outside the back door. Gwen balanced her phone on it. It gave enough light. 'It's not going to last very long though.'

'Right, well let's get on with it. I'll take him under the arms and step backwards, you grab him under his knees. And watch your step.'

Gwen left the phone and hurried over to slide her arms under Toby's knees. Grunting, they half-dragged, half-carried his body across to the raised bed. The soil Misty had removed made the surface uneven and Gwen stumbled as she stepped back, windmilling her arms to keep her balance.

'Careful,' Misty warned. She wiped a muddy hand over her forehead. 'It's not going to be easy getting him inside.' She squatted, got her arms under Toby's armpits, and hauled him up into a sitting position. 'Okay,' she grunted. 'You need to grab him under his knees again, and when I say go, we lift. Once we get him on the top, we can simply push him in.'

Gwen looked at the height of the flat edging stones. Three feet, at least. 'We're never going to do it.'

'Not with you standing there like a bloody spare wheel we're not! Just do as I say.'

The mobile phone light had gone out, Gwen set it running again.

'Quickly now,' Misty said. 'Wait for my signal.'

Toby wasn't a big man, but no lightweight either. A memory of his weight pressing Gwen into the mattress suddenly shot into her head, making her groan as she pushed her arms under his knees.

'Now,' Misty said, grunting as she pushed up with Toby's upper body clasped in her arms. Gwen staggered under the weight, her head bent almost to his crotch, stumbling when they managed to get the body onto the flat top and falling forward. For a horrifying second, her face was buried in his groin, making her pull away with a cry of despair.

'We did it.' Misty's voice was almost gleeful. 'Right, let's get on with it.' Without waiting for Gwen's help, she put her hands on the body and pushed.

Gwen stared, her mouth slightly ajar as nothing happened, the body seemingly wedged in place. Then with a soft shushing sound, it slipped inside.

Misty grabbed the spade to begin the task of putting the soil back on top.

'Wait.' Gwen held a hand up to stop her. 'The holdalls. There's room for them alongside.' At the nod of agreement, she hurried through the gate and around to the front door where Toby had dropped his bags only a short time before. *A lifetime before.* Gwen shivered, then looked up and down the street. It was so quiet. The surrounding houses in darkness, the occupants all sleeping peacefully. They wouldn't be having bad dreams of bodies buried in their gardens.

The bags were heavy: filled with all the expensive clothes Toby had loved, the handmade shoes, the silk ties, the monogrammed gold cufflinks. They banged against Gwen's legs as she took them down the dark passage to the back garden.

Misty hadn't waited. A mound of soil already covered Toby's face and chest. Gwen had a pang of regret she'd not said a final goodbye.

'Hurry!' Misty hissed.

Gwen pushed the holdalls beside Toby's legs, squashing them down as much as she could.

Using the spade to balance, Misty jumped on top of the bags and stamped them down with her feet. 'Better.' She climbed back onto the edge. 'Let's get this finished.'

In the darkness, Gwen couldn't read Misty's expression. She guessed it was probably the same as hers, horror mixed with relief. A sudden thought had her squeak, 'Stop! What about his mobile? We can't have it ringing from his grave.'

'I have it, don't worry. I'll get rid of it later.'

'Okay.' There was no further reason to delay. A spadeful of soil was thrown in and landed with a splat on the bags, the noise loud in the silence of the night. As everything was covered it became soil-on-soil quiet.

Finally, the shrubs were planted back in a line and pressed in place with the heel of muddy hands.

Misty brushed the soil from the edge. 'Looks as good as new.'

'What about this?' Gwen indicated the mound of extra soil that still remained on the ground.

'I'll get a trug from the shed and get rid of it. There's a compost heap behind the shed, most can go there.' The lower legs of Misty's trousers were laced with soil, her shoes caked. She used the side of the spade to scrape the encrusted mud away. 'I'll tidy up and it will be as if we've never been here.'

Never been here? They'd buried a man. Gwen almost admired the woman's coolness.

'Now, all you need to do is go home and forget that this ever happened. Toby never arrived at your house and you assume he changed his mind. You've never been in this garden. We've never met.'

Unable to think of words to suit this crazy, bizarre situation, Gwen settled for parroting what Misty had said. 'We've never met.'

There were no more words between them. Leaving Misty to tidy up, Gwen took a final look at Toby's resting place, then put her mobile into her pocket and left.

51

GWEN

'And that is it.' Gwen used two hands to lift the disposable cup to her lips where it trembled against her front teeth as she tried to take a sip. It was almost cold, but perhaps it was something she'd have to get used to. Letting her standards drop.

She looked across the table, smiling despite the situation when she saw surprise in the wide, heavily kohled eyes of the younger detective and the look of... was it sympathy... in the eyes of the other. 'It all sounds crazy, doesn't it?'

'A bit.' Hopper folded her arms across her chest and stared at Gwen. 'So according to you, Toby Carter simply keeled over like a domino.'

Gwen took one hand from the cup and rested the heel of it on the table. 'Like this...' She let her hand drop flat. 'No sound, nothing.' She remembered thinking he'd wanted to have sex there in that dark, damp side passage and had been turned on by it, had even reached down for him, her hands creeping over his body. The detectives didn't need to know that. 'While I was standing there, wondering what to do, Misty turned up. I suppose I must have looked shocked because she took over immediately and bent down to feel for his pulse. It felt like an eternity but it can't have been more than a few seconds before she got to her feet and confirmed he was dead.'

'Why didn't you ring the police? You could have explained he'd fallen over. It was probably a heart attack or stroke. A post-mortem would have proved that and you'd have been off the hook.'

Gwen put the cup down and pushed her fists into her eyes. How could she explain that she hadn't wanted the police digging into her past, into George's death, maybe adding two and two together and coming up with the correct answer. 'It would have got into the papers.' She took her hands away. 'Can you imagine the headlines? *Art gallery owner, Gwen Marsham, discovered in seedy tryst with dead man.*'

'So, instead, you decided to bury him?'

Gwen sighed again. 'It was Misty's suggestion. She made it sound like a good idea.'

A sneer curled the painted lips of the younger detective. 'A good idea?'

Gwen eyed her with dislike. 'You had to have been there.' She pulled the cup back and sipped the dregs of the cold coffee.

Hopper tapped the desk, bringing Gwen's attention back to her. 'Let me get this straight. You and Misty Eastwood buried Toby Carter in the garden on Myrtle Road.'

Gwen was staring into the coffee, she looked up with a frown. 'No, not Misty Eastwood.' She flapped a hand. 'I'm sorry, I should have explained. When the woman joined me, I assumed it was Misty. Not a sister as Toby had led me to believe, but a girlfriend, lover, whatever you want to call it.'

'Hang on.' Hopper raised a hand, her face twisted in lines of confusion. 'Are you saying the woman who helped you bury Toby Carter wasn't Misty Eastwood?'

'Yes, that's right. I didn't realise my mistake until the next day when I called around to the house and a woman I'd never seen before answered the door.' Gwen smiled at the memory. 'You can imagine my shock. I had to think on my feet to spin a believable tale but she seemed to accept what I told her without question.

'I could have left it at that. After all, when we buried Toby we'd agreed never to speak of it again, as if it had never happened. But...' She sighed. 'I was worried she might have changed her mind. That's why I'd called to the house, to get confirmation that what we'd done would stay between us, to swear her to secrecy.'

Gwen had lain awake the whole night, horrified at what they'd done. She'd gone around to the house, not only to swear her partner in crime to secrecy but to get reassurance that what they'd done had been the right thing to do. To be faced with a stranger had rattled her but she'd recovered and by the end of her conversation with Misty, she knew exactly who had helped her dispose of Toby's body.

52

GWEN

The discovery that Misty Eastwood wasn't involved in burying Toby Carter's body seemed to throw both detectives. Their reaction brought a brief smile to Gwen's lips. She saw DI Hopper's eyes fix intently on her face and wasn't surprised when the astute woman said, 'You found out who it was, though, didn't you?'

'It wasn't hard really in the end. It had to be one of Toby's women and when Misty told me about the previous girlfriend's violent attack, she seemed to be a likely candidate. I called around and sure enough I was right.'

'Babs Sanderson?'

'That's right.' Gwen shook her head and frowned. 'After we buried Toby, Babs had said we'd never speak of it again, never acknowledge what we'd done, that it would be as if it had never happened. And it was bizarre. In the twenty minutes or so that I was in her apartment, it was never mentioned. I tried to ask her how she knew so much about Misty's back garden but she wouldn't even allow that question. I left, thinking that our secret was safe and that everything would be okay.' Gwen lifted both her hands and let them drop noisily to the table. 'It was my idea to put the bags in with Toby, thinking it was better to get rid of them. If I hadn't you'd never have known about me.'

'No, we'd have arrested Misty Eastwood instead.' Hopper's voice was sharp. 'You should be pleased you've prevented that injustice.'

'Pleased?' Gwen huffed a laugh. 'Nothing about any of this pleases me, detective, but yes, I wouldn't have wanted her to suffer for what we did. Tell her I'm sorry.'

'I will. You need to get yourself a solicitor. A good criminal one, okay?'

'Yes, of course.' Gwen shook her head. 'What happens now?'

'We're still waiting for the results of the post-mortem to see exactly how Mr Carter died. When we do, we'll discuss your case with the Crown prosecutor and decide what charges will be brought against you and Ms Sanderson.'

'I can go?' Gwen felt a surge of hope that quickly sputtered and died in the face of the detective's emphatic head shake.

'We'll need to keep you for a while yet, I'm afraid.' Hopper tilted her head towards the younger officer. 'DS Collins will take you to the custody centre and you'll be given a room to stay in overnight. We have twenty-four hours before we are obliged to charge or release you, Ms Marsham, but I'm convinced we can proceed before that.'

Gwen felt her legs wobble when she stood. Unwilling to show weakness, she held onto the table for a few seconds as if lost in thought and ignored Collins who stood impatiently waiting.

'I suppose there is nothing else to say,' Gwen said finally. She took her hands away, straightened her shoulders and followed the rigid back of DS Collins deeper into the bowels of the police station.

~

Gwen was handed over to what she considered to be an inappropriately cheerful custody sergeant where she answered a ream of questions and handed over her handbag and her stiletto heels. In case she attacked someone with them? She couldn't imagine doing so, but then she could never have imagined being back in a custody centre.

'I need to ring my solicitor,' she said when he wanted to keep her phone.

'Right. I'll give you a minute.' He moved an inch away, his jowly chin sinking onto his chest, a bored look in his eyes.

She turned her back to him and rang the solicitor who'd been handling her business affairs for years. 'I need help,' she said when the assistant put Gwen through.

If the solicitor was taken aback at the abruptness of the request, she didn't comment, merely saying, as she always did, 'We're here for you.'

'I'm in police custody. I may be charged with burying a body.' *They couldn't charge her with killing Toby, could they, it had been an accident.* 'A man died, but it wasn't my fault.'

'Okay.' One word dragged out to give the solicitor time to gather her shocked thoughts. 'We have a criminal defence solicitor in the company. Her name is Heather Fitt. She's one of the best. I'll contact her and ask her to get there as soon as possible.'

Gwen felt some of the tension of the last couple of hours ease a little. 'I'm in Croydon police station, in the custody centre.'

'Fine, don't speak to anyone until Heather gets there.'

There seemed to be no point in telling the solicitor that Gwen had already emptied her soul to the police. 'Okay, thank you.' She handed the custody sergeant her phone, signed a slip for her belongings and was brought into a cell. It wasn't luxurious, by anyone's idea, but they'd improved since her only other stay in a cell some twenty-odd years before. She'd still been high, she remembered, and had giggled for hours before falling into such a deep sleep they'd had to shake her hard to wake her the following morning.

She wasn't giggling this time.

The thin mattress on the built-in bed didn't look too enticing but she was weary. She took the single blanket, put it underneath the flat pillow and lay down with her arm across her eyes.

Voices, shouts and other unidentified noises drifted from outside but inside the small cell, the silence pressed down on her. The creeping darkness of inevitability was filling her head. There was no way out of this mess that didn't reflect badly on her, that wouldn't destroy her business and her reputation.

The tears started, trickling from the corners of her eyes to run into her hair.

Foolish tears.

From a sad, pathetic woman who had believed that this time... *this time...* she'd found a love that was the stuff of dreams, of fairy tales, of the happy ever after she seemed to have been searching for all her life.

Sad, pathetic and foolish.

53

BABS

B abs sat in the interview room with her hands clasped behind her head. She tried to fix her expression into one suitable for the occasion... sorrowful, maybe even distraught... anything but the smile that insisted on appearing despite her best intentions. The two detectives opposite didn't have the same problem, they both looked grim. Babs dropped her hands, pushed them into her coat pockets and waited with little interest to hear what they had to say.

'The body of Toby Carter was discovered buried in the garden of a house on Myrtle Road,' DI Hopper said when the formalities had been completed. 'Gwen Marsham says it was your idea to bury him.'

Babs barked a laugh. 'Does she? Such an elegant woman but such a liar.'

Hopper took a sheet from the file in front of her and slid it across the table. 'For the record, I'm showing Ms Sanderson a photograph of the spade that was found in Misty Eastwood's garden shed.'

The legal aid solicitor who'd been assigned to Babs reached

for it first and examined it knowingly before handing it to her client.

'Your fingerprints are on the handle of this spade, Ms Sanderson,' Hopper said. 'It was found in the garden shed. And the soil on the blade is consistent with the soil around Mr Carter's body.'

The solicitor held a hand up. 'Is there a question there anywhere, detective?'

Hopper glared at her. 'This isn't a damn courtroom.' She waited until the solicitor dropped her eyes before turning her attention back to Babs. 'We have a witness who puts you in the garden, and your prints are on the handle of a spade that was used to dig the grave where Toby Carter was buried. It's pretty cut and dried really.'

Babs looked from one detective to the other and sniffed. 'There doesn't seem to be any point in my saying anything then, does there?'

'It's your opportunity to give your version of events on the night Mr Carter died, Ms Sanderson.'

'I think I'll pass, if it's all the same to you.'

'That's your prerogative, of course. We'll have the post-mortem results tomorrow, following which we'll be discussing what charges to bring. Until then, make yourself at home in our custody centre.'

Babs allowed the smile to break through then. Did they really think she'd be intimidated by spending a night in a cell? Nothing mattered anymore. Not the charges they'd be bringing. Not the loss of her job or the final demands that had necessitated putting her Streatham apartment on the market. The sale of it wouldn't be sufficient to cover her debts but she found it hard to care about that either.

They'd found Toby's body.

Babs wasn't a fool. She knew what that meant.

54

MISTY

I sat in the interview room with my face resting in my cupped hands. There was no solace in the darkness: characters, real and imagined, ran through my head in a full-colour continuous loop.

The solicitor had left an hour before but as she'd barely spoken to me since the detectives had left, her absence made no difference. 'Nothing is going to happen tonight,' she'd said, leaving me her card. 'You can leave a message and I'll be in touch in the morning. We can go from there.'

It was another hour before the door opened suddenly, startling me. I dropped my hands to the table, my eyes wide as I watched the two detectives come in. Their inscrutable expressions gave no indication as to what was happening outside the room.

They resumed their seats as if only seconds and not hours had passed. It was momentarily disorientating and only Hopper's calm voice as she spoke for the record stating the time grounded me.

'Sorry for the delay, Ms Eastwood. For the moment, you're free to go.'

I blinked, unsure if I'd heard correctly. 'What?'

'I said you're free to go.' Hopper held a hand up. 'Unfortunately, your home is a crime scene so you'll not be able to return to it for another day or two.'

'A crime scene. Yes, yes, of course.' I was saying yes but didn't understand what was happening and shut my eyes briefly in the hope it would reset my thought processes. Opening my eyes, I shook my head. 'I feel like I've been kidnapped by characters in my books, Detective Inspector Hopper.' I reached up and pushed a lock of hair behind my ear feeling the tremble in my fingers as I did so. 'Are you able to tell me whose fingerprints you found?'

'Let's say we have a couple of people helping us with our enquiries and leave it at that.'

'Of course, you can't tell me, I know that.' I wanted to cry, felt a sob building and swallowed hard, unsure if I was crying for myself, Toby or for whatever unfortunates were caught in this nightmare. 'I'm feeling a little...' I shrugged, unable to think of an appropriate word.

Hopper seemed to understand. 'Is there someone you can call? Somewhere you can spend the night?'

There was easy sympathy in her voice now I was no longer a murder suspect. 'Yes. Thank you.' I snuffled noisily, felt in my pocket for a tissue and blew my nose. 'I can go to my sister's.'

'Good.' Hopper pulled out her notebook. 'If you'll give me the address. We may have more questions for you.'

And I was free to go. It felt so strange I wondered if it were a trap. If they were waiting for me to attempt to leave, then they'd shoot me and say I was killed while trying to escape. Or was that the storyline of a movie I'd seen a long time ago?

Hopper got to her feet but she must have seen the confusion in my face. 'There's a constable outside, she'll show you to reception when you're ready to go. Take your time.'

Befuddled, I stayed seated until the detectives left, their footsteps fading as they walked down the corridor, doors banging behind them somewhere in the distance.

I don't know how long I sat there. Perhaps I'd have stayed longer if a young man pushing a mop and bucket hadn't opened the door.

'Sorry, I need to wash the floors if you're ready to go.'

'Yes, of course.' I jumped to my feet. 'Sorry, I didn't mean to sit so long. I'm ready to go. I–'

I stopped myself from talking with difficulty, gave a silly laugh that might have been a titter and left with another murmured, 'Sorry.' Outside, a bored constable leaning against a wall straightened when I appeared and I apologised again. 'I've kept you waiting. I'm so sorry.'

Sorry for everything. For being so stupid. For being so very, unbelievably stupid.

55

MISTY

I took a taxi from the police station to my sister Ann's house. It was a toss-up as to which sister to descend upon, either would have been delighted to have opened their doors to me, but Ann was the more pragmatic of the two and likely to be the more sympathetic.

It was late by the time the taxi pulled up outside the house in Hounslow. I paid the fare, got out and walked up the short garden path to the front door where I took a deep breath to gird my loins. It was an expression my editor had recently highlighted in garish yellow. Perhaps she'd been right but here, after the day I'd had, it seemed curiously appropriate. I'd gird my loins and tell my conservative sister everything.

The ring of the doorbell was answered almost immediately by my brother-in-law, Derry, who took one quick look through the two inches allowed by the safety chain, shut the door and opened it wide again a moment later.

I guessed my dilemma was written across my face because he pulled me into his arms and shouted up the stairway behind for his wife. The quick sympathy was my undoing and I slumped in his arms, burying my face in his shirt as I sobbed.

'What's happened?' he said, leading me to the family room at the back of the house.

The sound of Ann's feet thudding on the carpeted stairway gave me time to draw a breath and I had myself in control again before she appeared, hair tousled and wearing a crumpled pair of pyjamas. Her scrubbed clean face creased in worry when she saw me. \

'My God, what's happened?'

'I'm sorry.' I pulled away from Derry's arms and held a hand towards her. It was caught between her warm ones and I was tugged, unresisting, into a tight hug that was another undoing. 'I'm sorry,' I said again, my words thick with tears. I snuffled against her shoulder. 'I'm sorry for descending on you but I'm not allowed home for the moment.'

Derry hovered and reached a hand to pat both our shoulders. 'I'll get some brandy. You look like you could do with some.'

Ann kept her arms wrapped tightly around me, swaddling me in comfort as she whispered in my ear. 'Whatever it is, we're here for you, okay?'

The family ties that bound us together, my anchor in times of trouble. My sisters had always been there. They always would. This was my life. Toby Carter had been an anomaly. I listened to reassuring repetitive words of comfort, ones I remembered our mother saying many years before when we were distressed for any reason – a scraped knee, the cruelty of friends, our first loves, our failures – and all the tension of that day and the days before left me in a whoosh.

Only when we were sitting around the table, with Derry's idea of a healthy amount of brandy in tumblers in each of our hands, did I tell them everything. I kept my eyes on the brandy, taking miniscule sips as I spoke. 'So that's where I stand,' I said, lifting the glass and emptying the last drop.

'Here,' Derry said, stretching behind him for the bottle. 'I don't think one is enough, not for this.'

'I knew that Toby guy was trouble. I said it to you, didn't I?' Ann looked to her husband for agreement. When he nodded, she turned back to me. 'So they don't think you've anything to do with it, despite your daft confession?' She reached a hand for my arm and patted it gently. 'Honestly, how silly you were to think such a thing. You haven't a violent streak in your body. I bet it was that old girlfriend of his, the woman who attacked you months ago. I bet she's responsible.'

'But why bury him in my garden?' *The garden of my lovely house, where I'd expected to stay forever. It was spoiled now. I'd have to move.* 'I'll have to sell up,' I said aloud. 'I can't stay there not knowing what has happened.'

'Don't do anything rash.' Ann's hand closed around mine. 'Stay here with us for as long as you like, then, since you can work from anywhere, maybe it would be a good idea to go away for a few months. Rent an apartment with a stunning view somewhere warm and sunny. Afterwards, when all the fuss has died down, you can get on with your life. It's not as if the body is still going to be there, after all.'

I met Derry's eyes and we both laughed at Ann's prosaic way of looking at things. But she was right. Toby was gone. It was foolish to allow him to cause me any more pain.

56

MISTY

Ann's spare bedroom was a pretty room with a comfortable single bed and a large window overlooking the sprawling garden at the back of the house. To my surprise, I slept better than I had in a long time. I'd liked to have believed it was a clear mind, but I think it was the generous amount of brandy I'd consumed.

We had talked until the early hours. I'd told them the full story again, adding bits of detail as I remembered.

Ann had dismissed the idea that I had lost a few hours the night Toby was killed. 'You were writing,' she pointed out. 'You always lose hours when you're deep into your characters' lives, especially when you're almost finished a book. And as for the paperweight being on the floor... didn't it sit on that shaky pile of papers on the edge of your desk?'

It did. 'Yes.'

'Well then. It probably rolled off days before and you never noticed.'

Ann's common sense was what was needed to put my fears into perspective. Anyway, her version of events was as believable as mine, and hers was the one I desperately wanted to believe.

I pulled a borrowed robe over matching PJs and went downstairs in search of coffee. Ann was sitting at the table in the family room with the salmon pink pages of the *Financial Times* open in front of her. She closed it and smiled at me. 'You're looking much better this morning,' she said, getting to her feet. 'Sit, I'm going to make you your favourite breakfast.'

'Coffee and toast will be fine.' I reached for the newspaper and turned to the front page looking for any reference to Toby's death. But it appeared the lofty pages of the *FT* weren't concerned with the death of one man buried in a suburban garden.

Ann bustled about the kitchen, opening cupboards and the fridge, maintaining a steady stream of inconsequential chatter as she worked as if afraid to leave a second's silence. It was a soft lullaby that kept me calm without requiring more from me than the occasional yes or no. I had no idea what she was making, having no clear recollection of having a *favourite* breakfast. It didn't really matter, it was nice to be fussed over and I'd eat whatever it was she was troubling herself to make.

'There you go,' Ann said, putting a plate of pancakes in front of me with a jug of what my nose told me was maple syrup.

'Oh wow! I can't remember the last time I had this. How lovely.' I looked up from the plate to her smiling face. 'I can't believe you remembered.' On a family holiday in Cornwall, many years before, I had insisted on pancakes every morning, telling everyone they were my favourite breakfast.

Ann put an arm around my shoulders and pulled me in for a hug. 'That's what big sisters are for.'

I poured a little syrup onto my plate.

'You may as well finish the lot,' Ann said. 'It'll only go to waste.'

'We can't have that.' I emptied the jug and handed it to her with a smile. 'This is so good,' I said, and proceeded to clear the plate. Finally, I sat back with a groan. 'That was yum.'

'You ate them as if you've not eaten in days.' Ann took the plate away and came back with a pot of coffee. 'I'll have to feed you up while you're here.' She poured two mugs of coffee, pushed one and the milk jug towards me before sitting beside me. 'I told Ursula everything. She sent her love.'

'I guessed you would.' I smiled. No secrets. It was the way it had always been in their family until recently, until Toby's arrival in my life made secrets necessary.

'She wanted to come over but I asked her to wait a day or two, give you time to recover.'

'I'm surprised she listened to you!'

Ann laughed. 'It took a bit of persuading.' When the doorbell pealed, she looked up to the kitchen clock and got to her feet. 'Probably the postman, back in a tick.'

A deep male voice was followed by Ann's, then silence before the male voice came again. More urgent this time. I was so relaxed that it didn't strike me as strange that my sister would be having a protracted conversation with the postman. It wasn't until I heard her coming back that I paid attention. One set of footsteps had gone out, more than one was returning.

I had pushed back the chair and got to my feet before they came through the door.

Ann was first, her hands clasped together in front of her chest as if in prayer. Worry lines creased her forehead and her lips were pressed tightly together. Two uniformed officers filled the space behind her, their expressions neutral.

'We need you to come with us, Ms Eastwood,' one of them said politely.

Politely. I wondered how fast that would change if I refused to go. 'What's this about?'

As if they had to take turns to speak, the other officer replied,

'We were simply asked to bring you in and don't have any details I'm afraid.'

Ann had walked to stand beside me. She pulled her hands apart, clenched each into a fist and rested them on her hips, elbows sticking out. 'That's not good enough. So basically, you're a taxi service!'

I might have found my sister's aggressive mother stance amusing had I not been worried by the unexpected arrival of the police, but then I saw fear flicker on her face and hurried to reassure her. 'It's okay, Ann. Detective Inspector Hopper said she might have more questions for me. These guys are simply doing their job.' I looked back to the two officers. 'I'll need to dress. Five minutes, okay?'

'Take all the time you like, miss. There's no urgency.'

'Go, have a shower.' Ann gave me a gentle shove. 'I'll make them some coffee, they'll be fine, I won't eat them.'

The two officers didn't look reassured but I knew my sister's flashes of anger never lasted longer than a blink. She was more likely to insist on cooking them breakfast.

DI Hopper had said that she might have more questions, but I'd assumed she would visit me to ask them, not that I would have to go back to the police station. Unless, of course, they'd had the post-mortem results and there was something that pointed a finger directly at me.

Fear uncurled. I had been fooling myself, lulled by my sister's belief that I couldn't have done anything so violent as to throw that damn paperweight.

But what if I had?

What if I *had* killed Toby and then rung someone to help me? Who would I have called? I stood under the shower and let the water cascade over me. It washed away my confusion.

~

I don't love you anymore, Toby had said, the words poisonous barbed arrows he'd aimed without care.

They had hit their target and spread a devastating toxin to every cell in my body. I'd disintegrated and reached for something solid to hold on to, my fingers closing over the cold, smooth glass paperweight. I wasn't a violent sort, Toby wouldn't have expected me to hit back and it was reaction rather than action that sent it sailing through the air. I hadn't deliberately aimed to hit him... at least not consciously.

He hadn't time to duck out of its way. The paperweight hit the side of his forehead and fell to the floor with a thud.

I could still see Toby's comical surprise, his mouth a wide O, eyes bugging. He'd raised a hand to his head and grinned foolishly as it came away dry. With a laugh, he picked up his bags and walked away. Leaving me.

The shower in Ann's main bathroom was powerful; I held my face up to the spray and let the water whip me as I remembered that night. His words... my actions. I *had* thrown that damn paperweight, but I hadn't killed him. Relief made me laugh, an edge of hysteria creeping in as the laughter continued. Tears washed down my face, fell into the shower tray and raced away.

57

MISTY

It was a different interview room, slightly smaller and shabbier, more akin to the ones described in my books. I tried not to see it as a demotion indicating bad news. I checked my watch again. It was a minute later than the last time I'd looked. Fifteen minutes I'd sat there, tension creeping around me and tightening its hold on my heart and stomach so that one beat loudly and the other tightened and burned with an acid sting.

I'd rung the solicitor on my way. She arrived shortly after me looking, if possible, paler than the last time I'd seen her. She dropped a slim briefcase on the table and sat in the chair beside me. 'Have you spoken to anyone yet?'

'No.' I twisted my hands together. 'But there's something I need to tell you.' My tale was hesitant, faltering. 'I meant it when I told the police I couldn't remember what had happened, but this morning it came back to me. I did throw that paperweight at Toby and I think it did hit him, but not hard, there was no blood or anything and he picked up his bags and left me.' I threw the solicitor a smile.

It wasn't returned. Pale eyes considered me for a moment.

'They would have brought you in today for a reason.' She pushed a lock of heavy ginger hair behind her ear, reached for her briefcase and withdrew a plain A4 pad and pen. 'No doubt they'll soon enlighten us.'

I sighed, it was probably silly to be looking for reassurance from a woman who was there simply to look after my legal rights, but I wished she were a little more supportive, a little friendlier.

I wished she'd been chattier too. Efforts to start a conversation were met by monosyllabic answers that made me give up after the third attempt. For the next ten minutes we sat in silence and when the door opened, I jumped to my feet and greeted the two detectives like old friends with an inappropriately cheerful hello. I immediately felt foolish, especially when the younger one, Collins, curled her lip. Her disdain, Hopper's obvious sympathy, I didn't like either and took my seat, keeping my eyes down.

Introductions were done again for the record and I was reminded that I was under caution.

'Yes,' I said, although an answer wasn't really required. I met DI Hopper's eyes and decided to be blunt. 'Why am I here?'

'We appreciate you coming in to help with our enquiries,' Hopper said, as if I'd had a choice. 'We've had some reports come in which have thrown up a few issues we need to resolve.' She opened the file she had brought with her and took out an A4 sheet that she slid across the table. 'You recognise this?'

I looked at the photograph. 'Yes, it's my paperweight. I should tell you–'

The solicitor held up a hand to stop me, then leaned over to whisper in my ear.

I pulled away from her and shook my head. 'No, I don't agree, it's best to let them know.' I took a deep breath, looked across the table and met Hopper's eyes with a slight smile. 'This morning, I finally remembered what happened that night.' The smile faded as I put my hand on the photograph and imagined I could feel the chill of the glass the moment before I flung it across the room.

'I did throw the paperweight at Toby and I think it must have hit him a glancing blow because he raised a hand to his head.' The memory of that last moment seeing him alive almost overcame me. I supposed it would linger for a long time. I took my hand from the photograph and rubbed my head the way he'd done that night. 'He took his hand away, looked at it, then waved the same hand at me. There was no blood. He didn't speak to me again, simply picked up his bags and left.'

Hopper reached for the photograph and returned it to the file. 'Apart from your fingerprints, there was no blood or trace evidence on it.'

'As my client said, it was merely a glancing blow.' The solicitor spoke as if attempting to justify her need to be there.

'Indeed,' Hopper said. Opening the file again, she removed a second sheet and slid it across the table. 'You might find this a little distressing. It's a copy of the X-ray of Mr Carter's head.' She reached forward and placed a finger on one section. 'He sustained a compressed skull fracture of his frontal bone here.' Her finger tapped the paper. 'It was caused by a blunt-force trauma such as being hit by a smooth, heavy glass paperweight.'

My breath caught as I eyed the concave indent on the skull X-ray. 'B-b-but, he walked away.' I looked up, fear filling my eyes and pressing my lips together. 'I swear to you, he walked away!'

'It appears that with this type of brain injury the repercussions may take a few minutes to be obvious. Mr Carter may have been able to walk away, exit your home, chat to someone else. But then the brain injury that was sustained made itself felt, causing him to keel over.'

My hands crept over my mouth as the reality of that one

moment of meltdown dawned on me. I'd killed someone. I'd killed Toby. The three words ricocheted painfully inside my skull. But when I said them aloud, 'I killed him,' the real horror sank in.

Hopper pulled the X-ray back. 'It's not as clear-cut as that, I'm afraid, but it looks as if this blow certainly led to his death.'

'Perhaps you could explain, detective.' The solicitor spoke sharply. 'Either my client killed Mr Carter or not. It seems to me it should be simple.'

'You would think,' Hopper said, picking up the file. 'But sometimes things are never as simple as they look.' She got to her feet, Collins following like a reflection. 'We've a few things to sort out. We'll be back. For the moment, sit tight.'

When they'd gone, I dropped the hands from my mouth and released the howl I'd been holding back. I was unsurprised when my solicitor drew away as if disgusted by this as she hadn't been by hearing that her client was a murderer.

58

GWEN

The lights in the custody suite never went completely out. They dimmed for a few hours, when Gwen supposed some might manage to sleep, before being restored to their glaring brightness at seven. It didn't matter to her; she hadn't managed to sleep at all.

She lay on the thin mattress with an arm over her eyes and barely stirred even when the hatch on the door was slid back and forward at regular intervals during the night. She could have told them she wasn't a suicide risk; she'd come through too much over the years to leave now.

That she might lose all she had worked for was something she might have to come to terms with. Her gallery... some of the artists she'd supported over the years might stand by her but others would take inordinate delight in what they would no doubt see as the great Gwen Marsham being brought down to size. Their size, their level. The reputation she'd built up with hard work and tough decisions, the respect that work had earned. They'd be lost. Those who said there was no such thing as bad publicity didn't move in the same circles she did.

A tray was brought into her at eight. There was no choice:

too-strong, barely warm tea; rubbery toast covered with a luminous yellow spread that neither looked nor tasted like butter and a bowl of cheap-brand cornflakes. None of it was appetising but Gwen ate everything and drank the tea. She'd been a fool, now was the time to be sensible.

At ten, she was led into the same interview room she'd been in the day before. Her solicitor, Heather Fitt, was already there looking elegant and sophisticated in a jacket Gwen recognised as Armani. She was conscious of her own grubbiness, the faint stink of body odour from her silk shirt, the creases in her skirt and jacket.

Heather got to her feet and came around the table to greet her, enveloping her in a hug that Gwen drew comfort from as she inhaled the cloud of scent that had accompanied the embrace. Coco, one of her favourites.

'You keeping it together?'

'Just about,' Gwen said and with a final hug, pulled away and sat. 'What happens today?'

'We have to wait and see what more information the detectives have and whether they're prepared as yet to go to the Crown prosecutor. If so, we should know what charges you're likely to face.'

'I will go to prison?'

The solicitor sighed. 'You concealed the death of a man and assisted in preventing that man's lawful burial. But on the plus side, you run a successful business, are an upstanding member of the community, and apart from a minor drugs misdemeanour, you've never been in trouble before so...' Fitt see-sawed her hand. 'It also depends on what Barbara Sanderson says, and whether she supports your story. You were obviously in shock having seen Mr Carter collapse the way he did, so I could argue you were vulnerable to being led astray.'

'I did want to ring the police.'

'It's a shame you didn't.' Fitt shook her head. 'I'll do my best for you, of course, but this might be a messy one.'

The door opened and focused both women on the arrival of the detectives.

'Morning,' DI Hopper said, slipping onto a chair opposite, DS Collins taking the one beside her.

Gwen, deprived by circumstances of her usual Tom Ford lipstick, found herself curiously fascinated by Collins' red painted lips.

'Gwen... Gwen?'

Only when Fitt reached to grip her shoulder did Gwen realise they were all staring at her with concern.

'Are you all right?' The hand squeezed gently.

'Yes, I'm sorry, I didn't sleep last night.' She saw Hopper look to the solicitor for guidance and sat up straighter. 'I'm fine, can we get on with this.'

'We can wait until later if that would be easier for you?'

'No!' Gwen lifted a hand in apology. 'I'm sorry, I didn't mean to shout. No, please, I would really like to get on with this. Please.'

'Okay.' Hopper tapped the file she held on the top of the table. 'We've had some reports back and have discovered more about what happened the night Toby Carter died.'

'Right.'

'Ms Marsham, can you run us through what happened after Mr Carter collapsed?'

'Is this absolutely necessary?' the solicitor said. 'My client has already told you what occurred. That's not going to change.'

'If this weren't important, Ms Fitt, believe me I wouldn't be wasting your time... or ours.'

Gwen put her hand on the solicitor's arm. 'I don't mind going over it again.'

'Fine,' Fitt said. 'I think, though, that we could do with something to drink.'

'No problem, we can get whatever you like.' Hopper looked at Collins and jerked a thumb towards the door. 'DS Collins will do the honours.'

Five minutes later the small room was filled with the aroma of bitter coffee. Gwen wrapped her fingers around the disposable cup and described the night Toby Carter had died. 'His fall was so dramatic, I thought he was kidding around at first. I waited for him to start laughing... *to pull her down on top of him and fornicate in that damp, dark passage...* to start laughing,' she repeated, trying to swallow that other thought. 'It was only when I bent over him that I realised something wasn't right. I think I must have shaken him but he didn't respond. I was hunkered down beside him when Misty... Babs... appeared.'

Gwen glanced towards her solicitor, remembering what she'd said earlier. This was an opportunity for damage limitation. 'His collapse had been so unexpected, that I was shocked and panicking. Babs took control. I remember saying we should ring the police but she persuaded me it was a bad idea. She bent down and tried to find his pulse.'

Hopper held a hand up to stop her. 'You're sure about that?'

Gwen frowned. 'Yes... yes, I'm absolutely certain. I remember she pushed up his sleeve to find his pulse, then when she couldn't find it–' Gwen brushed her fingers down her neck. '–she felt here, but she said she couldn't find one. That he was d-dead.' She could still remember the horror she'd felt at that moment. 'It was awful. I wanted to ring the police but she said it would be better to bury him there.'

'Why?' Hopper asked. 'I know I've asked this before but I'm struggling to understand why you couldn't have rung the police?'

Gwen shook her head slowly. 'It all happened so quickly.

Babs went on about how bad it would look for me to have been in that passage with him, the seedy spin the press would put on it. She said it would take a few days for the post-mortem to show he'd died of natural causes and until then I'd be under suspicion. The more she talked, the more convinced I became that burying him in the garden was a good idea. And don't forget,' she reminded them, 'I thought it was her garden. That he'd stay hidden forever.'

'Okay, what happened then?'

Gwen went through the rest, stumbling now and then. 'Then I saw Babs bent over him. She was checking to make sure there was no pulse.'

Hopper held a hand up. 'She checked his pulse again?'

'Yes, she said she wanted to make sure she'd been right.'

'And did she check the pulse at his neck this time?'

Gwen tilted her head, trying to remember. 'N-no, I think she only tried his wrist the second time. She seemed satisfied that he was dead, though, and together we half-lifted, half-dragged him across the garden to the raised flower bed.'

'And you both rolled him in.'

'Not exactly. We both lifted him up. The raised bed is probably three feet high so it wasn't easy. We managed to get him onto the flat edging stones. It was Babs who pushed him from that. It was then that I remembered the bags so I told her to wait and ran to get them. When I got back, she'd already covered his face and chest with soil. I put the bags in by his legs and squashed them down. Babs was standing on the edge, she pushed them down with her feet, then finished filling it in.'

'Okay,' Hopper said slowly. She played with the edges of the file on the table. 'We've had some reports back.'

Gwen sat forward, alert. 'The post-mortem. Do you know what made him collapse? Was it a heart attack?'

'No, it wasn't. It was a head injury.' Hopper sucked in her

lower lip. 'He had sustained a blow to his head a short time before.'

'A head injury?' Gwen looked from one detective to the other, then back to her solicitor as she tried to make sense of this information. *Toby died from a head injury.*

59

BABS

Babs spent a restless night in the custody suite. Her head ached with the conflicting thoughts that banged noisily around the inside of her skull. The breakfast they brought her made her heave – she took a sip of the coffee, spat it out and pushed the tray away.

Her belongings were returned to her before she was brought back to the interview room mid-morning. She grabbed her coat, slipped it on and belted it tightly. The tweed cap was still in the pocket, her fingers closed around it bringing an instant feeling of calm.

She was brought to the same interview room, surprised to find the legal aid solicitor already waiting when she entered. 'Morning.'

'Good morning. You don't look too well. A bad night?'

Babs shrugged and sat in the chair beside her. 'It's not the Ritz, that's for sure.' She looked around, her nose twitching. 'It stinks in here.'

The chairs were fixed to the floor. Unable to move, the solicitor leaned away from Babs as far as she could. 'I think it's coming from that coat.'

Babs ran her hands over the Burberry raincoat. It had been Toby's. One of three he had, she didn't think he'd missed it. She'd worn it almost daily since he'd left, wearing it and the tweed flat cap on her jaunts to Hanwell to spy on Misty.

Maybe it did smell a little, she didn't care.

It was another fifteen minutes before the two detectives who'd interviewed her the previous day came into the room and took the seats opposite. The older detective looked tired, the younger with perhaps even more make-up than the day before, her lips a garish red.

Babs, aware of the dark tramline down the parting of her dyed blonde hair was sorry, despite the heat, that she'd not put on the flat cap. Like a lot of things, it was too late.

'Right,' DI Hopper said when formalities were completed. 'As you're aware, Ms Sanderson, we've placed you at the crime scene and your fingerprints are on the spade that was used to dig the bed where Toby Carter's body was buried.'

It was the solicitor who replied. 'My client admits that she dug out the raised flower bed after she was begged to do so by Gwen Marsham.'

'Dug out the bed, rolled Mr Carter's body into it and put the soil back on top to bury him.' Hopper looked at Babs. 'Is that correct?'

Babs glanced at her solicitor. There didn't appear to be any help coming from that quarter. But it was her word against Gwen's, wasn't it? 'She made me help her. I wanted to call the police but she said no, that the bad press would destroy her business.' She sniffed. 'She begged me, and stupidly I decided to help her.'

'Help her,' Hopper repeated. 'Right, I see. Were you still in love with Toby Carter?'

Babs' laugh sounded false even to her ears. 'Of course not! Don't be ridiculous. I told you, he left me broke.'

'Yes, you did tell us that but, you see, it's a bit odd.' Hopper smiled. 'What were you doing at the house where he was living the night he died?'

Babs regretted skipping breakfast. Maybe if she'd eaten something, she'd be able to come up with a reasonable answer for being in Hanwell that night.

Hopper's arms were resting on the desk in front of her, she leaned forward pushing them closer. 'You'd been keeping an eye on him, hadn't you?'

'I...' Babs couldn't find the words and shook her head.

'You'd been keeping an eye on him but you didn't know he was leaving Misty Eastwood for another woman. You didn't find that out until you met Gwen Marsham in the side passage of the house on Myrtle Road.' Hopper's voice softened. 'It must have made you angry.'

'Must it?' Babs sneered. 'You don't know anything.'

Hopper pulled a photo from her file and pushed it across the desk. 'Do you recognise this?'

The solicitor pulled the photo closer, then slid it sideways to Babs who picked it up and dropped it a second later. 'It's a watch.'

'Toby Carter's Rolex watch, inscribed with *To Toby, love Babs*. It must have cost a pretty penny.' Hopper pulled the photo away. 'Ms Marsham stated that you took Mr Carter's pulse, his wrist and–' Hopper patted the side of her neck. '–because you've medical training, you knew to check the carotid if you can't get a radial pulse.'

Babs' face tightened. 'I never did. That Marsham woman told me he was dead and I took her word for it.'

Hopper turned to look at her colleague. 'That's not what Ms Marsham is saying, is it, DS Collins?'

'Nope.' The painted face looked at Babs with a raised eyebrow. 'She says that you checked the radial and carotid pulse when you arrived and before you dragged his body over to bury it, you checked his radial pulse again.'

'Rubbish. You can't prove anything.'

'Well, d'you know,' Hopper said. 'Sometimes we can prove the oddest things.' She opened the file, pulled out a photo and sent it sliding across the table. 'This is a fingerprint lifted off the bracelet of that expensive Rolex. Your fingerprint, Ms Sanderson, when you pushed the bracelet out of the way to take his pulse.'

The legal aid solicitor pulled the photo over, looked at it briefly before sliding it back. 'Perhaps you could tell us the relevancy of this, detective. Whether or not my client took his pulse seems to be a moot point since the man was dead.'

'But that's the problem, you see, he wasn't.' Hopper hid a smile when she saw the solicitor's rapid change of expression from boredom to dismay. 'Exactly. Now you understand the importance.

'Your client buried Toby Carter alive.'

60

BABS

Babs saw the satisfaction on the detectives' faces. It looked like it was all over for her. She found she didn't care.

'You can still tell us your side of the story, Ms Sanderson,' DI Hopper said.

'My side of the story?' Babs sat back and shoved her hands into the pockets of Toby's Burberry. 'I suppose I might as well.'

The night that Toby Carter died, Babs had been watching the house on Myrtle Road, as she often did since he'd left her. Sometimes she watched for hours. Over the weeks, she'd learned the gardens she could shelter in, the walls she could sit on, the places to hide. It was a quiet street, most of the residents were retired, people who rarely left their homes at night. No curtain-twitchers either, in all the weeks she'd stalked the street not one person had challenged her.

Now that she wasn't working, she was free to visit any time of the day. Once, she'd even followed Misty to the local shops. Mostly, though, she preferred the quieter evenings. She'd go to her favourite vantage point, a gate pillar in a garden across the road from where Toby was living and lean against it. In the off-white Burberry with the tweed flat cap covering her blonde hair, she blended in with the weathered sandstone.

Her visit was never wasted. If nobody entered or left the house, it didn't matter, she'd wait for that glimpse of either Toby or the woman at one of the windows. The first evening Babs had visited, she'd figured out that the woman worked from a room in the front of the house. Her back was to the window, the glow of a computer screen in front. It took Babs a few minutes to puzzle out the strange, deformed shape of the woman's head, then she banged her forehead with the heel of her hand. Headphones!

The nights when she caught a glimpse of Toby gave her more pleasure. She saw him most days, of course, following him when he left his office, keeping her distance on the train, getting off at the same stop and walking several feet behind him until he reached Myrtle Road.

Seeing him at home, though, was different – there was a curious intimacy about seeing him cross a room, shirt collar open, sleeves pushed up. Sometimes, he'd stand at the window with a drink in his hand. He couldn't see her but she could see him and memories of being with him would come flooding back. The way he would unexpectedly grab her for a hug, a kiss or more. The smell of him, the feel of his skin.

Sometimes her desperate need for him would almost overcome her and she would grab onto the pillar for support. And when the stars blinked into existence, she'd wish on each one that he would see sense and come back to her.

The nights when she'd watched Toby and the writer woman leave by taxi were the worst. It would curdle Babs' brain to imagine all the wonderful places they were going. Once or twice, she waited until they returned, slumping to the ground in a gap between the gate pillar and a privet hedge behind. She kept a

61

BABS

Babs was ready to forgive and welcome Toby back, more than happy to take up exactly where they'd left off before he'd been lured away. She opened her mouth to call him, but before she uttered a word, before she'd moved away from the pillar, the quick clip of footsteps dragged her attention from the man she loved to the figure rushing toward him... an elegant, beautifully dressed, obviously wealthy woman.

Babs looked back at Toby in time to see his cheating, lying face break into a smile that said he knew this person intimately. Anger doubled Babs over and made her gag followed by a wave of nausea that sent her stumbling against the pillar. But she couldn't drag her eyes away from the scene unveiling across the street.

Toby leaned forward as the woman reached his side and Babs braced herself to see them kiss. Anger and jealousy twirled in a painful dance that left her weak, blurring her vision for a moment. When it cleared, she wondered if they had kissed and she'd missed it, because Toby had dropped his bags, had taken the woman's arm and together they walked to the passage at the side of the end-of-terrace house.

Babs had already explored the side passage and knew it led to a generous back garden. Weeks before, while on one of her early morning visits to the house, she'd seen a van pull up and a tall, well-built man climb out. The van proclaimed him to be a gardener but her suspicious eyes saw the muscled body and was instantly convinced that the writer was cheating on Toby.

Her suspicions increased when the man didn't knock on the front door. Instead, with an air of entitlement that shouted he'd done it before, he sauntered down the side passage and vanished from sight. He'd not been carrying any tools of his trade nor did he return to his van over the next hour. Neither was there any sign of Misty at her desk. *Gardening, pah!* Toby needed to know what was going on behind his back. Filled with the anger of an avenging angel, Babs crossed the road and made her way to the side of the house.

It was a sunny morning, but the narrow passageway was bordered on one side by the house and on the other by a high wall so little light filtered through. A wooden gate separating it from the garden beyond was shut with a simple lever catch. No lock. She pressed her ear to the rough surface of the gate wanting to hear grunts and groans of passion. She pictured herself breaking the bad news to Toby, then offering him consolation. But if the gardener and writer were fornicating in the garden, the sound was smothered by loud music. Babs needed to know... she needed proof she could take to Toby.

Her fingers closed over the lever and pressed gently. It was the point of no return. She pushed the gate open. It creaked loudly but the sound was smothered by the music and she stepped into the garden with high hopes. What she wanted to see was a tawdry, compromising scene involving a naked gardener and a cheating, sluttish, wannabe writer.

So certain she was of what she was going to find, that it took a few seconds for Babs' brain to process the mundanity of what she was seeing. The gardener was on his knees with his attention on what he was doing – but he wasn't doing any naked female. His frowning concentration was on the spirit level he was holding on the top of a low brick wall.

Her grunt of annoyed disbelief was louder than she'd intended and before she could step back into the passage and disappear, the gardener looked her way.

Babs pasted on a smile and stepped forward. 'Hi, I'm sorry to bother you.'

Keeping his eyes on her, he reached a dirty hand behind to switch off the radio. The same dirty hand pushed thick curling hair from his eyes as he got to his feet. 'What can I do for you?'

'I live up the road–' Babs waved a hand towards the front of the house, the gesture deliberately vague. '–and saw your van. I was thinking of having work done and wondered if I could have a business card.'

'Sure.' He brushed dirt from his hands, reached into a pocket and pulled a pile of cards out. Separating one, he shoved the rest back. 'Here you go, my mobile and website.'

'Thanks so much.' Babs took it, looked at it with feigned interest and slipped it into her coat pocket. 'This is a nice garden.' It was. She hadn't expected it to be so large.

'It was a bit flat and boring so the owner came up with an interesting plan.' The gardener nudged the wall he was building with the toe of his shoe. 'This is going to be a raised flower bed and there'll be another on the other side with grass or maybe AstroTurf in between.' He smiled again. 'I'm not keen on the fake stuff but the final decision isn't mine.' He pointed towards the shed. 'Between this area and that, there's going to be a wild flower bed. There'll be a path through it to the shed which is going to be painted in pastel shades so that it blends in a bit.' He prodded the half-built flower bed again. 'There's going to be hardy fuchsias in here. They'll give nice colour all summer and are fairly easy to maintain.'

Babs struggled to keep an interested expression in place. 'It's going to be lovely. I know Misty, of course. The noise doesn't bother her?' Babs indicated the radio.

'No.' He held his hands cupped over his ears. 'If she's working, she uses headphones, can't hear a thing. I don't need to bother her when I come around. Everything I need is there in the shed.' Obviously keen to reassure a prospective client that he was a thoughtful, conscientious worker, he indicated the neighbours on one side with a jerk of his thumb. 'I don't bother the neighbours either, they're away on that side.' His dirty thumb moved to the other side. 'I spoke to the elderly couple on that side, they said I could hold a rock concert in here and they wouldn't hear it.'

Babs gave the laugh that he seemed to expect. 'Right. That's great.' She'd heard enough. 'Thanks for your card, I'll be in touch.'

Back on the road, she took the card out, tore it into pieces and tossed it into the breeze. She'd no use for the stupid man's services. She'd wanted a tawdry affair, something she could wave under Toby's nose.

Still, her time hadn't been wasted, she'd learned how easy it was to access the back garden. Over the next few weeks, she visited several times, waiting until it was dark to sneak around the side of the house, open the gate and hurry inside. She discovered the shed was never locked but there was nothing of interest in it and, behind it, a nasty-smelling compost heap didn't encourage further exploration.

Once, the light had been left on in the kitchen. Babs crept up to the windowsill and peered into the room, then slid along the wall to the French doors. She wanted to sneer at the candles that sat in the middle of the dining table and on the shelving unit behind... she wanted to but she couldn't, not with tears running down her face...

Once, she saw Toby's jacket draped over the back of one of the chairs and she was filled with a desperate longing to bury her nose in it. She stood with her face pressed to the glass for a long time until, startled by the opening of the kitchen door, she jumped back to blend in with the shadows and slink away.

62

BABS

That Saturday night Babs waited for the distinctive creak of the wooden gate to tell her that Toby and the woman had gone through to the garden. When it didn't come, curiosity forced her across the street. She stepped around the bags Toby had carelessly dropped and crossed the small front garden to the side of the house. Muffled groans coming from the side passage fell into the silence and painted a clear picture for her. They twisted her heart and brought her to a standstill, a hand over her mouth to stop the cry of despair.

She should leave. Put a stop to the heartache she was causing herself. Face the truth that Toby wasn't coming back to her. He'd never intended to.

She should leave, she knew she should, but her obsession was deep-rooted and her feet moved forward. At the edge of the house, she stopped again, her ears tuned to the sound of passion that drifted on the night air from the dank side passage. Had they been overcome with lust before they managed to open the gate?

Babs edged nearer, gripped the quoin brick and leaned

forward to peer down the passageway. Little light filtered through to the end but enough to show her the figure of the woman straddling Toby. The groans were coming from her. The rhythmic sound of passion. Conflicting emotions of love and hatred kept Babs immobile, her eyes fixed on the woman as she got to her feet, still groaning.

Babs waited for Toby to get up and when he didn't, when it finally struck her that the woman's continued moaning was bizarre, she stepped forward.

The woman turned with a gasp when she saw her. 'I think he's dead.'

No, it wasn't possible. Babs rushed forward, squatted down and pushed back Toby's sleeve to feel for a pulse. There was one but it was faint. She dropped his wrist, then reached a hand to his face, her breath catching as her fingers, almost despite themselves, lingered in a caress. She swallowed the sob and moved to the still warm stretch of skin between Toby's jaw and the collar of his shirt to feel for his carotid pulse. It was stronger.

The woman was standing close by, lines of worry on her face. But any sympathy Babs might have felt was wiped away by the sight of the elegant, classy clothes and the scent of expensive perfume that cut through the dank smell of the side passage. The holdalls made sense then. Toby was leaving the writer woman all right but he was moving on, not returning to Babs. *This* was the woman Toby had chosen. A more elegant, sophisticated, and wealthier woman.

Despite all the behaviour management courses Babs had done, anger always simmered beneath the surface waiting to erupt or, as in that moment, to ooze insidiously as the woman hovered anxiously, shuffling from one expensive shoe to the other. Each movement sent her scent wafting over Babs, triggering a memory of Toby nuzzling her neck, telling her how much he loved her natural smell. How much he loved her. How she made his life worthwhile... all the lies he told and she foolishly believed.

All the lies.

She felt Toby's heart beating under her fingers, a tiny dart of pain shooting through her as she finally acknowledged that despite all her work and years of planning, despite all his words, all his promises, his heart didn't beat for her.

'He is dead, isn't he?' The woman's voice, soft, educated, thick with sorrow and shock.

Babs felt the anger oozing from every pore, felt herself bathed in its toxic mess as she struggled to her feet. 'Yes, I'm afraid he is.'

Later, when the grave was ready for its occupant, Babs picked up Toby's wrist again, shocked to find the radial pulse stronger. Strong enough to worry her. She sent Gwen to lift the legs so she wouldn't feel the waft of his breath as they carried him to the side of the raised flower bed. Babs felt his warm breath on her cheek as she struggled to get him upright and she was almost sure she heard him grunt when he landed inside.

With Gwen gone to fetch the holdalls, Babs acted quickly and shovelled the soil in over Toby's face and chest as quickly as she could. It was easy to ignore the faint cough she heard, easy to aim the next loaded spade of soil to land on his face. There were no further sounds after that.

Babs looked across the table at the two detectives as she finished her story. She guessed neither the severe-faced older one or the one with the clownish make-up had a clue what loving someone like Toby was like. The gut-wrenching pain of seeing the man you loved so desperately cast you aside and move on to someone else.

It seemed ironic to Babs that a Rolex watch which had contributed to her financial disaster was now proving her guilt. She remembered pushing it out of the way to take Toby's pulse, the idea that she should remove it dismissed instantly when her fingers felt the steady beat that told her he was still alive.

'I paid eight grand for that watch. Extra to have it inscribed. He told me I was spoiling him, that it was too much.' Babs laughed briefly, the sound lacking humour. 'He didn't mean that, of course. Toby never thought money spent on him was too much.' She looked down at her bare hands. 'I hoped he'd ask me to marry him, that we'd be together forever. Even when he moved on to that writer, I thought he'd come back to me. He told me...' She met the older detective's eyes. 'Lies. He told me lies and I believed them.'

'You still loved him?'

Babs thought she heard a touch of sympathy in the question. 'Loved him or hated him. To borrow from the great John Dryden, *thin partitions do their bounds divide.*' She dropped her eyes to her hands again. 'At that moment, I suppose hate had the upper hand. I hated him for wanting Gwen more than me.'

'And if you couldn't have him, she wasn't going to?' Collins said with a sneer.

Babs looked at her. There was no hint of sympathy in the younger detective's cold eyes. This wasn't a woman who was going to obsess over a man, who would ever understand the way love could consume you. For a second, Babs envied her, but only for a second. It might have been an obsession but for a while it had been paradise.

'No, it wasn't quite that simple,' she said, staring into the heavily made-up eyes. 'More a case of, if I couldn't have him, *nobody* was going to.'

63

MISTY

It had been four hours since the detectives had left the interview room. The solicitor shrugged and raised a ginger eyebrow when I asked her if this was normal practice.

'There's no *normal* when it comes to murder, I'm afraid. Best thing is to sit back and try to relax.' She opened her briefcase, took out a neat laptop which she opened on the table and sat glued to it, ignoring me.

Maybe I had to pay extra for polite conversation. For a while, I sat and thought about Toby. I'd killed him. An accident, my wild anger-driven throw hitting a mark I'd not aimed for.

Now and then, bored and uncomfortable with sitting on the hard chair, I stood and paced the small room.

The only distraction came when the door opened and a young constable asked if she could bring us drinks.

'What's happening?' I asked, not really expecting an answer.

'I'm sorry, I don't know. I can try to find out for you but first, would you like something to drink?'

I asked for tea and the solicitor took her attention briefly from her laptop to request the same. The constable returned minutes later and set disposable cups on the table before looking at me. 'The detectives in charge of your case said they'll be with you shortly.' Colour flared in her cheeks. 'I'm sorry that was all I could find out.'

'That's okay,' I said, grateful she'd bothered. 'Thank you for trying and for the tea.'

It was another hour before the door opened again and the two detectives walked in.

'Our apologies for the long delay, Ms Eastwood,' DI Hopper said, taking the same seat she'd sat in earlier. 'We were waiting for information from a medical consultant regarding Mr Carter's head injury.'

I felt a band of tension tighten around my chest. The next minute might affect the rest of my life. I wanted to hear what the detective was going to say but I didn't want to hear... the repercussions could be devastating.

Hopper rested her forearms on the table and linked her fingers together. 'The medical consultant agrees with the original report, that the injury Mr Carter sustained from the paperweight you threw could have caused him to collapse a short time later. However–' She unclasped her hands. '–the consultant also states that the head injury was treatable. Mr Carter may have been left with some residual problems but the injury itself would not have resulted in his death.'

I blinked, unsure if I was hearing correctly. My mouth was suddenly dust dry. I reached for the almost empty cup and took a sip of cold tea before managing to ask, 'I didn't kill him?'

'Your action contributed to his death,' Hopper said. 'But no, the medical reports seem quite clear. You didn't kill him.'

The solicitor had shut her laptop when the detectives came in. She tapped manicured nails on the lid. 'Elaborate please, detective, on how my client's action contributed to his death?'

Hopper sat back. 'The investigation is ongoing so I'm not at liberty to go into the details. Suffice to say that when Mr Carter collapsed as a direct consequence of the blow to his head, other people took advantage. It was their subsequent action that resulted in his death.'

I thought I understood. 'These people killed him and buried him in my garden?'

Hopper stared at me for a second but instead of answering, she got to her feet. 'I've spoken to the Crown prosecutor. Based on the medical report, and that it was in any case an accidental rather than deliberate act, I recommended that no charges be brought against you and she agreed. There is, therefore, no reason to keep you any longer.'

I wasn't sure I was hearing correctly and looked to my solicitor for confirmation. 'I'm free to go?'

The solicitor was sliding her laptop into her briefcase. 'Indeed you are.' She turned with the first smile I had seen. 'Good luck.' And with that she got to her feet, nodded to the detectives, and left.

'I'm free to go.' I shook my head. 'Sorry, it's all hard to process.'

'You've had a tough time, Ms Eastwood. But you are free to go and your sisters are waiting in reception.'

'My sisters?'

'They've been there for hours. They'll be relieved to see you.'

My sisters. I swallowed the lump that had suddenly appeared in my throat and got to my feet. 'Thank you both.' I shook my head, still unable to believe my ordeal was over. 'Mrs Carter... Dee... is she okay? She must have been devastated.'

'She was, but her daughter has come back from Aberdeen to be with her so I think Mrs Carter will be okay. You've no need to worry about her, she'll be informed that you had nothing to do with her husband's death.'

I remembered the woman's hysterical cries that I had killed Toby. She was almost right. 'I don't want her to be prosecuted for assaulting me.' I smiled briefly. 'I know I can't ask for the charges to be dropped, but you can, can't you?'

'Yes,' Hopper agreed. 'But as it turns out, I don't have to. The CPS has decided it's not in the interest of justice to pursue the case against Dee Carter.' The detective smiled. 'Sometimes, the law shows common sense.' With a final nod, she left the room.

I felt lighter as I walked down the corridor towards the reception and stood in the doorway looking to where my two sisters sat. They were holding hands, their faces twisted in worried concern. When they looked up and saw me, they jumped to their feet and rushed over to envelop me in hugs.

'It's okay,' I said, wrapping my arms around them. 'I'm free to go. Everything's okay.' I pulled back from their embraces and reached to brush tears from Ann's cheeks. 'Everything's okay and what's more, I have a brilliant idea for my next book!'

I walked out with a sister on each side, their arms linking mine. This was all I needed. In future, men would be relegated to the pages of the books I wrote. It was much safer that way.

And if I fell in love with them, at least they could never hurt me.

64

GWEN

Gwen stopped at a local Indian restaurant on the way home from the police station and picked up a takeaway. By the time she pushed open the front door of her apartment, it was late and she was past weary. She sat in the living room where she slumped on the sofa and ate samosas and vegetable pakora directly from the containers with her fingers, chewing and swallowing without tasting.

After a few mouthfuls, she got up, wiped her greasy hand on a towel and grabbed the first bottle of wine that came to hand from the rack. She didn't care what it was and poured a glass. It was white, and warm.

It didn't matter.

She might yet face charges for her part in burying Toby, but her solicitor, Heather Fitt, was confident that in view of Babs Sanderson's confession, Gwen would escape lightly.

Babs... she had assumed Gwen's distress that fateful night was caused by Toby's death but Babs had been wrong. It wasn't distress either. It was fury that he had died before Gwen had got her revenge for the lies and the betrayal. Bubbling anger that he'd got away with treating her like a fool, something she'd never allowed before.

Her lying, cheating husband, George, had learned his lesson the hard way. There'd never been any hint of her involvement in his death.

Gwen sipped the sickly warm wine and smiled. Nor had there been any question of her involvement in that sleazy con man's death. It had taken her weeks to find Sam Burke, assuming, rightly, that he'd stick to generally the same area to choose his prey.

They'd never found his body, it was unlikely they would at this stage.

She filled her glass and sat back. There was some consolation in knowing Toby hadn't died that easily, that he'd been alive when they'd dragged him across the garden and shoved him into that brick grave. She hoped he was aware of what was happening... that he came to in time to feel the soil hitting his face.

After all the lies he told, it was a fitting end.

THE END

ACKNOWLEDGEMENTS

As ever, grateful thanks to all in Bloodhound Books especially Betsy Reavley, Fred Freeman, Tara Lyons, Heather Fitt, Morgen Bailey and Ian Skewis.

A special thanks to Heather Fitt for the use of her name for one of the characters and to Beverley Hopper, who runs the Facebook group The Book Lovers, for her continued support – she gets to be detective in this novel!

When you work so hard on a story you want people to read it – so a huge thanks to all the bloggers who get the word out. Thanks to all who review – always such a relief to see when people enjoy what you wrote. And a big thanks to all who contact me to tell me they love my writing – that never gets tired.

The support from the writing community is always fantastic and an author's world would be a lonelier place without it – so a big thanks to all my fellow Bloodhound authors and a special thanks to the writers Jenny O'Brien, Leslie Bratspis, Pat Gitt, Pam Lecky, Michael Scanlon and Jim Ody for your continued support and encouragement.

A huge thank you to the artist, Scott Naismith, from whose Blog, Art Speak: Arty Nonsense Exposed, I borrowed the over-flowery art statements in Chapter 17 and for allowing me to 'hang' his paintings in my fictional gallery. He can be found here: scottnaismith.com.

Thanks to my husband, Robert, my sisters, brothers, extended family, and my friends for always being there for me.

I love to hear from readers – you can find me here:

Facebook: www.facebook.com/valeriekeoghnovels

Twitter: www.twitter.com/ValerieKeogh1

Instagram: www.instagram.com/valeriekeogh2

A NOTE FROM THE PUBLISHER

Thank you for reading this book. If you enjoyed it please do consider leaving a review on Amazon to help others find it too.

We hate typos. All of our books have been rigorously edited and proofread, but sometimes mistakes do slip through. If you have spotted a typo, please do let us know and we can get it amended within hours.

info@bloodhoundbooks.com

Made in the USA
Las Vegas, NV
26 September 2021

30874462R00163